A McCORD SISTER ROMANCE

COWGIRL AT HEART

CHRISTINE LYNXWILER

BARBOUR
PUBLISHING

DEDICATION AND ACKNOWLEDGMENTS:

To Cocoa and Beauty and all my four-legged friends who went before them. You have selflessly given me comfort and happiness during the bad times and the good. Even though you'll never read or understand these words, I've loved you all.

To Kevin—because no book would ever be finished without you, my inspiration and support. By your example, you help me stay focused on God when I would tend to turn inward, especially during tough times. I thank you for that and so much more. I love you.

To my girls—Words can't express the love and joy in my heart when I see how you are growing up. I'm very proud of both of you and love you more than life itself.

To my family and friends—Thank you for your support and encouragement, big and small. Each of you is precious to me.

3 1969 01986 3272

© 2010 by Christine Lynxwiler

ISBN 978-1-60260-151-2

Scripture quotations are taken from the New King James Version®. Copyright © 1982 by Thomas Nelson, Inc. Used by permission. All rights reserved.

This book is a work of fiction. Names, characters, places, and incidents are either products of the author's imagination or used fictitiously. Any similarity to actual people, organizations, and/or events is purely coincidental.

Cover design: Müllerhaus Publishing Arts Inc., www.mullerhaus.net

Published by Barbour Publishing, Inc., P.O. Box 719, Uhrichsville, OH 44683, www.barbourbooks.com

Our mission is to publish and distribute inspirational products offering exceptional value and biblical encouragement to the masses.

ecpa Member of the
Evangelical Christian
Publishers Association

Printed in the United States of America.

CHAPTER 1

Elyse McCord guided her Jeep down the gravel road for another slow pass. The white frame house on the corner lot hid its secrets well. Just as the guy at the café said, the tall privacy fence didn't allow even a peek of the backyard. And driving back and forth all day wasn't going to change that.

With no hard evidence, she was going to have to take his word about the starving dog in the backyard that could only be seen from his woods. And about the big, mean-looking guy who lived in the house, rumored to be fresh out of prison. She shuddered.

Elyse turned down the side road and followed the privacy fence until it disappeared into the brushy thicket. The dark brushy thicket. Maybe she should just go home and call someone. Her hand hesitated on the gear shift knob. What if it was a false alarm? She'd look like an idiot. Or what if it was true and the dog couldn't wait that long?

Her new Jeep bounced as she pulled onto the shoulder of the road and parked. That was her idea of living dangerously—buying a Jeep and not gripping the steering wheel with two white-knuckled hands whenever she hit a bump. This crazy mission she'd undertaken on the spur of the moment was just that. Crazy and out of character. Except that a dog was depending on her. Her cell phone was fully charged and in her pocket. Once she saw the dog, she'd call the sheriff. She snagged a dog food pouch and water bottle from the console and climbed down.

In the woods, her heart pounded out a rhythm with her feet as she eased between the trees. She counted the dogwoods and maples as she went, their already changed leaves making them bright red beacons among the autumn mix of color. "One, two, three," she whispered, moving forward on trembling legs. It was a trick she'd learned before she even learned to read—using mundane tasks, such as counting or sorting things by colors, to take her mind off her fears.

She stepped out from the shadow of a giant cedar tree and tiptoed across the thick bed of brown needles. Ahead, a battered, sagging chain-link fence, about three feet tall, marked the beginning of a backyard. Another step forward. A limb snapped beneath her foot. She stopped, letting the cedar scent calm her, fighting the need to bolt back through the woods to the safety of her Jeep.

Then she saw the dog. Yellow lab from the look of him. Dust caked his ridged sides, each rib distinctly visible. He tucked his tail and watched her, big soulful eyes fearful as though begging her to be kind.

In a flash of emotion almost foreign to her, Elyse wanted to hit something hard with her fist. What kind of monster would treat a dog this way? "Hey, boy," she said softly as she walked up to the fence.

His tail relaxed and he gave a feeble wag.

She pulled the water bottle from her pocket and poured it

through the wire into a dusty bowl.

The dog lapped at the stream, not letting it hit the bowl first.

Hot tears pricked against Elyse's eyelids. If she hadn't overheard the hunters talking at the café. . . If she hadn't come out here today. . . She shook her head, blinking hard. She'd learned a long time ago not to live in "what if" land.

The dog had stopped drinking and was regarding her curiously, one dusty ear raised. His collar hung loosely around his neck. A heart-shaped name tag dangled from it.

She bent down to read it. Pal. At some point, someone had cared about this dog. "Hey, Pal. I brought you some food." She forced a smile. Better to stay alert than to give in to emotion. Keeping a wary eye on the house, she knelt down near a spot where the ground dipped and slid the open pouch of dog food under the fence. "I wish I could have mixed you up some of my special recipe, but it was short notice."

Her dogs always smelled their food before they ate it, but Pal gulped this down, barely chewing.

While he ate, Elyse considered the house. One faded green shutter was missing. The other hung askew into a window box full of dead, brown flowers, giving the impression of a distorted wink. Was someone watching her now? She squinted at the windows. The blinds were down. And even though the back screen door gaped open, a wooden door behind it appeared to be solidly closed. Jagged glass framed a broken basement window. No movement anywhere.

Relief pushed air into her lungs, and she slowly exhaled. She hadn't realized she was holding her breath. She squeezed two fingers through the nearest diamond-shaped opening in the chain link and scratched the dog's head. "I'm going to call someone and get you help," she whispered.

He cowered away from her.

"Don't be afraid. We'll get you out of here."

His tail wagged as if he understood. He stepped closer to her again, allowing her to scratch his head. Then he moved a few feet away and watched her.

Empathy welled up inside her. He wanted to trust her, but he wasn't sure if he could. She remembered that day sixteen years ago when Jonathan and Lynda McCord had reached out to her. She'd been afraid to believe that they would really love her. "It's hard to let go of the fear, isn't it, Pal?"

He smiled at her. She'd taken a lot of teasing in her life for thinking dogs could smile. But he did smile. And his smile hooked her.

"I'm going to get help," she said softly. "Right now." She pulled her cell phone from her pocket and slid it open.

Without warning, the dog barked, took a step back, and bared his teeth. The dirty hair along his spine stood up like a porcupine's quills. A low growl sent shivers up Elyse's own spine, and she froze.

"What's wro—" A hard tug on her hair yanked her to her feet. "Oww!" Pain raced along her scalp. She twisted around to face her attacker and stared down the barrel of a pistol.

At the sight of the gun, her legs collapsed, but the grizzled man held her up by her hair with one meaty fist. He kept the snub-nosed pistol pointed at her with the other and gave her a shake as if she were a dog toy. "You snoopin' around here, tryin' to butter the dog up so he won't growl when you break in later?"

She shook her head. The bright sunlight seemed to fade.

"He. . .he. . .he was hungry." The gun in her face was too much to bear. She almost wished she'd just pass out. But even as uncontrollable shaking worked its way through her body, her vision came back into focus. No escape.

The man's eyes, beady and mean above a bulbous red nose, narrowed further. "You tryin' to tell me you're just a good S'maritan?"

She swallowed hard, still trembling all over. If she didn't answer him, he'd kill her. She knew it. "I just wanted"—she gulped again—"to give him some food and water."

He let out an obscenity of disbelief.

She gagged at the strong smell of alcohol on his breath. *Think*, she commanded herself. *Think. Don't give in to the fear.* She needed to calm down and assess the situation. Her attacker was obviously mentally unbalanced and drunk as well. Her only hope was to be rescued. Her phone, still clutched in her hand, caught her eye.

"Seriously." She winced at her fearful voice, but she continued, "You. . .probably didn't realize how hungry he was." She nodded toward Pal.

He glanced instinctively at the dog.

She worked her fingers slowly, trying not to call attention to her hand: 9-1—

He snatched the phone from her and threw it on the ground. She gasped as it broke into pieces. He shoved her hard against the fence. The sagging chain link molded around her like an upright metal blanket and dug into her sides. She couldn't hold back a groan. Behind her, Pal growled low in his throat.

"I heard what you said about gettin' help," the man snarled. "You're nothing but a liar." He waved the gun at her. "Now on your feet."

Elyse closed her eyes. *Please, Lord, help me.*

"On your feet." He grabbed her by the arm.

Pal gave three short excited barks then resumed growling, louder this time. "It's okay, boy," she murmured as she stumbled to a standing position. If she couldn't make the dog calm down, the man might snap completely and kill them both. "He needed food and water."

The man gave her another rough shove. "I've heard all that garbage I want to hear from my sister. 'Feed Pal, Zeke. Make sure he has water, Zeke.' "

His high-pitched mimic sent a fresh shiver up Elyse's spine. Pal jumped against the sagging fence, snarling at the man but unable to get to him.

"A bullet through his head is what he needs. And that's what he's gonna get."

She glanced back at Zeke just in time to see him turn the gun toward the dog. "No!" she roared and threw herself at him.

He grabbed her by the shirt collar and shoved the gun against her throat. Madness and rage glittered in his eyes, his foul alcohol-saturated breath hot on her face. "You're gonna pay for that." He yanked her hair and shoved her forward again, pushing her along the chain-link fence toward the privacy fence that spanned the sides of the backyard.

She'd almost forgotten what gut-wrenching fear felt like, but dizziness and nausea brought the memories rushing back. The last thing she saw as she stumbled around the corner next to the privacy fence, the gun jabbing in her back, was Pal, watching. At least she'd gotten Zeke and his gun away from the dog for now.

"I'm gonna teach you a lesson you won't ever forget," Zeke said, his voice slightly slurred.

"You're not teaching her anything," a deep voice drawled from behind the man. "Not today or any day."

Behind her, Elyse felt Zeke swing around to face the voice. She knew she should probably run for the road, but she spun around, too, just in time to see the newcomer kick the gun from Zeke's hand.

Zeke grabbed his hand and swore. "I oughta. . ."

The other man narrowed his eyes and shook his shaggy blond head. The instant she looked into his deep blue eyes, her panic subsided. She was safe. She silently thanked God for answering her prayer.

Her rescuer looked like a good-looking beach bum in his paint-splattered cutoff jeans and pocket T-shirt. But he stood like a martial arts expert, his hands as ready as a pair of deadly knives.

Zeke paused as if considering hand-to-hand combat. Then he fell to his knees, scrambling around for the gun.

With one muscled arm, the young Chuck Norris grabbed him by the back of his shirt and pulled him upright. He held the wiggling man easily and reached down to pick up the gun. The weapon looked comfortable in his hand.

For the first time since the young man's arrival, a tendril of unease curled up Elyse's spine. "Um, thanks. . ."

The man nodded. "You're welcome. I'm Andrew. I'd shake your hand, but I'm a little busy. What's your name?"

"Elyse." The unease evaporated as quickly as it had come, and she didn't even stammer.

"Elyse, why don't you tell me what's going on here?"

"I'll tell you what's goin' on," Zeke broke in, his face red and splotchy. "She's trespassin'. I ain't done nothin' wrong."

Andrew's presence gave Elyse courage to be angry again. "There's a dog starving to death here, and I came to feed and water it." She glared at Zeke. "Just for the record, I was outside of your fence when you grabbed me." And thanks to her eavesdropping this morning, she knew the woods belonged to the guy in the café.

"Besides," Andrew said, shoving Zeke toward the front yard, "last I heard, convicted felons couldn't own guns."

"How'd you—" Zeke started then snapped his lips together in a grimace.

Andrew shrugged. "Small town."

Elyse stared at him. Yes, Shady Grove was a small town. So why had she never seen either of these men until today?

Zeke slumped his shoulders.

Andrew pushed him around to the front of the house and up the wooden porch steps toward a straight-backed plastic chair. "Sit."

Zeke sat.

Elyse walked slowly up the steps to stand beside Andrew.

Andrew pulled out his cell phone and punched in 911. "This is Andrew Stone. I interrupted a possible kidnapping and assault with a deadly weapon at the corner of River Road and River Trail." He listened intently. "No. I've got him here." He held the gun steady, aimed at Zeke. "He's not going anywhere right now."

Zeke swore under his breath.

Andrew flipped the phone shut and glanced at Elyse. "You okay?"

Elyse nodded and considered her knight in paint-splattered denim. Was he a local? Someone she knew? His shirt and shorts weren't the only things dotted with paint. His unruly blond curls had a few flecks of white enamel in them, and his tanned face was lightly speckled, too. His starburst blue eyes returned her scrutiny with an amused expression. She looked away. He wasn't someone she was likely to have forgotten.

"That's my sister's gun," Zeke said. "I've never seen it before in my life until I found it when I saw this nosy. . ." His face twisted into a snarl.

"Watch what you say." The steel in Andrew's voice left no room for argument.

Zeke blew out his breath. "Anyway, I saw this girl messin' with our dog." He shifted his gaze back to Andrew and gave him a slightly off-kilter smile. "For real. This is my sister's house. That's why I said no when you came by asking about painting it. I'm just here taking care of her while she's sick."

Taking care of her? Like he took care of the dog? A sudden shard of terror pierced Elyse's heart. "Where's your sister?"

He shifted in the chair but didn't answer.

Andrew took a step toward him. "Answer her question, Zeke. Where's your sister now?"

Zeke tossed his head toward the house. "She's in bed. Not doin' too well. I was about to call an ambulance when I got distracted by Miss Nosy here."

Elyse took off for the front door.

"Wait." Andrew held the gun out to her. "Take this and watch him. I'll go in the house."

She stopped. "You think it's a trap?"

"You'll have to be wondering that for the rest of your life, girl," Zeke muttered, his earlier ingratiating manner gone in a flash. His eyes flamed with hate. "I'll get you for this if it's the last thing I do."

Elyse shivered.

Andrew shook his head and trained the gun back on the man.

"Don't listen to him, honey," he said softly. "Take the gun." He stepped back as if waiting for her to step in front of him and put her hand on the gun.

She stared at the weapon in his hand, memories making her legs go weak. "I can't."

"Yes, you can. All you have to do is shoot him if he moves." His voice was as hard as the gun metal.

Her breath closed off and she whimpered. "I. Can't." She hated her weakness, but she could feel her body start to shake.

"Whoa," Andrew said softly as if she were a frightened pup. He kept the gun aimed at Zeke and squeezed her shoulder with his free hand. "It's okay."

They stood without speaking for a few seconds.

Finally, Elyse found her voice. "I'll go check on his sister."

He nodded. "Holler if you need any help."

She started for the door.

"Wait!" Andrew's voice stopped her again. He kept his gaze and gun trained on Zeke as he stepped over to the door and pushed it open then waited. From behind him, Elyse could see a foyer, just like a million other foyers, a mirror on the wall and a small bench beneath it. She saw Andrew's shoulders relax, and he stepped back to allow her to enter.

"Thanks." In the foyer, she stopped and wrinkled her nose. The house smelled of mildew and ruined food. "Hello?" Her voice sounded unnaturally loud. The only answer was the faint hum of the refrigerator.

Her heart slammed against her ribs, but she squared her shoulders and started down the hall. If the painter out on the porch could kick a gun out of a man's hand and not even break a sweat, she could surely check on a sick woman without fainting.

Andrew Stone stared into the beady eyes of the man he'd been staking out for the past two weeks. He'd painted every house within a mile radius dirt cheap just to be able to keep an eye on this guy without arousing suspicion. Lie low and watch. That had been the plan. But all it had taken was a beautiful brunette on the wrong side of a gun to change his plan.

Keeping the gun steady, he pulled the gold and amethyst necklace from his pocket and inspected it one more time before holding it up in the sunlight. It looked exactly like the one Melanie had worn all the time. If he knew for sure it was the same necklace, he wouldn't be able to trust himself with a gun on this guy. "Where'd you get this?"

Zeke's eyes widened, but he quickly looked down. "Never saw it before in my life."

Red hot anger bubbled at the edges of Andrew's consciousness, but he ignored it and subtly pushed the gun a little closer. "That's not what the guy at the pawn shop said. He got a real good picture of you on his security camera when you came in to pawn it."

Zeke grunted. "Why do you care? Who are you anyway?"

Andrew stepped closer, his anger and frustration spilling over. "Your worst enemy if you don't tell me where you got the necklace," he growled through gritted teeth.

Beads of sweat glistened on Zeke's round face as sirens sounded in the distance. "It was my mother's. My only inheritance."

"Yeah, right."

"Andrew!" Elyse's voice was shrill with panic. "Help me!"

CHAPTER 2

Hurry!" Elyse screamed.

"Coming!" he yelled then stared at Zeke. "Stay put. The cops will be here in just a second. It'll go worse for you if you run."

The sirens grew steadily louder. But Elyse could be in danger. He'd found Zeke once; he could find him again if he had to. He had no choice but to tuck the gun in his waistband and run in the house. "Elyse, where are you?"

She stepped out of a door at the end of the hallway. "I don't think she's breathing!"

He sprinted down the hall and brushed past her into the small crowded bedroom. Furniture lined every wall, and a bed was centered under the only window. A woman with short salt-and-pepper hair lay on the bed, her face an alarming shade of blue.

Elyse looked up at him. "She was breathing when I came in, pretty raspy. But then she quit."

Andrew felt for a pulse, and his gaze met Elyse's frightened brown eyes. "It's thready but she's still alive." The woman's chest rose and fell slightly. The loud noise of sirens filled the house. "Just in time," he murmured. "Let's go see if they sent an ambulance."

She stood by the rumpled bed without moving, just staring at the sick woman.

He gently took her hand in his and tugged her out of the room. The shock of the last hour was taking its toll on her.

On the porch, he was thrilled to see an ambulance pulling in but not really surprised to see that Zeke was gone. Andrew quickly located the sheriff and gave him a rundown on the situation, leaving out the fact that he'd been staking Zeke out.

The EMTs rushed the house, and the deputies scattered out over the property, searching for Zeke.

Andrew kept Elyse close to his side. She seemed to be glad of his presence.

When the EMTs came out after about ten minutes with Zeke's sister on a stretcher, Elyse touched his forearm. "Do you think they'd tell us if she's going to be okay?"

Happy to hear her speak, Andrew nodded. He guided her toward the ambulance, and they waited until the uniformed workers loaded the sick woman into the back and shut the door.

"How is she?" Andrew asked.

The man shrugged. "Too soon to tell. Maxine's tough. Good thing you two found her when you did though. I don't think she'd have made it much longer."

They stood and watched as the ambulance sped away, lights flashing and siren screaming.

Sheriff Jack Westwood walked over to them. "Elyse, what are you doing here?"

She kept her gaze on the ground. "I overheard some guys at the diner talking about a mistreated dog."

Jack slapped his forehead with his palm. "I should have known there was a dog involved."

Elyse didn't answer.

"You okay?" Jack asked gently.

She nodded but didn't speak.

"She's had a rough time. Zeke shoved her around and threatened her with a gun." Andrew slipped the gun from his waistband, and Elyse shuddered. "This gun, actually."

Jack pulled a large Ziploc bag from his pocket and held it out for Andrew to put the gun in. "I'll need you to come by the station next time you're in town and be fingerprinted so we can separate yours from anyone else's."

Andrew dropped the gun in the bag. "Sure."

Jack shook his hand. "Thanks for being here. Elyse is really important to a lot of people."

Andrew was glad the sheriff didn't question him closer about why he was there. He'd long ago crossed the line from "investigating" into "obsession" as far as most lawmen were concerned. Jack Westwood seemed like a nice enough man, but Andrew would rather keep the local officials out of it. "It was nothing."

Elyse seemed to snap out of it a little. She looked at Andrew, her olive complexion still ashen. "You saved my life."

He ducked his head. "I just did what anyone else would have done."

"I doubt that," she said. "Most people I know can't kick a gun out of someone's hand."

Jack looked from Andrew to Elyse then back to Andrew. "You kicked the gun out of his hand?"

Andrew shrugged. "Adrenaline."

"And years of karate lessons, I'm guessing," Elyse said softly.

"Well, that, too." A sheepish grin played across Andrew's mouth. Even in shock, she was sharp.

She looked up at the sheriff. "Can we go check on Pal?"

Jack shook his head. "Not as long as Zeke's out there. But as soon as we catch him, you can take the dog home with you. I know Maxine will be glad for you to take care of him while she's in the hospital."

Andrew shook his head. "I'm sorry about letting Zeke get away. Hopefully he won't get far."

"On foot?" Jack snorted. "Not likely."

A deputy ran up to them, his radio in his hand. "Sheriff, we've got a problem."

"What's that?"

"Dispatch has had three calls from people on River Road about some guy driving like a maniac."

Andrew slapped his hand to his forehead, and his gaze met Jack's. "He stole a car," they said simultaneously.

"A blue Jeep Wrangler to be specific," the deputy said.

"Put out an APB on the man and the vehicle," Jack barked.

Elyse swayed on her feet.

Andrew grabbed her forearms to keep her from falling down. "Whoa there. You okay?"

She shook her head and let him lead her the short distance to the porch and sit her down on the wooden plank step.

Guilt rushed him. Maybe he'd made the wrong decision running into the house when she'd screamed. Now thanks to him, she had to worry that her attacker was on the loose. "It'll be all right. They'll find him."

Jack cleared his throat. "Elyse?"

She looked up at him, her brown eyes huge.

"Did you drive here today?" the sheriff continued.

She nodded, looking so nauseous that Andrew wanted to put

his arm around her and hold a cool cloth to her forehead.

"Where'd you park?"

"River Road. At the edge of the woods," she mumbled.

"Keys in it?" Jack asked.

Her shiny brown curls bobbed up and down, and realization hit Andrew like a pouncing ninja. "You have a blue Jeep." Andrew didn't even bother phrasing it as a question.

"Brand-new," she muttered. Suddenly she looked up at him and Jack, her eyes panic-stricken. "My insurance—will it pay since I left the keys in it?"

Jack cleared his throat, hesitation in his eyes. "Let's cross that bridge when we come to it. Right now, we need to get you home."

"I'll handle that," Andrew said then glanced at Elyse. "If that's okay."

Doubt clouded her face.

"The sheriff needs to go see what he can do about finding Zeke and your Jeep," he added.

She nodded.

"I just live about a quarter of a mile away. We'll go get my truck, come back, and pick up the dog, and I'll run you home. Okay?"

"Okay."

"Thanks, Andrew." Jack cast a concerned glance at Elyse. "I'll send a deputy back to stake out the house in case Zeke comes back. Not that I'm expecting—" He broke off as a white van pulled into the driveway. CHANNEL SIX NEWS was emblazoned in huge black letters on the side. Jack frowned. "How did she find out about this so quickly?"

The van doors opened and a dark-haired woman in a suit climbed out, followed by a man with a video camera.

"Blair, what are you doing here?" Jack growled.

Elyse scooted over on the porch as if trying to hide behind Andrew.

"We were across the road at the River Fest when we heard the sirens. Wasn't that lucky?" She walked over to the porch. "I got the basic facts of what happened on the police scanner on the way over. I can fill that in at the station. Let's just get to the interviews."

Andrew heard Elyse gasp softly. Her face had lost even the slightest bit of remaining color.

"You're Elyse McCord, aren't you?" Blair asked curtly.

And just as quickly as it had paled, Elyse's face flamed. She nodded.

"We'll start with you."

"Now wait a minute," Jack said, but Blair held up her hand and motioned to the cameraman to start recording.

"I'm here at the scene of the crime with local legend Elyse McCord. Many people in the Channel Six viewing area have heard of this mysterious woman who some call our very own dog whisperer. Elyse, why don't you tell us what you were doing here today?" She stuck the microphone in Elyse's face.

Elyse pushed the microphone away and shook her head, panic as evident in her eyes as it had been when Zeke was shoving his gun in her face.

Andrew stepped in front of her. "She was here trying to feed a dog she'd heard was starving."

Blair's eyes lit on him like a dog's gaze on a juicy steak. She turned the microphone on him. "And who are you?"

"I'm just a house painter who happened to be in the area."

"And what did you see?"

Andrew looked at the sheriff, who gave him a curt nod and motioned toward the reporter. "Blair, if you have any more questions, ask me. You're done harassing innocent citizens today."

She made a cut motion to the cameraman and narrowed her eyes. "Sheriff, I know you aren't trying to stand in the way of freedom of the press."

He shook his head, looking way more relaxed than Andrew guessed he felt. "Nope. Just volunteering for an interview."

"Very well, we'll come back to you two," she said to Elyse and Andrew.

As soon as the cameraman started rolling, Andrew slipped his hand under Elyse's arm and helped her to her feet. She was trembling. "Let's go," he whispered.

Her brown eyes widened. "Really?"

He tugged her down the porch steps and over past the property line away from the news crew. "Hurry before they see us." At the road, he released her arm. "Are you okay to walk?"

"I think so. Sorry about earlier." Her color had evened out, and she seemed to be breathing better.

"No problem. Lots of people have stage fright."

"I have it whether there's a stage or not," Elyse mumbled as she hurried down the road, her brown curls blocking her face from his view.

"Porch fright then."

"How did you happen to be in the right place at the right time?"

His brain whirred with possible answers. Finally, he settled on the truth. With all the extra details pared away. "I'm painting a house right down the road. Sometimes I take a shortcut through the woods on the way home." He frowned. "Almost didn't today."

They walked in silence for a minute. When she spoke, her voice was so quiet he had to strain to hear her. "I'm thankful you did."

CHAPTER 3

Y ou always loved dogs?" Andrew's blue eyes bore into Elyse's.

She ducked her head. "As long as I can remember. . .especially after. . ."

"After?"

She shrugged, angry at herself for giving so much away so quickly. "After I got old enough to take care of them."

He accepted her evasion as if it were nothing and glanced down at the gravel road they were walking on.

Even though he'd saved her life and rescued her from making a fool of herself on television, she felt odd going home with a man she'd just met today. "Is your house much further?"

He shook his head.

"So do you have a dog?"

A grin tipped his lips. "'Fraid not. Sorry to disappoint." Something unreadable flashed through his eyes. "Not anymore."

"What kind was it?"

"Collie."

Sympathy came easily to her. The man had obviously lost a dog that meant a great deal to him. She used her hair to shield her face and cut a glance at him. Or had he just known that would be the quickest way to get her to trust him?

"You only trust people with dogs?"

She drew in a soundless breath. There was more than a grain of truth to his observation. "Zeke had a dog," she evaded. "Didn't make him trustworthy."

"Wasn't his dog, either."

They rounded the curve, and River Road Campground entrance lay directly to the right.

To her surprise, Andrew guided her into the gates. "I need to run in and get the keys. You want a bottle of water?"

"You live in a campground?" she blurted out.

"Something wrong with that?" He walked ahead of her, leading the way to a small camper near the river.

She wouldn't have thought she was capable of smiling, but the sight of the satellite dish on the roof of the tiny camper tilted her lips upward. "Nothing at all wrong with it. Looks like you've got all the comforts of home."

He followed her gaze and nodded. "And none of the hassles."

She stared at his back. What was his story? "There's more to home than just the hassles."

He fished a lone key from his pocket and glanced over his shoulder at her. "Really? Nice to know there are people who still believe that." He turned back to slide the key in. "Not that I'd expect any less from someone who would risk her life to save a dog. Why did you do that, anyway?"

"He was starving. How could I have just ignored that?"

He waved his free hand as he turned the key in the lock. "I mean, why didn't you just report it to the authorities?"

"Oh." Now it was her turn to feel sheepish. "I thought it

would take too long."

He held the door open for her, and she stepped inside. Cool air hit her in the face. He motioned to a small plaid couch that ran the width of the camper.

She sank down gratefully. A small painting on the wall by the couch caught her eye. It was a bird's-eye view of a man breaking a horse. The way the artist had perfectly captured both the humor and the humanness in the scene reminded her of Norman Rockwell, but at the same time the style was unique. She looked around. The whole camper was sort of like that, unique and cozy.

Without asking, Andrew pulled a bottle of water out of the small fridge and tossed it to her. "So you make a habit of this? Rescuing mistreated dogs?"

"No! Not usually." A slight grin teased at her lips as she thought of her menagerie at home. "Most of the time people just bring them to me." She looked up to see Andrew regarding her strangely.

"How many dogs do you have?" he asked.

"Three right now."

"So you find them good homes instead of keeping them?" She nodded.

"You have a cape and an alter ego? Wonder Woman, maybe?"

She laughed. "Nothing could be further from the truth. I'm just a simple dog groomer who does some training on the side." As she said it, she knew it wasn't the whole truth. In her heart— and according to the certificates that hung on her wall—she was a dog trainer. The grooming business came because she didn't have to deal with people as much when she just groomed their dogs. But that wasn't something to tell a stranger. Even one who made her feel so relaxed.

"And risks your life performing rescue missions in your spare time."

In spite of the frigid air blasting over her, her face grew hot again. "This was the first time I rushed in unprepared."

"Your secret's safe with me." A crooked smile broke across his tanned face. "At least until today's adventures hit the Channel Six news."

"I don't even want to think about that. New subject. What about you?" she asked. "That was pretty impressive back there. Are you some kind of Walker, Texas Ranger?"

His smile died as abruptly as it had come. "Nothing could be further from the truth." He parroted her earlier words back with no inflection. "I'm just a simple house painter."

"Who rescues damsels in distress on the side."

He turned back to the refrigerator and retrieved another bottle of water. "Only when I can't get out of it."

His words had a ring of truth to them.

※

"So where's your TV?"

He jerked his attention back to the brunette on his couch. "I don't have one."

Her arched brows drew together. "What about the satellite dish?"

He shrugged. "Computer."

She wanted to question him—he could see it all over her face. But her mama had apparently raised her not to be nosy.

She took a long drink of her water and set the bottle on the small side table. "You know, I can call someone to come help me get Pal. You've done enough. First rescuing me from Zeke, then from Blair."

He cleared his throat. "A princess is never really rescued until she's back home in her castle."

She pushed her thick brown curls back and raised one arched eyebrow. "Did you learn that from fairy tales?"

"Video games," he said dryly.

Laughter erased the tension from her face. "Never let it be said that Elyse McCord stood in the way of getting to the next level of the game. Do you get extra points if you rescue the princess and the dog?"

"No doubt." He snatched his truck keys from a hook by the door and led the way out of the small camper before she changed her mind. He opened the passenger door of his bright red four-door truck and waited until Elyse was seated before heading around to the driver's side.

"Do you think she's gone?" Elyse's voice as she spoke from the passenger's seat was small.

He gripped the steering wheel and glanced across at her. "I think you're more worried about the press still being there than you are the possibility of Zeke coming back."

She leaned forward in her seat. "Drive slowly by to make sure the van's gone." She looked over at him. "If you don't mind."

He nodded and did what she asked. "Looks like the coast is clear." He backed up and eased into the now empty driveway.

Elyse unbuckled her seat belt and slipped from the vehicle just as he came to a complete stop. She was wasting no time getting to the dog.

Andrew sprinted along behind her and caught up when she

had trouble opening the wooden gate. He lifted the latch easily and stepped into the dusty backyard.

The yellow dog shuffled to its feet, and Andrew winced at how skinny it was. He took a step forward, and the dog growled low in its throat.

A touch on his shoulder stopped him. "Let me go first, if you don't mind."

He glanced back at her, keeping a cautious eye on the dog. Her gentle tone belied the note of authority in it. He stepped back, and she slid past him.

She walked slowly toward the dog. "Hey, Pal." Her voice was like a soft breeze. "I told you I'd come back." She squatted and held out her hand. "C'mere, Pal."

The dog ambled over to her, his tail wagging.

"Good boy." She retrieved something from her pocket and let him eat it from her hand.

Andrew grinned. "You keep treats in your jeans pocket?"

She tilted her head without breaking eye contact with the dog. He could see the corner of her mouth tilt up. "Doesn't everyone?" She pushed to her feet and patted Pal's head. "Let's go meet Andrew."

Andrew took a step forward, but she put her hand up.

"Let him come to you, if you don't mind."

"'If you don't mind?' Is that your way of covering up the fact that you're telling me what to do?" He grinned.

Her eyes widened and she opened her mouth then shut it again. She chuckled. "Maybe. But it really would be the best thing if you would wait and let him come to you."

He squatted down and held out his hand.

Pal took a couple steps toward him.

"Will he bite me when he finds out I don't have a treat?" he whispered.

"I've got your back." She patted her pocket.

He turned to the dog. "Wanna go for a ride?"

Pal bounded toward him, his skinny body wagging all over.

Andrew jumped to his feet and threw up his hand, just in time to keep from being knocked over. "I'll take that as a yes."

"Down," Elyse said, that note of authority back in her voice.

Pal stopped leaping and sat, his tail thumping against the dusty ground.

"I think he wants to G-O," Andrew whispered. "Should I carry him?"

"Why don't we check in the house and see if there's a leash? I think he's up to a short walk, aren't you, boy?"

Pal pressed his head against her hand in a nodding motion. Andrew did a double take. For a second, it looked as if the dog was directly responding to what she'd said.

"Long day," he muttered then suddenly realized she'd handed him a golden opportunity. "I'll get a leash."

She nodded, already engrossed in the dog.

His heart pounded as he walked around and up the porch steps. Did he dare do a quick search for Melanie's jewelry? If he found it, he'd know that Zeke was his man. His search would have a real purpose again.

His footsteps sounded loud in the foyer, and he hurried through the living room to the first door in the hallway. He yanked it open. Steps led down to a dark basement. He flipped on the light by the door. Everything had a fine covering of dust. Definitely not lived in. He turned off the light and shut the door then walked on down the hallway. The next door was open. A small bathroom with floral wallpaper. And Maxine's room was at the end. That left only one door. Closed tightly. He felt positive that this was Zeke's room. He put his hand on the doorknob and twisted it slowly.

"Hey, I found a leash." Elyse's voice in the living room flooded him with guilt.

He dropped his grip on the knob. The question in her brown eyes could have been his imagination, but he quickly shifted his gaze to Pal, still emaciated but looking happy to have the leash on.

"Oh good." His gaze fell on something in her right hand. "What's that?"

She opened her hand to reveal three pieces of an electronic device. "My cell phone. Zeke threw it on the ground earlier. The good news is that it looks like the battery just came out." She shoved the pieces into her pocket. "I may not have a car, but at least I won't be completely cut off from the world."

"Got to keep our priorities straight," he said, grateful she hadn't questioned him about the room he'd been about to go into.

They walked outside toward the truck. "You need to call your vet?"

"Great idea." She pulled her phone out of her pocket and popped the battery back in then carefully slid the back plate on. As soon as the phone powered up, she hit one button and mashed it to her ear.

He opened the truck door for her. "You have your vet on speed dial?" He remembered the dog treats in her pocket and grinned. "Oh wait. Let me guess. Doesn't everyone?"

She helped Pal in and turned back to him with twinkling eyes. "Thanks," she mouthed.

He walked around the truck and climbed in just in time to hear her say, "Matt?"

The male voice on the other end resonated through the cab, every word plain. "Elyse! Where are you?"

Andrew frowned. This vet took it a little too far looking out for his patients' owners.

"I'm sorry," Elyse said softly. "I didn't realize the news would travel so fast. I'm on my way home to tell you in person."

On her way home to tell him in person? She was married to a vet? That would explain so many things. Yet. . . Andrew looked across at her. She hadn't given off a married vibe. His gaze fell to her hand. No ring. He started the truck motor, the muscle in his jaw jumping. What difference did it make to him?

The man's voice on the other end of the phone had muted, but Elyse glanced at Andrew. "Jack was right. I'm with him now. We just got the dog in the truck, and we're heading there." She paused. "No, you don't need to come. See you in a few minutes."

She flipped her phone shut and turned to Andrew. "Apparently everybody and their brother heard on their scanners about the incident with Zeke and a blue Jeep Wrangler being stolen. All it took was a phone call to Jack to confirm it was me and that I was with you."

Andrew nodded. If she was his wife, he'd be looking frantically for her, too.

"I can't believe I didn't call home first thing," Elyse murmured. She gave him directions to her place. "You might want to let me out at the end of the lane."

Uh-oh. Was he about to have to deal with a gun-wielding maniac and a jealous husband in the same day? "If that's what you want. I don't want to make things hard for you."

She smiled. "It's not me I'm worried about."

"I can take care of myself." He turned down the road she directed.

"Your martial arts won't help you in this situation. I'm just trying to warn you there might be a lot of people there."

"So it's not that your husband will mind me bringing you home?" In spite of what she'd said, he didn't want to make her already difficult day worse.

She jerked her head around to stare at him. "My what?"

CHAPTER 4

He kept his eyes on the road. "Your—Matthew. The vet?" What had he told himself a million times about jumping to conclusions?

She put her hand to her mouth but not before he saw the smile. "I'm sorry if you misunderstood. Matthew—the vet—is my brother. One of four. And unless I miss my guess, at least two of them will be at the house. And so will one of my sisters and her fiancé. And Mama and Daddy and the ranch hands and no telling how many neighbors. But no husband."

"Okay then." His face burned. How long had it been since he was embarrassed? He hadn't even known it could still happen.

"My lane is the next one on the left, but we might as well go on to the main entrance. Everybody is waiting at Mama and Daddy's house."

He glanced down the little lane as they passed and could see a small house with a fenced-in yard and a couple of weeping willows. "So you don't live with your parents?" Was it his fault that she was so confusing?

She shook her head. "I have my own place next door. Still on the ranch but all mine."

"Cool." He pulled into the wooden gates and drove down the long driveway.

The front door to the sprawling ranch house flew open, and people began streaming out.

Elyse handed Pal's leash to Andrew. "Will you hold him here for a minute? I don't want him to be overwhelmed."

"Sure." He took the leash, grateful for an excuse to get his bearings before he met her family.

Elyse climbed down and ran around the truck.

An older, sandy-haired man scooped her into a big hug and held her tightly then passed her to a pretty petite woman about the same age.

After everyone gathered had hugged her and she'd talked to them for a minute, she came back over to his truck window. "Why don't you leave Pal in here while you meet everyone?"

He stepped out of the truck, and Pal moved over to the driver's seat.

The older man stepped forward and stuck out his hand. "I'm Jonathan McCord, and this is my wife, Lynda."

Andrew nodded at the blond woman and returned Jonathan's handshake. "Andrew Stone."

Jonathan smiled. "My daughter tells me you're quite the hero."

Elyse cleared her throat and quickly introduced him to her sister, Crystal, and Crystal's fiancé, Jeremy. Crystal smiled at him. "We're so thankful you were there this morning."

The tall, dark-haired man behind Elyse spoke up. "Wish I'd been there."

Elyse turned around. "I should have called you, Luke. I'm sorry."

"I'm just saying. . ."

"You would have gone with me, I know." She turned back to Andrew. "This is my brother, Luke, who is going to be hurt for the rest of his life that I didn't call him before pulling such a 'stupid stunt.' "

Luke shook Andrew's hand then touched his knuckles to his sister's shoulder. "Sorry. We were just worried about you."

"Besides, Luke never likes to be left out of stupid stunts," the brown-haired man said and stuck out his hand. "I'm Matthew."

Elyse's smile grew broader, and her eyes twinkled as she looked at Andrew. "Yes, my *brother* Matthew who is just waiting for the results of his exams to hang out his veterinarian shingle."

"Nice to meet you, man." Andrew clasped Matthew's hand, not caring that Elyse was needling him. Anybody would have been glad to avoid a run-in with a jealous husband.

Matthew looked a little confused. "You, too. So, sis, let's go check on your newest project."

As they walked toward the truck, Andrew heard her say, "His name is Pal. . . ."

He looked to her family. "It was nice meeting all of you."

"Thanks again, man." Luke turned to his dad. "I'm going to run down to the bunkhouse and tell Slim and the guys that everything's okay."

"We'd better get going if we're going to keep our appointment with Mama Ruth," Crystal said.

"It's not too bad if you're late to the wedding planner's, as long as you're not late for the wedding," Lynda said and hugged her daughter. "Love you," she murmured.

Andrew's heart clenched as Crystal turned to tell her dad good-bye. Elyse probably had no idea how blessed she was to have been born into a family who hugged and spoke of love so easily. Maybe things would have been different at his house if his father had remarried after his mother died instead of pinning all his hopes and dreams on Andrew. That had proved to be a bigger burden than a seven-year-old could bear.

His mouth twisted into a grimace. Who was he kidding? Even at twenty-seven, he couldn't be what his dad wanted him to be. But he'd learned to live with it. Sort of.

"We'd love to have you." Andrew jerked his attention back to the present. Crystal and Jeremy were getting into their truck, and Lynda McCord was looking expectantly at him.

"I'm sorry. What did you say?" For the second time that day, his cheeks burned.

Lynda smiled. "I invited you to come to lunch after church tomorrow. As far as that goes, we'd love for you to attend worship with us."

He nodded. "Thanks. I appreciate both invitations, but I'm not sure if I can make it."

She waved a breezy hand in a way that reminded him of Elyse. "You don't have to let us know."

Jonathan shook his head. "No, there's always room for one more at our table. Especially considering what you did today."

Lynda's clear blue eyes flooded with tears. "Don't get me started." She looked toward where Elyse and Matthew had gotten Pal out of the truck and were examining him. Then she met Andrew's gaze. "When I think of her being in that kind of danger. . ." She shook her head. "I'm sorry. I'm just a mess today. I think I'll go in and find a good book to read. Keep my mind off what might have happened if you hadn't shown up."

When she was gone, Jonathan McCord kicked at the dry

grass with his boot toe then looked up at the cloudy sky. "Might get that rain we've been needing."

Andrew nodded. "Weatherman said there's a 50 percent chance."

"Jack says you're from Texas."

"Born and raised," Andrew said.

"You just passin' through?"

Andrew felt like a young man standing on a front porch on Saturday night being grilled by a protective dad. "I'll be around for a while." Until he found Zeke again and got some answers. Or another lead turned up. "But eventually, yeah. . .I'll be leaving."

Jonathan nodded and considered the road for a moment, then looked back at Andrew. "Thanks again for protecting Elyse."

"I just did what anyone would have."

Jonathan smiled. "I wish we lived in a world where that was true."

Andrew shook the man's hand one more time and walked to his truck.

"Andrew, wait." He heard Elyse's voice behind him.

He stopped until she caught up with him. "So what does your vet think?" He smiled. "Pal going to be okay?"

She ran her hand through her tangled curls and nodded. "It'll take awhile, but I think we rescued him just in time."

"I'm glad."

"Me, too. Thanks again for being there."

"Anytime." He climbed into the driver's seat.

She gave him a little wave and walked back over to the dog.

He put the truck into reverse. A flash of irritation at his reluctance to leave made him accelerate quickly on his way out. It was nothing personal, he reminded himself. But until they found

Elyse's Jeep, she was his main link to Zeke. With that in mind, it only made sense that he keep an eye on her for a while.

❧

Elyse held Pal's head up and scrubbed under his neck. She glanced at her sister. "I guess this is a far cry from Broadway."

Crystal smiled. "I'm not complaining."

"Thanks for helping me bathe him. I know I groom dogs by myself all the time, but Pal and I are both still a little jittery."

"Who could blame you?" Crystal sprayed the water carefully on the dog's chest and shoved her shoulder-length blond hair away from her face with her other hand. "It's nice to be able to take care of something." She frowned. "Even if it is a terribly scrawny dog. I don't want to think about what would have happened if you hadn't found him today. Or what would have happened to that poor woman, for that matter."

"Or what would have happened to me if Andrew hadn't found me." Elyse hated the quaver in her voice.

Crystal stopped the water and stared at her across the trembling dog's head. "How does it feel to have a real-life hero of your very own?"

Elyse blushed and bent down to soap Pal's stomach. "He's not my very own hero. I can't believe Mama invited him to lunch tomorrow."

Crystal didn't move. "Well, he did save your life."

Elyse raised up and arched an eyebrow. "Can I get some water here?"

She heard something that sounded suspiciously like a snicker. "I get it. Work, not talk."

Elyse shrugged. "I don't mind talking. Just not about Andrew."

Crystal squeezed the trigger on the sprayer. "In honor of how relieved I am that you're okay today, I'll let you choose the conversation topic."

"What's going on with you and Jeremy?"

Elyse barely saw the surprise on Crystal's face before her sister's acting skills kicked in. "We're planning a wedding. What do you mean?"

Elyse considered repaying the favor and dropping the subject Crystal was obviously playing dumb about. But she had a feeling her sister needed to talk. "Y'all have been deliriously happy ever since you left Broadway and came home. But the last few days. . . I can tell something's different."

"Expecting deliriously happy to last forever is unrealistic."

Elyse stepped back and considered her sister's suddenly drawn face. Maybe so. But it wasn't too much to expect it to last until the wedding at least, right?

Crystal laid the sprayer down and ran her hand down Pal's wet back. "Okay, I know what you're thinking." She sighed. "And you're right. Jeremy and I just have some things we need to work out."

Elyse grabbed a towel and wrapped it gently around the dog. "It's okay, sweetie," she murmured. She looked at her sister. "I'm here if you want to talk."

Crystal's smile was only a little strained. "And we have your hero to thank for that."

"If you don't quit saying that, you're going to need a hero to save you," Elyse growled, mostly kidding. She lifted Pal out of the tub and wrapped him in a towel, anger welling up in her again that he was so lightweight.

An hour later, when they were settled in the living room with the dogs around them, she looked up to find Crystal staring at her. "What?"

"I have one question I just have to ask."

"Shoot."

"It's about Andrew."

Elyse sighed. "Go ahead."

"Were you actually *teasing* with him? I couldn't tell what it was about, but when you were introducing Matthew, your voice sounded like you were about to laugh, and it looked like you winked at Andrew." The incredulous tone in her sister's voice would have been amusing if it wasn't for her own disbelief at her reaction to this stranger.

"I didn't wink at him," she protested quickly. "But I was playing around with him. That's why I hope he doesn't come to lunch tomorrow. It's too dangerous for me to be around him."

"You don't feel safe with him?"

Elyse looked into Crystal's worried eyes and shrugged. "I know it sounds crazy, but I feel *too* safe with him."

"What does that mean?"

"You know how I'm all tongue-tied and flustered around people outside the family. But it's not like that with him. He's easy to talk to."

"And that's a bad thing? I remember when we were teenagers you said that if you ever met a man you felt comfortable around immediately, you were going to. . ." Crystal put her hand to her mouth. "Oh! I get it. Oh."

Elyse didn't answer. She remembered, too, her silly adolescent vow to marry the first man she could talk to easily. All these years, there'd never been any danger. And there still wasn't, really. Just because the drifter didn't make her a nervous wreck didn't mean she was attracted to him. Maybe she was just finally getting over her shyness some and hadn't noticed it.

But if he came to lunch tomorrow, the whole family would realize immediately that she wasn't reacting normally. She loved her family, but the last thing she needed was for them to make more of this than it was.

"So are you going out with Jeremy tonight? Or are you and he and Beka going to stay home and watch *Sleeping Beauty*?"

Crystal's face clouded. "I'm not sure what we're doing, to be honest."

"Crys, I'm sorry. Is there anything I can do?"

Crystal shoved to her feet. "Pray for us. I really don't know what's going on. It just feels like he's shutting me out suddenly."

Elyse shook her head and stood, gently moving Pal's head from her lap. The other three dogs had let the newcomer have the place of honor tonight. Elyse would show her appreciation with extra attention for them when Crystal left. "Y'all have been through so much. I thought after Beka was found and you moved back here, everything would be perfect."

"God doesn't promise us perfect." Crystal's rich voice trembled slightly. "You and I both know that."

"I'll be praying for you." Elyse hugged her. "I'm so glad you're my sister."

"Same here."

When Crystal was safely in her car, Elyse locked the door behind her then whistled softly. Three dogs. . .no, four dogs. . . came running down the hallway to her. "Want to go outside?"

They hurried to the back door, and she let them outside into the fenced-in yard while she got a bottle of water out of the kitchen. She left the door cracked a little, and when Missy, the black lab, pushed it open with her nose and bounded in, Elyse jumped. The other three followed behind her. "Good girl, Missy. Ready for bed?"

Her three turned as one and went to her bedroom, leaving poor Pal behind looking at Elyse.

She knelt down and hugged him. "There's a place for you, too." Standing, she clicked her tongue. "C'mon, let's go."

He followed her down the hall and into the room. The other three dogs were bedded down on their individual rugs.

Elyse took a couch throw and laid it on the floor not too far from Majesty. The golden retriever was a natural caretaker, and she'd look out for the new kid on the block.

Pal smelled the blanket then curled up on it.

Elyse turned off the light then turned it back on. For some reason, tonight she didn't want to be in the dark. She slid from the bed and turned her bathroom light on and closed the door. Then she switched her bedroom light off. That was better. She snuggled under the cover. "Good night, guys."

It was hard for her to shut off her mind, but she finally settled down enough to say her prayers. Right before she fell asleep, she thought of Andrew and his daring rescue of her today, just at her darkest hour. She wouldn't admit it to Crystal, but as far as she was concerned, he was the epitome of a hero.

❧

Back in her childhood room, Crystal McCord flopped onto her twin bed and pulled out her phone. Should she call him? How crazy was it that she'd be uncertain about contacting him first? Especially considering they'd spent the afternoon with a wedding planner.

The wedding was in three months, and today they were supposed to choose and order invitations. Instead, for every one that she or Mama Ruth suggested, Jeremy gave some inane reason why that particular one wouldn't work. Then he refused to point out an invitation that would suit him. By the end of the time, Crystal's face was hot from the constant embarrassment. On the way home, she'd confronted Jeremy, questioning him as gently as she could about whether he still wanted to marry her. And he'd clammed up.

She played with the fringe on a throw pillow. Okay, that wasn't exactly true. He'd said yes, of course he did. And yes, he definitely still loved her. But then he'd refused to give any reason for his crazy behavior. She hugged the pillow to her. So now what? Would he call her? Should she call him?

She pulled up a blank text message and typed in "Hey."

In less than a minute, the reply came back. "Hey."

She put her pounding heart on the line and let her fingers do the walking. "Do you want to do something tonight?"

Then she waited. And waited. Finally, the light flashed. She pulled up his reply, feeling sixteen again.

"I think Beka and I might just stay in tonight if that's okay."

She hugged the throw pillow to her stomach and blinked against tears. What was happening? One thing she'd always loved about Jeremy was how easy he was to talk to. She'd wracked her brains but couldn't think of anything she'd done to offend him. Yet for the last few days, he'd hardly spoken to her. And Friday when she'd offered to come get Beka and keep her a few hours, he'd made an excuse. It was almost as if he was slowly easing away from Crystal and taking his precious little girl with him.

Before she could stop herself, she fired back a text. "Okay.

See you at church then."

In a few seconds, she punched in another message. "I'm going to eat lunch here tomorrow since all the fam will be here." Why should she go to his folks if he wasn't even going to talk to her?

Again, at least a full minute passed before the answer came back. "Sounds like a plan. Good night."

"Night." She slammed the phone shut and toyed with the idea of throwing it against the opposite wall. Her mama and daddy would probably come running, and then she'd have to explain. On second thought, she grabbed her old Bible off the nightstand and flipped it open to where she'd stopped reading this morning. She needed a reminder that there was One who was constant and never-changing.

CHAPTER 5

Elyse's breath caught in her throat, and she bolted upright in the bed.

Nikki, her small white bichon frise, gave a sharp yap.

Elyse blinked and looked around the dimly lit room at the dogs blinking sleepily back at her. It had been a bad dream. She'd seen Zeke again, holding the gun on her. And then she'd had the gun in her hand. That had been even worse.

She flexed her hand now, stretching away the feeling of that cold, heavy weight. In the dream, she'd been about to shoot Zeke. Just as her finger had tightened on the trigger, he'd changed into her daddy. She frowned. Or maybe it was someone else. It was fuzzy now, fading further into confusion with every second of wakefulness.

She put her palm to her chest. Her heart raced beneath her fingers. Just a bad dream. She used to have nightmares all the time after she was put into foster care and before the McCords adopted her. And she had a few after Cami died and Crystal went away. But she hadn't had one in a long time.

"It was a hard day," she murmured to the dogs, all still watching her in the dim light. "Want to get on the bed?" She had a king-sized bed for this very reason. Sometimes she just needed the comfort of having her family all together.

Missy, Nikki, and Majesty leapt onto the bed without hesitation, but the skinny yellow lab shoved to his feet and looked at her, as if unsure.

"C'mon, baby." Elyse patted the top of the covers. "You can get up here."

Finally, he climbed up slowly. She and the other dogs watched as he settled down right at the edge of the bed. Elyse lay back down and left her own dogs to find their places. Nikki nuzzled her hair then trotted down to nestle against the curve of her legs. Majesty stretched out on Elyse's right side and Missy on her left. By morning, they'd be sandwiching her tightly, but tonight she didn't care. She appreciated their calming presence. A reminder that she wasn't by herself.

A mental picture of Andrew, alone in his camper, flitted through her drowsy mind. She ran her hand down Majesty's soft fur as she drifted back to sleep. He needed a dog.

❧

Andrew shook hands with the preacher and walked out into the sunshine. From the front steps of the tiny building, he could see the river sparkling through the trees.

He felt a hand on his shoulder. "Andrew. How are you, my boy?"

He turned around to smile at an older man. "Hi, Mr. B.T."

"We saw you on the news this morning. You and that McCord girl. It's a cryin' shame about Maxine's no-good brother. But they said you're a real hero. Everybody's talking about it."

That explained why people were even friendlier than normal this morning. "It was nothing."

"That's not how Sheriff Westwood made it sound on TV."

Andrew didn't know what to say.

The older man seemed to sense he was uncomfortable with the subject. "Martha can't quit bragging about what a good job you did painting our house. Especially the price. She still thinks I need to pay you more."

Andrew shook his head. "I told you before you paid me plenty."

B.T. looked back over his shoulder. "I'd better go tear Martha away from the other ladies, or we'll never get to eat. You have plans for lunch?"

Andrew remembered Lynda McCord's invitation. Tempting, but too many complications for someone just passing through. "I'm going to throw together a ham and cheese sandwich and grab my rod and reel. Who knows? Maybe I can catch supper while I eat lunch."

B.T. laughed, his silver tooth glinting in the sunlight. "You sound like the luckiest man alive."

How ironic, Andrew thought, as he walked out to his truck. For the past three years, he'd considered himself one of the unluckiest men alive.

❧

"I'm sad he didn't come. I was dying to meet him." Kaleigh tossed the dishcloth into the sink.

"Must be your journalist's curiosity. Because I don't see what the big deal is." Elyse retrieved the rag, wrung it out, and draped it across the divider between the two deep aluminum sinks. She rinsed her hands and dried them.

"You're kidding me." Kaleigh lifted her mop of red curls off her neck. "He rescued you." She sat down at the bar and took a long sip of iced tea. "It would just be cool to get to meet a real knight in shining armor."

"This must be your lucky day then," Luke said wryly as he lifted the garbage bag out of the can and tied the ends. "If you're talking about Andrew, he just showed up."

Elyse's heart thudded against her ribs. "He's here?"

"In the flesh." Luke set the full bag down and deftly tucked another one into the can. "Or at least, in the living room," he said over his shoulder as he walked out the swinging door.

Elyse sat down beside Kaleigh.

"Aren't you going out there?"

"I don't know. Today has been so stressful."

Kaleigh put her hand on Elyse's shoulder. "Because of Blair's news report?"

Elyse nodded. "Everyone at church wanted to ask me about it. At once."

"Grr. . .Blair gives journalism a bad name." Kaleigh's green eyes shone with sympathy. "Did you have a panic attack?"

"No. I just froze up like I did in front of the camera. Then Luke dragged me out of the line of fire."

"Our brother—a hero in his own right," Kaleigh drawled.

The kitchen door swung open again, and Crystal walked in. "Andrew's here."

Elyse looked at her oldest sister. Her usual bright smile was missing. Jeremy and his six-year-old daughter, Beka, had been conspicuously absent at lunch today. Usually the couple and Beka took turns eating with the parents on Sundays, but today, for whatever reason, they'd gone their separate ways after church. As far as Elyse knew, no one had asked why. "Are you okay?"

Crystal's brows tugged together, but she ignored Elyse's question. Her blue eyes had dark circles under them. "Did you hear me? Andrew's here."

"Luke told us," Kaleigh volunteered.

"So why are you sitting in here?"

Kaleigh sipped her tea. "We're just not sure we're up to facing Superman today."

Elyse shook her head. "I wouldn't exactly call him Superman. His hair's not dark. But he does have kind of a chiseled jaw."

Crystal poured herself a glass of tea. "What then? Batman?" She lifted the pitcher toward Elyse. "Want some?" she mouthed. Elyse nodded. Crystal got another glass from the cabinet.

"Not unless he has pointy ears. What about Spiderman?" Kaleigh suggested.

"You know the weird thing about him is"—Elyse said as Crystal set a full glass of iced tea in front of her—"he's not like anybody else. He's unique."

"Call Marvel Comics," Kaleigh quipped. "A new superhero."

Crystal pursed her lips. "He may not *be* like anybody else, but he *looks* like a mix of Owen Wilson and Matthew McConaughey."

Kaleigh pushed to her feet so fast she almost knocked her stool over. "This I've got to see."

Elyse gulped down a big drink of the cold liquid as if it were a shot of courage. She slammed the glass back down on the counter. "Let's do it." She followed Kaleigh and Crystal into the living room.

"Where is he?" Kaleigh whispered as they hovered in the doorway.

Elyse glanced around. Her mom was talking to Matthew on the loveseat. Chance, Kaleigh's twin, lay sprawled on the couch, eyes closed and mouth open. Luke was slumped in his favorite chair watching a muted baseball game. Elyse stepped up and slapped him gently on the head. "I thought you said Andrew was here."

"He's out at the pole barn with Dad."

"Why?"

Luke never took his eyes off the TV. "Something about getting him to paint it?"

"It's a beautiful day for a short walk before Sleepyhead and I head back to campus," Kaleigh pronounced.

Elyse protested, but within less than a minute, she and her sisters were outside "walking," coincidentally in the direction of the barn. The only consolation she had was that it was also in the direction of her house. "I don't know what you two are doing, but I'm on my way home to check on Pal."

"Great idea. We'll all go," Kaleigh said. "And just our luck that we have to walk right past the barn to get there."

Crystal absently nodded. Elyse could tell that her heart was a few miles down the road at Jeremy's parents' house. But she just as obviously didn't want to talk about it.

They walked up over a hill, and the pole barn came into sight. Beside it, Andrew was talking to their daddy, making big sweeping gestures with his arm toward the side of the building.

"He's serious about his painting, isn't he?" Kaleigh whispered.

Even though they couldn't hear what the men were saying, the enthusiasm on both their parts was palpable.

Crystal frowned. "Daddy seems to be excited, too. Weird."

"Just keep walking," Elyse said quietly as they got closer.

"Maybe they won't notice us."

"Are you teasing?" Kaleigh hissed. "What purpose would that serve?"

"Girls!" Daddy spun around, a smile lighting up his face. "Out for a walk?"

"We're on our way to check on Pal." Kaleigh's smile radiated innocence.

Too much innocence, Elyse thought. She should have let Crystal answer. As a professional actress, she knew how not to overact.

"How's Pal?" Andrew said, his gaze meeting Elyse's.

"He's doing better. Finally getting rehydrated."

"Good."

"So are you going to paint—" Kaleigh stopped abruptly, and Elyse knew the twenty-two-year-old had done again what she so often did—speak without thinking. "I'm Kaleigh, by the way."

"I'm Andrew." He looked at their dad. "And as far as painting, I'm going to give an estimate, and then we'll see."

Daddy nodded. "You'll be out Thursday, right?"

"Yes. See you then."

"I think I'll head back up to the house, then, and see if it's too late for my Sunday afternoon nap."

"I'll give you a ride if you want," Andrew offered, nodding to his truck.

"No, thanks. My girls have inspired me to walk." And with that, he strode confidently back up the hill toward the house.

Andrew walked over to where Elyse and her sisters stood.

"So you came by to look at the barn?" Elyse asked, cringing at how stupid the question sounded.

His blue eyes twinkled. "Not really. I came to see you."

"Oh." She didn't dare look at Kaleigh. No telling what kind of reaction her little sister would have to that news.

"Yes, I wanted to know if there'd been any word on your Jeep."

"Oh." Okay, not exactly the same as just coming to see her, but at least he was concerned. "No, no news."

He nodded across the field to her little cottage. "Your dad said that's your place over there."

Elyse smiled, keenly aware of her sisters both watching her interaction with this painter. Even though he didn't make her nervous, their obvious fascination with her reaction to him did. "My humble abode."

"It looks cozy."

"Thanks. See you later." She locked her arm in Kaleigh's and spun the redhead around toward the path to her house. Crystal followed.

When they were several yards away, she glanced back to see Andrew getting in his truck.

"I can't believe how you talked with him." Kaleigh skipped along backward in front of her. "There wasn't a shy bone in your body."

For the first time that day, Elyse saw Crystal smile. "That's exactly what I was thinking. It's amazing."

Elyse laughed. "You two are making a big deal out of nothing."

"Trust me. How he looked at you wasn't 'nothing.' " Kaleigh's bow mouth tilted into a wry grin. "I've been waiting forever for a man to look at me like that."

Crystal snorted. "Men look at you like that everywhere we go."

"The right man, I mean," Kaleigh said, her grin fading.

Her words froze in Elyse's heart. In spite of the fact that she didn't get nervous around Andrew, there'd be no "right man" for her. She may have had childhood illusions of fairytale endings, but by the time she'd become an adult, she'd accepted that her life would be a solitary one, filled with four-footed friends rather than human companionship. And unless she found a time machine that let her go back and rewrite history, that wasn't likely to change.

CHAPTER 6

Kaleigh McCord glanced across the car at her twin brother. "Who are you taking to Crystal's wedding?"

"Huh?" Chance looked over at her for just a second then brought his gaze back to the road. "Who am I taking?"

She smacked her forehead with her palm. "A date."

"Oh." Still clutching the steering wheel with both hands, he shrugged. "I don't guess I'm taking a date."

"You're kidding!"

He frowned. "Crystal didn't mention that we had to bring dates, did she?"

"No. But everyone single brings a date to a wedding party."

His frown grew deeper. "Really? Which book did you read that in? *The Singles' Guide to Weddings*? Or *Wedding Dates for Dummies*?"

She sighed. "Forget it. You don't have to bring anyone." She stared out the window for a minute. "But I do."

"Why?"

"There are three McCord sisters. Crys will have Jeremy." She looked over at him. "Obviously."

He nodded. "Even I'm smart enough to know that."

"And now Elyse has her hero."

"That Andrew guy? You think Elyse is interested in him?"

Kaleigh sighed again. Having four brothers, she really should have the inside track on how oblivious men could be. So why did it never cease to amaze her? "Yes. She'll take him to the wedding."

"So?"

"So that just leaves me, without a date."

"Harding is a big school," he said. "You'll find someone before Christmas."

"You think so?"

"Sure, you can start as soon as we get back to campus." He smirked. "But this is just September. The trick will be keeping him until time for the wedding. Maybe you're starting too early."

"Chance! That was mean."

He pulled into the Bulldog Drive-In. "I'm going to get a cherry malt."

"We're just ten minutes from campus. You can't wait and get something there?"

He just looked at her. "Do you want anything?"

"Yeah, a nicer brother."

He shrugged and slid out. "You're out of luck."

While she was waiting for him to get back, she pulled a little notepad out of her purse. At the top of the page, she wrote Operation Wedding Date. Under it, she started to list the names of guys she knew.

Chance came back with two Styrofoam cups. He handed her one.

"What's this?"

"Strawberry-banana malt, just like you always get."

"Aw, thanks. I take back what I said about you not being nice."

"Uh-oh. What do you want?"

She tossed him a smile. "Just to pick your brain on the rest of the trip."

"We've only got ten minutes."

She wanted so badly to say, "That should be plenty of time," but she bit her tongue and said, "Then we'll have to hurry." After all, she needed his help.

She used her tiny penlight to read the list to him. On the first several names he just said no. She didn't feel like arguing, so she marked them off. "Nathan Manchester?"

He shook his head.

"Why not?" She was tired of just taking his word for it.

He glanced at her then back at the road. "You really want to know?"

"Yes!"

"He can't stand you."

"Why?"

"You humiliated him last year when you trounced him in the intramural Ping-Pong tournament."

"Humph." She remembered now. He hadn't wanted to play the third game just because she'd already won the first two. "Sore loser." She put a big black mark through Nathan's name.

"Tristan Jones."

"No."

"C'mon, he really liked me."

"He canceled your last date, remember?"

"Because he had strep throat."

Chance made a funny noise. "Not exactly."

"Why then?"

"Because you sang karaoke when y'all went out to eat."

"It was karaoke night!"

"Yeah, but you sang three songs."

"And got a standing ovation every time." Kaleigh couldn't keep the righteous indignation from her voice. "They were still yelling 'encore' when he hustled me out of the restaurant."

"I think he was probably just jealous," Chance said softly. "But you *were* going out to cheer him up after he auditioned for that small singing group on campus and didn't make it."

"Oh. Yeah." They rode in silence for a few minutes. A grave realization hit Kaleigh like a speeding bus. "I'm going to have to change."

Chance tapped the brakes. "What?"

"I'm going to have to change who I am, unless I want to end up like Granddad did."

"Living on a houseboat on the Mississippi River?" Chance asked.

"Old and alone," Kaleigh said. She ripped the list off the notepad and wadded it into a tiny ball. Then she got out her pen again. "Operation New Me," she said aloud as she wrote it in bold letters.

"Oh no," Chance muttered.

Kaleigh ignored him and started making her new list.

❧

Andrew stared at the woman lying in the hospital bed. What secrets slept within her unconscious mind? Maybe none. Or maybe the key to solving Melanie's murder and finally clearing his name after all these years.

He looked down at the rumpled bouquet of flowers in his hand. They seemed like a poor weapon against the antiseptic smell of the room. He ran his finger around the neck of his shirt. He didn't know which was harder to bear, his guilt at coming for a hospital visit with ulterior motives or the disappointment of finding her still semicomatose.

He'd found out from his preacher that Zeke's sister's name was Maxine Moser and she actually used to attend the tiny little congregation in the woods. She was in her sixties. Since he wasn't family, he'd not been able to get any information from the nurse. A no-nonsense woman, she'd looked as if she considered throwing him out just for asking. Thankfully, she'd gone to get him a vase instead.

Over the sound of the beeping machines hooked up to the woman, he could hear muted voices from the hallway. A tap on the door was quickly followed by the door being pushed open. Miss No-Nonsense waltzed in, waving a plastic vase made to resemble crystal. She shoved it under the sink faucet and filled it with water. "When she goes home, the vase stays here," she announced and set it on the nightstand next to the bed.

Andrew stood and stuffed the flowers into the water, watching Maxine's face for any sign of wakefulness. "When do you expect that will be?"

"She's going to have to wake up first, don't you think?" The nurse shook her head as if some people's ignorance was more than she could bear.

"So this isn't drug-induced?"

"This is just her body being so dehydrated and so exhausted from the pneu—" The nurse snapped her lips together and stood up straight and tall. "If you need anything, call for me." And with that, she left the room, her soft-soled shoes whispering across the tile floor.

CHRISTINE LYNXWILER

A few seconds later, another tap sounded on the door. When no one entered immediately, Andrew stood and pulled it open.

Elyse McCord stared back at him, her brown eyes wide above a brilliantly colored bouquet. He hadn't seen her in three days. Somehow he'd convinced himself that, in his mind, he'd exaggerated how beautiful she was.

He hadn't.

"Andrew. I wasn't expecting to see you here." A big smile spread across her face. "It was so sweet of you to come check on Maxine."

He nodded. Could he feel like more of a worm?

"How is she?"

"She's apparently suffering from pneumonia," he said, as if he were in the inner circle of information and not gathering from the fringes of cutoff words and abruptly ended sentences. "And dehydration." He shrugged. "I'm sorry I don't know how she's really doing. They won't tell me anything since I'm not family."

Elyse nodded. "I understand. I wonder if the police know about any other family besides Zeke."

"My preacher said something about a nephew she's really proud of who lives around West Plains, Missouri."

"Maybe you can find out his name and give it to Jack Westwood."

"I'll try." He motioned toward the flowers still clutched tightly in her hands. "Do you want me to ask the nurse to find another vase? Or do you want to put them in with mine?" He glanced at his pitiful excuse for a bouquet, mostly baby's breath and greenery. "Or maybe I should just throw mine out and let you have the vase for yours."

"Don't be silly." She walked over and put her flowers in the roomy vase with his, did some quick movements with her hands, and stood back. "Voilà!"

"Wow. That looks amazing."

"Thanks. But half the credit goes to you." She turned to Maxine and held up the flowers. "Ms. Maxine, if you could just open your eyes, you'd see some really pretty flowers." She looked over at Andrew. "And two people who are eager for you to wake up."

He met her gaze. Was there a double meaning to her words? Did she guess that he had a hidden reason for coming here? Her eyes were guileless, though, as they looked back at him. Her motives were pure, and she assumed his were, too. He cleared his throat. "Would you like to go to lunch?"

"Oh, I. . ." She smiled. "I'd love to."

Spur-of-the-moment plans weren't like him, but maybe it was time he changed a little. "Good. There's a new little Italian place across the street. We can just walk if you'd like."

"Considering I had to bring the old farm truck, that sounds perfect." Elyse turned back to the woman in the bed. "Ms. Maxine, I wanted to tell you that Pal's staying at my house until you get better. He's doing great, but I know he wants to see you." She patted the woman's arm. "I'll bring him to see you when you wake up. Bye-bye for now."

She turned around, and Andrew held the door open for her.

In the hallway, they met a beautiful dark-haired woman and a smiling man. The teenage boy with them had a golden retriever on a leash.

Elyse's face lit up. "Hey, it's good to see y'all! Out getting in some therapy hours?"

The boy nodded and patted the dog, who was sitting calmly by his side.

Elyse smiled at her friends. "This is Andrew Stone, a friend of mine."

She turned back to Andrew. "This is Dylan Worthington and his dog, Charlie. Charlie is a therapy dog."

"Thanks to you." Dylan's grin was shy but genuine.

"No, thanks to lots of hard work from both of you." She motioned toward the brunette. "And this is his mom, Victoria. And her friend, Adam Langston."

Victoria and Adam both shook hands with him. "Nice to meet you," they said almost in unison.

"That was a great thing you did, rescuing Elyse." Adam grinned. "And surviving Blair."

Victoria gave Adam a hard look.

He shrugged. "What? She may be a big shot on TV, but she's a menace to society, and you know it."

Elyse put her hand on Victoria's arm. "Don't worry. Andrew and I know firsthand how Blair can be."

Victoria smiled. "Don't we all?"

Elyse motioned toward Charlie. "We'll let y'all get back to business. Charlie has been patient long enough."

"Now it's time for him to see patients," Dylan said.

Adam groaned. "And time for you to get some better jokes."

The three of them said good-bye and left laughing together.

Andrew watched them walk into a room down the hall. "They seem like a happy family."

Elyse chuckled. "Victoria is Dylan's mom, but Adam is just a family friend."

"Oh, sorry."

"Sometimes it's easy to misunderstand relationships."

He looked at her. Was that a warning? Or was he paranoid today? Probably the latter.

Outside, Elyse tilted her face to the sun. "There's something freeing about walking out of a hospital."

"I agree." Andrew put his hand lightly on the small of her back and guided her across the street. "I don't see how you can talk so naturally to someone unconscious. I was impressed."

She laughed. "It's tons easier than talking to people who are awake." She looked over at him. "That's where I have a problem."

"You indicated that before, but I think you do a fine job of relating to conscious people. Unless I'm comatose and don't know it."

She gave him a sheepish grin. "Trust me. You're the exception."

"Good to know." He didn't know why it pleased him so much to hear her describe him as the exception, but it did.

They passed the outdoor dining area with small umbrella-covered tables and neared the dark green door of the restaurant.

Elyse gasped and stumbled a little.

He grabbed her arm to steady her. "What's wrong?"

Her eyes were panic-stricken, but she shook her head as if to clear it. "Nothing. I'm fine."

He guided her into the foyer of the restaurant. The smell of garlic and Italian spices made his mouth water. He glanced at the specials of the day listed on a blackboard held up by a tripod.

"I'm sorry, Andrew," Elyse said softly. "I'm going to have to take a rain check. Suddenly I'm not feeling well."

"Why don't I drive you home? One of your brothers can ride back with me to get the truck."

"No, I'll be fine. You go ahead and eat."

"I'm at least walking you to your truck." Together they started retracing their steps from minutes before. "You look like you saw a ghost."

"Something like that," she said, her mouth twisted into what was probably supposed to be a grin. "But I'm too old to believe in ghosts."

"It wasn't Zeke, was it?"

"No!" She narrowed her eyes at him. "Why? Do you think he's coming for me?"

"I don't know," he said honestly. "Do you?"

"He'd be crazy to."

Andrew nodded. That was what worried him.

CHAPTER 7

For once, Elyse relished the bouncing of the old, beat-up truck on the washboard ruts of the lane to her house. Maybe the vibration would shake some sense into her. Her hands were still clammy on the steering wheel, and her heart beat somewhere slightly above her normal rate. She couldn't believe she'd acted like such an idiot in front of Andrew, of all people.

How many times in the last eighteen years had this happened? Ten? At least. She'd see someone in a crowd, usually from the back, which was the case today, and the set of a person's shoulders or the way he or she walked would throw Elyse backward into a time warp. More often than not, it was a woman. Which was ridiculous. Because eighteen years ago, Elyse had seen for herself the impossibility of that when she watched, hidden, while the coroner covered the body with a white sheet. But sometimes, like today, it was a man. And that scenario, though highly improbable, was possible if he'd been released and somehow found her after all these years. Or if he'd just happened through Shady Grove by accident.

She'd been so engrossed in her thoughts that she'd parked in front of her house without realizing it. The dogs were probably going crazy inside wondering when she was coming in.

All three of her dogs came to greet her at the door. She'd trained them not to jump on her, but they ran to her and sat, each one watching her expectantly.

She knelt down in front of them and smiled at the *thump thump thump* of the bigger dogs' tails on the parquet floor. Nikki was technically sitting, but her whole body was wagging. "Hello, little precious," Elyse said and lifted her into her arms. "Are you keeping everyone in line?" Nikki gave a one-bark answer. "I'll take that as a yes."

Elyse set her down and moved on to golden Majesty, who sat in a very queenly manner, waiting patiently for her loyal subject to approach her. Elyse put her arms around her and buried her face in the sweet-smelling fur. "It's been one of those days," she whispered next to the dog's ear. Majesty nuzzled her head against Elyse's head as if comforting her.

A short, deep bark interrupted, and Elyse looked up to find Missy watching her. "You want your share, don't you, honey?" Elyse cooed and scooted over toward the black lab. She rubbed the soft underside of Missy's ear, and the dog pushed against her hand, grunting in a purring-like way.

After a minute, Elyse patted her lap and Nikki leaped up there. Majesty took the cue to move closer, and Missy smashed up against her on the other side. Elyse sighed. The two big dogs were trained therapy dogs, and Nikki was working on it, but for now they were all therapy for her. She relaxed against them and let the remnants of her earlier upset fade away.

Finally, she set Nikki gently on the floor and stood. "Time to check on our visitor," she announced. The three dogs followed her as she walked through the house to the grooming area in the back. It had an outside entrance so that customers didn't have to come through her house, but Elyse loved the convenience of being able to go straight from home to work without leaving the building. And the big open area made a perfect place to keep rescued dogs before they were placed, or at least—she thought of how Nikki had chewed so many things during her first days here after being rescued—before they had time to get acquainted with the house and the house rules.

Pal ran happily over to greet first the other dogs and then Elyse. He was amazingly well mannered and extremely affectionate. Two signs of a well-loved dog. Elyse's heart went out again to Maxine. How awful it must have been—knowing that her beloved dog wasn't being taken care of and not being able to do anything about it.

Just as she brought the dogs back in from the fenced-in backyard, the front doorbell rang. "Y'all stay here and play," she said and closed the four of them in the grooming area.

Maybe Andrew had come by to check on her. That seemed like something he would do, as thoughtful as he was. She'd been so surprised to see him in Maxine's room this morning.

She peeked out the door blind and saw Matthew standing on the step. She unlocked the dead bolt and the door lock. "Hey! Come in."

He hugged her and stepped back. "How's it going?"

She was happy that he'd walked down to see her, but at the same time the special effort concerned her. Usually when he was in, they just visited at the main house. Unless there was a problem they needed to discuss privately. "Same as it was last night when we left Mama and Daddy's. What's going on?"

"Cut to the chase, don't you?" He gave a little laugh.

She frowned. "Is something wrong, Matt?"

He shook his head. "I just wanted to talk to you for a few minutes. It's kind of important."

She led the way to the living room and motioned to the chair next to her small rocker. "Have a seat."

She studied Matthew. Handsome in a scholarly way, he was the most ambitious of her brothers, determined to make his mark on the world. He'd zoomed through veterinarian college with high honors. Sometimes Elyse wondered how much of his ambition stemmed from a need to make sure their parents were proud of him and how much came from a true desire inside himself. Either way, he was on a quick track to success, and she was very proud of him.

"What's up?"

"You know I've been here the last few days scouting out office locations?"

She nodded. "We can't wait to get you back closer to home."

He straightened his shoulders and leaned forward slightly. "Here's the bottom line, Elyse. I want you to consider sharing the office with me."

She frowned. "Move my dog grooming business into your office?"

He shook his head. "I want you to join McCord Veterinary Clinic as a dog trainer."

She sat back and stared at him. "You know I can't do that."

"Why not?"

He was her brother. One of six people who knew her better than anyone. "Matt, you've seen me around strangers. It's all I can do to hand them their freshly groomed dogs and take their money. I can't talk to people I don't know. Training takes a lot of interaction between the owner and the trainer. That's why I don't do it much anymore." She smiled to take the sting out of her blunt words. "But I'm honored that you'd like to have me."

He held up his hand. "I'm not planning on taking no for an answer. At least not yet. It'll be at least two months before I have to make a final decision on a building. I want you to promise me that you'll think about this and pray about it. Then, at Thanksgiving, you can give me your final answer."

She stared at him. Hadn't she just given him her final answer? How much plainer could she be?

"You know this is what you've always wanted, Elyse." His voice was soft. "And it's within your reach."

She sighed. "I'll let you know for sure at Thanksgiving."

He pushed to his feet. "That's what I wanted to hear."

He hugged her and was gone, leaving her to daydream about the possibilities.

❧

On Thursday afternoon, Andrew shook Jonathan McCord's hand. "I'll be able to start Monday. I'll do the outside first before the weather turns too cold to paint then move to the inside. I should have it all done by Thanksgiving."

"Perfect."

"I have one more question. I noticed there are water hook-ups and electrical outlets on the outside of the barn. I like to live as close to work as possible. With that in mind, I'll knock 10 percent off the price I quoted you if I can hook my camper up here."

Jonathan's eyebrows drew together, and he stared at Andrew

for a moment without speaking. "Before I give you an answer, I have a question for you. How much of your desire to live here has to do with being close to my daughter?"

Andrew considered his options. The truth seemed to be the only viable one. "Quite a bit, to be honest. I don't know if you realize it or not, but Zeke made some terrible threats to Elyse the day he stole her Jeep. He swore he'd get her if it was the last thing he did." Much as Andrew had sworn he'd get the man who killed Melanie if it was the last thing he did, but Jonathan McCord didn't need to know that.

Jonathan frowned. "She didn't tell me."

"I'm sure she didn't want to worry you. It's obvious that any member of her family would gladly take a bullet for her. But it seems like it wouldn't be a bad idea to have one more person between her and Zeke who will do whatever it takes to stop him from getting to her. That would be me."

"Maybe I should talk to her about moving into the main house for a while."

Andrew shook his head. "You and I both know she wouldn't be happy with that idea."

"I have to agree with you on that. For someone so shy, she's as independent as they come." Jonathan gave him one more measuring glance. "I'll tell you what. You can park your camper here as soon as you want to. There's even a bathroom with a shower inside the barn you can use. And I appreciate you keeping an eye on Elyse. But if you're still planning on moving on, you'd better make sure you don't take her heart with you when you go." He grinned. "I'd hate to have to hunt you down."

"Yes, sir. In that case, I'll go ahead and move over here this afternoon. Then when I finish the house on River Road, I'll be ready to start here." He wished he could explain that, as far as Andrew was concerned, Elyse's heart couldn't be safer if it was in a monastery. He would never get involved in another relationship as long as the cloud of suspicion from Melanie's death still hung over his head.

Two hours later Andrew was under his camper leveling it when he heard someone say his name. He scooted out on his back and looked up to see Luke standing over him.

"You need any help?" he asked.

"No, I'm used to doing it by myself."

"Kind of a loner, aren't you?"

Andrew decided this might be the kind of conversation where he'd prefer to be on his feet rather than his back. He stood before he answered. "Kind of, I guess."

"Elyse doesn't normally talk to strangers much."

Andrew nodded. "I get that. Maybe I'm different because I saved her from Zeke."

Luke shrugged. "Maybe."

Andrew walked over and checked the level. If Luke wanted this conversation to go a certain direction, he was going to have to be the one to take it there.

"She usually keeps her defenses pretty high."

He looked over his shoulder at Luke. "Why?"

Luke shrugged again, a habit that could quickly become annoying. "Sometimes a danger can come in under the radar, and before you know it, they're right in the middle of your home territory, looking like one of you."

"I'm no danger to Elyse."

Luke snorted, but at least he didn't shrug. "You are if you break her heart."

What was it with these McCords and their assumptions that he was a heartbreaker? If only they knew he hadn't so much as looked at a woman in three years, and before that, he'd been too busy with work for romance until he met Melanie. "I'm not planning to break her heart."

"Good." Luke turned to walk away.

"Hey."

He turned back around. "Yeah?"

"What if she breaks mine?"

Luke grinned. "Then we'll help you pack."

Andrew nodded. "Nice," he muttered as Luke walked away. "Real nice."

After Luke left, Andrew convinced himself that it was almost comical. But by the time Matthew showed up an hour later with the same warning—only in a more tactful manner—he was starting to see that the McCords were serious. He shook the vet's hand and sent him on his way with yet another promise that he wasn't going to break Elyse's heart, and went in to fix supper.

A tap on the door startled him. Elyse? Had she discovered his camper and come to tell him not to expect her heart in return for taking up residence on the property?

He pushed open the door and stared into Crystal's clear blue eyes. "Hello."

She held up a delicious-smelling basket. "A housewarming gift from Mama and me."

He raised an eyebrow. Arsenic-laced brownies, maybe? "Thanks." He took the basket and lifted the cloth. Brownies. So he was half right, at least. "Would you like to come in?"

She shook her head. "No thanks. I'd better get back to the house."

"Okay." He couldn't believe it. No warning?

"But before I go. . ."

This was more like it.

"Elyse is a really special person. And she's not usually relaxed around people like she is around you."

"So you're afraid that because she has her guard down, I'll take advantage of that and break her heart," he said in a wry monotone.

Her eyes widened. "Will you?"

He shook his head. "Your sister is already very important to me. The last thing in the world I'd ever do is hurt her."

A huge smile lit up her face. "Good." She gave him a little wave. "Enjoy the brownies."

"Crystal."

She spun back around.

"Would you do me a favor and tell the rest of your family that I'm not a lowlife player out to break Elyse's heart?" That might be the only way he'd ever have time to get any work done without constant interruptions.

She laughed. "I'll do that."

He closed the camper door and carried the brownies over to the table. Ironically, the one McCord he'd hoped to see this evening he hadn't. He really couldn't blame the McCords. There was a quality about Elyse that made him want to protect her at any cost. Even from himself. No wonder they felt the same way.

He walked back outside and arranged his favorite lawn chair under the porch awning. Talk about a view. To the left, he could see the McCord house and the livestock barn. To the right, Elyse's house, and farther on past her, the river, unseen but distinguishable by the row of trees that grew along the winding bank. In front of him, a little lane, shared by the barn he'd been hired to paint and Elyse's house, led to the gravel road two hundred yards away. But from here he could see beyond the road to the vast miles of rolling hills on the other side, dotted with cattle and unmarred by buildings.

A place of peace. That was his first thought as he sat in the chair and surveyed his surroundings. Peace was something he'd had very little of since Melanie's death. He'd convinced himself that it would come if he could only find her murderer and clear his name once and for all, but sometimes he wondered if he'd lost the ability to be at peace.

He watched as the sky changed from a dusky pink to a deep gray blue and a few twinkling stars popped out. In the distance, he heard a motor puttering, and headlights came into view on the road. Even traffic out here was unobtrusive, thanks to the buffer of land between the barn and the road.

At the end of the lane, a motor slowed then stopped. Just as quickly, the lights went out. Andrew sat quietly in the gathering dusk, his ears straining for the sound of a car door opening and closing. Crickets chirped, and in the distance a cow bawled. But no other sound.

He eased to his feet and glided across the driveway to the fence line. Staying close to the tall posts, he made his way down the rutted pathway toward the road. Halfway down, he could make out an old yellow Toyota pickup parked sideways directly across the road from the entrance to the lane. Probably somebody studying a map or kids looking for a place to park. But he needed to find out.

As he reached the main road, he could see there was just one person in the truck. It looked like a man, but he couldn't be sure. Apparently the driver saw him at the same time, because the truck sprang to life and spun onto the road and away, leaving a thick trail of dust. Andrew frowned. Had Zeke switched vehicles and come to get revenge on Elyse? Or was it a coincidence that a man who obviously didn't want to be seen had stopped on this stretch of a lightly traveled road?

He walked back up to his camper. Elyse had been gone somewhere earlier, but she was home now, and her house had a few lights still burning. Maybe he should warn her. He remembered the parade of McCords to his camper. On second thought, there'd probably been enough warnings for today. He'd just sleep with one eye open tonight and decide tomorrow what to do about the little yellow truck.

CHAPTER 8

Crystal barely touched a bite of supper. She couldn't stand to see the pity and concern in her mama's eyes, so as soon as the dishes were done, she started up the stairs to her room. Suddenly she stopped. She'd spent a ridiculous day waiting to hear from Jeremy. She'd even made brownies in anticipation of his calling to invite her to eat supper with him and Beka.

When he hadn't called by late afternoon, Mama had suggested she take half the batch to the barn and welcome Andrew to the neighborhood. While she was there, she'd tried to drop a subtle hint about how vulnerable Elyse might be. If Andrew's reaction was any indicator, subtlety wasn't her strong suit. So she wasn't even going to try subtle with Jeremy. She ran up the stairs and grabbed her purse and keys. She was going for blunt and to the point. There was no way she could go to bed another night not knowing what was wrong with him.

She prayed all the way to his house. Once parked, she took the half batch of brownies and walked slowly to the door. The echo of the doorbell inside made her heart beat fast. What if he didn't come to the door? A week ago she couldn't even have imagined something so crazy, but now standing in the dusky darkness, it seemed perfectly plausible.

The door opened, and he smiled.

Relief surged through her. He was glad to see her.

He stepped back to let her inside.

Before either one could speak, Beka came bounding into the room. "My Crystal!" She threw her arms around Crystal's legs and squeezed.

Crystal smiled at Beka's nickname for her.

"You brought brownies?" The little girl's eyes were big. "Can I have one?"

Crystal looked at Jeremy, and he nodded. She walked on into the kitchen that she'd already started thinking of as hers and took a brownie out for Beka. By the time she set it on the counter, Beka was on a stool.

Crystal poured Beka a glass of milk, set it down, and turned back to Jeremy, her resolve to be blunt melting away. Maybe the uneasiness had just been her imagination. A weird blip in an otherwise wonderful relationship.

She walked over to hug him. And he did lift his arms and put them around her. But her doubts flooded back, double and triple. This was not a normal embrace. He held her away from him as if he were afraid she'd break. Or contaminate him in some way. She looked up at him. "What's wrong, honey?" she whispered.

He motioned toward Beka with his eyes. "Let's talk later," he mouthed.

Crystal sat at the counter beside Beka, unsure what to do. "How's school going?"

Beka shrugged as she pulled her brownie apart with stubby fingers. "Okay, I guess."

"Are you still having fun in art?"

Beka nodded. "I drew you a picture." She looked at Jeremy, her gaze stern. "But Daddy made me give it to Grandma."

Jeremy turned toward the sink and started loading the dishwasher.

Crystal stared at his back, feeling as if the air had been sucked from her lungs. But she forced herself to respond to the little girl with a smile. "That's okay, honey. You can draw me another one later."

"Okay, I will."

"Finish your brownie and milk, Little Bit." Jeremy's voice was strained. "It's almost time for bed."

"Will you sit in my room and read me a story?"

Jeremy nodded.

"Will you make it a long one?"

Crystal waited for his answer. If he wanted to talk to her after Beka went to bed, he'd make the nightly ritual as short as possible.

When he answered Beka, his eyes met Crystal's, and the sadness there squeezed her heart. "I'll make it a long one." He tore his gaze away. "Now, come tell Miss Crystal good night."

It was all she could do to hug Beka and get out the door before the tears started.

❦

Elyse finished drying the little poodle and deftly put a tiny red bow in her topknot. "You really are a sweetie, aren't you, Sweetie?" The poodle pranced as if to agree. "Since we have a few minutes, would you like to work on something to impress Victoria and Dylan?" Sweetie pranced again and tossed her head.

Elyse spent the next ten minutes showing the tiny dog the finer arts of obedience. She used treats for rewards, but not every time, depending instead on praise to motivate dogs like Sweetie. When her friend Victoria Worthington came in the back door, Elyse was down on the floor with the dog.

Victoria laughed. "You do know that you should charge for teaching her to behave so well, don't you?"

Elyse shrugged. "It's fun." She grinned. "And we had extra time since she was so good while I was grooming her. This is her reward."

"Yes, well. . ." Victoria dug around in her oversized Jimmy Choo purse and pulled out some cash. She waved it at Elyse, leaving an aromatic trail of Obsession perfume in the air. "This is *your* reward, and I don't want to hear any arguments." She put it on the counter.

"Thanks." Elyse knew from experience it was useless to argue with her wealthy friend.

Victoria walked over to the steaming coffeepot, retrieved a ceramic cup from the shelf, and poured herself a cup of coffee. "When are you going to realize that you need to go into dog training full-time?"

"Have some coffee," Elyse said dryly.

"Why, thank you, I believe I will." Victoria sank down in one of the two cushioned chairs against the wall, and Sweetie jumped up on her lap. "Do you have time to drink a cup with me?"

Elyse nodded. "My eleven o'clock canceled." She poured herself a cup of coffee, fixed it to suit her taste, and joined Victoria. "How are things at Worthington Enterprises?"

Victoria wrinkled her nose. "I don't want to talk about me. We didn't get a chance to talk last night, and I wanted to. Are you sure you're okay? Blair made it sound like you almost died. Is that true?"

Elyse filled her friend in on the details of last Saturday morning's incident with Zeke. When she finished, there wasn't a trace of a smile left on Victoria's face.

"Wow. Did your life flash before your eyes?"

Elyse shook her head.

"Did it at least make you think, *I wish I'd focused on using my talent as a dog trainer instead of bathing*"—Victoria put her hands over Sweetie's ears—"*spoiled pooches?*"

Elyse burst out laughing. "No, I can't say that it did. I was more worried about Pal and keeping that awful man from shooting him."

"Thank goodness for your hunky hero."

"I never said he was hunky."

Victoria took a sip of her coffee. "You didn't have to. I saw him on TV." She set her cup on the table between the chairs and leaned forward. "How many years have we done 4-H meetings together?"

"Three?"

"Three years of you wasting your life teaching little kids how to make their dogs sit and stay."

Elyse gasped. "Victoria! That is so not true. I love working with the kids. And their dogs!"

"Okay, I overstated. Dylan probably would have been a neurotic only child of an overprotective single mom forever if you hadn't shown him how great it is to love dogs. And, thanks to you, he knows how to take care of them. So I'm not sorry you've done 4-H or started the Therapy Dog Foundation. But there's more to life than this. You're as good as that dog whisperer guy on TV. You could be famous."

Elyse laughed. "That's the last thing I want."

"Killjoy."

"So you want to stay for lunch?" Elyse asked. "I'll make some chicken salad."

"Actually, I have to go." She stood, and Elyse followed suit. "I'm meeting Adam for lunch." The color in her face heightened slightly, just as it always did when she mentioned her friend Allie's younger brother. "Business," she quickly clarified. "I'm thinking of investing in his video game company."

Elyse nodded. If she remembered correctly, Adam Langston had been graduating high school when she was starting junior high. That made him about six years younger than Victoria. In spite of the age difference, he'd been Victoria's sidekick ever since Elyse met her at the first 4-H meeting and who knows how long before. She remembered Andrew assuming they were a couple when he met them at the hospital. Sometimes Elyse sensed there was a spark between the two, but for whatever reason, the relationship was stuck in friendship mode. "Have fun. Thanks for the big tip, and thanks for drinking coffee with me."

"Thanks for inviting me— Oh wait," Victoria teased. "Guess you didn't really."

Elyse hugged her friend. "You're welcome at my coffeepot anytime."

After she closed the door behind Victoria, Elyse grabbed four leashes from the hooks by the door and went to find her dogs and Pal. When she passed the doorway of the den, she smiled.

Missy was in the corner chewing on a dog toy, keeping an eye on everything. Majesty lay on her stomach with her front paws crossed elegantly in front of her. Nikki was curled up in a tiny ball in her small bowl-shaped chair. In the middle of the floor,

Pal was sound asleep on his back, all four legs up in the air. The last observance was the one that made Elyse smile the biggest. Dogs lie like that only when they feel completely at ease and secure. Pal was recovering nicely.

"Who wants to go for a walk?" She held up the leashes, and her three dogs ran to her and sat in a row. Pal woke and joined them, jumping and barking. Elyse gave Pal a couple of simple instructions and showed him what she expected. When he sat and waited patiently for her to put the leash on him, she stroked his head. "Good boy."

Outside, she considered turning toward the river. Mama had called yesterday afternoon when she was on her way to the 4-H meeting to tell her that Andrew was hooking his camper up at the barn. When she got home, Elyse had skipped the dogs' evening walk so he wouldn't think she was strolling by just to see him. Since he was finishing up some jobs on River Road, he surely wouldn't be home in the middle of the day.

She guided the dogs down the familiar path to her parents' house. Just as she reached the camper, the door opened and he stepped out. She stopped, startled. Had he been watching from the window? He looked surprised to see her, so maybe it was just a coincidence.

He grinned. "What perfect timing. I was about to come down to your house and see if I could call in that rain check from Monday."

"Are you on lunch break?"

He ducked his head. "I had a hard time sleeping last night, so I'm getting a late start today. I only lack a few hours being done, so I thought that before I headed to work, I'd pick up the paint for the barn in town and satisfy this craving for Italian food. That is, if you have time and want to." He nodded toward the dogs.

"Are these your three?"

"Yes." She introduced the dogs one at a time, grateful for some time to process his invitation. "And of course you know Pal." The yellow lab had been straining at the leash, wagging excitedly to get to Andrew.

He reached and scratched his head. "Hey, Pal. How are you settling in? You're looking better."

Elyse looked at the dog. His ribs weren't standing out much at all. "He's doing amazingly well."

"So? What do you say? Will you take pity on me and go eat pasta with me? I'll take you by to see Maxine while we're there."

"I have an appointment to groom a dog at three."

"I promise to have you back in plenty of time. I need to be painting by three anyway."

"In that case, let me go put the dogs in the house and I'll be ready." She looked down at her jeans and turquoise pullover. "Do you think I should change?"

He shook his head. "You look beautiful." His eyes widened as if he was as startled by his own words as she was. He glanced down at his own jeans. "I'm pretty sure this place allows jeans. If not, we'll order takeout and go eat somewhere that does."

"Okay then. See you in a few minutes." She headed back toward her house, a smile tilting her lips. She'd been worried about it looking as if she was seeking him out, but he'd had no trouble admitting he was about to come to her house to ask her to lunch. Plus, he'd called her beautiful. And she hadn't even blushed. It didn't get much better than that.

Andrew pulled up in front of Elyse's house, and she came right out. He didn't know what to think. Melanie had always made him wait at least half an hour when they were dating. Not that he and Elyse were dating. He hastily corrected his thoughts. He'd asked her to go with him into town for two reasons: one, to keep her close in case Zeke showed up, and two, if Maxine was awake, she'd feel more comfortable if Elyse was there. And she'd be more likely to trust Andrew later if he came back alone to question her. The fact that Elyse was good company and he liked being around her was a distant third, if it rated at all.

As she climbed into the passenger seat, Andrew was struck again by how beautiful she was. But this time he wisely kept it to himself.

She buckled in carefully. "Thanks for inviting me," she said a little formally.

He nodded and backed up to turn around. "So how do you like living right in the middle of a cattle ranch?"

She cleared her throat. "Considering I'm terrified of cows, it's not so bad."

He gave a startled laugh and aimed the truck down the little lane. "So you're not a cowgirl?"

She shook her head. "Definitely not. Cowgirls are filled with courage and determination. That's not me."

To his surprise, she sounded serious. He frowned. "You may not know this, but I saw you throw yourself at Zeke and his gun when he was going to shoot Pal."

Her cheeks turned a slight pink. "I lost my head."

"I thought it was a classic example of courage and determination." He meant every word of it. He didn't think he'd ever forget her fearlessness in the face of danger. "I'd say that makes you a cowgirl at heart."

She laughed. "That's reaching, but okay. Between us, you can think I'm a cowgirl. But don't try to convince anyone else." She put her hand on her seat belt as they hit a big bump.

"What else are you afraid of. . . ?" His words drifted off as he caught sight of a little yellow truck at the end of the lane. "Have you ever seen that truck before?" he asked her, trying to keep the urgency from his voice.

She leaned forward. "Nope. Looks like a Toyota, doesn't it?"

Just as they reached the end of the lane, the Toyota accelerated, spinning gravel all over Andrew's truck.

Andrew gripped the steering wheel with both hands and pressed down on the gas.

CHAPTER 9

The grassy hills flew by as Andrew concentrated on keeping up with the smaller truck.

"What are you doing?" Elyse sounded as if she barely had enough air to get the words out.

Her voice distracted him for a second, but not enough to slow him down. "Just trying to keep you safe," he answered without looking at her, focusing on not losing sight of the yellow truck in the clouds of dust.

The Toyota disappeared around the last bend before the main highway. When Andrew cleared the same curve, the truck was nowhere in sight. He pulled up to the stop sign at the highway. He slammed his palm on the steering wheel. "Which way do you think he went?"

When Elyse didn't answer, he looked over at her. Her head was pressed against the back of the seat, both of her hands were tightly gripping the shoulder strap of her seat belt, and her face was white.

He jerked the truck into a turnaround at the edge of a field and killed the motor. "Elyse? Are you okay?"

She forced her hands loose from the seat belt and relaxed her shoulders. "To answer your question. . .about what else I'm afraid of. . ." She took a deep breath and blew it out. "That would be reckless driving."

"I'm so sorry." He felt like an idiot.

"That's okay," she said shakily. "With anyone else, I'd have hyperventilated." She unbuckled her seat belt. "As a matter of fact, I think I need more oxygen to my brain right now." She opened the truck door and jumped out.

He got out and walked around to where she was leaning against the front fender. "I'm sorry," he said again, hating himself for making her scared.

She waved his apology away like a pesky fly. "You think that was Zeke?"

He turned to look back at the empty highway. "I don't know. I saw the same truck in the same place last night."

She stared at a patch of grass near her feet. "Why didn't you tell anyone?"

"I just kept watch."

She jerked her head up to look at him. "All night?"

He shrugged. "Until the rooster crowed. Then I figured there was too much action for Zeke to show up."

She ran her hand over her face. "Boy, no wonder you're getting a late start today."

"Yeah, I'm hoping that if your dad notices, he'll blame it on artistic temperament."

She pushed off from the truck. "You're an artist? Like you paint pictures?" She grimaced. "Or did I just put my foot in my mouth again and you consider house painting an art?"

He smiled. "I guess house painting is an art. But yes, I paint 'pictures,' too." His smile faded. "Or at least I used to."

Her mouth dropped open. "That painting in your camper? Of the man breaking the horse? You did that?"

"Yes."

"You're amazing."

He couldn't believe how good it felt to hear her say that. Inside a little locked box in his heart, something pounded against the door, trying to get out. "Painting houses and barns pays more."

She shook her head. "Not with that kind of talent, not for long."

"I gave up on the starving artist life several years ago." Three years ago, to be exact. "For now, I'll stick to what pays."

"You don't paint anymore at all?"

His throat tightened at the sadness he heard in her voice. "Now and then. I have a few paints left, but when these run out, I doubt I'll buy any more." He'd actually promised himself he wouldn't. Some dreams were too silly to keep pursuing.

"I think that's a mistake. We have a really great art supply place in town."

He motioned to the truck. "If I promise to drive at little old lady speed the rest of the day, will you ride into town with me?" He opened her door for her and helped her in, then walked around to get in the driver's side.

"Little old lady speed, now, don't forget," she said solemnly. "You promised."

"Oh, I forgot to tell you," he teased. "My grandma was in the Indy 500."

"Yeah, right." She pulled her seat belt snug. "That had better be a joke."

In spite of the rocky start, Elyse couldn't remember when she'd had a better day. They'd eaten their pasta at an outdoor table under a large umbrella. Even the paint store had been fun. The only sad part had been finding out that Maxine still wasn't awake.

Andrew got Elyse back home by two o'clock, even going a sedate speed several miles per hour below the limit. He jumped out and ran around to open her truck door for her.

"You're going to spoil me." She stepped down next to him.

"I don't think that's possible. You're probably the most un-spoiled person I've ever met." His eyes were warm.

"Maybe you just don't know me."

He shrugged. "I guess that's a possibility. But I think I have a pretty clear picture of who you are."

As they slowly strolled up to her walkway, she considered his words. If he had a clear picture of who she really was, he probably wouldn't be nearly as interested in spending time with her. But at least he seemed to like who she wanted to be.

At her door, he turned to her and leaned forward.

Her heart pounded against her ribs.

He dropped a quick kiss on her cheek. "I'd better go get this paint unloaded at the barn so I can go to work."

"Thanks."

He grinned. "See you later."

After he drove off down the path to the barn, she slapped herself lightly. "Thanks? For what?" She slid her hand over her eyes. "Kissing me on the cheek? Taking the paint to the barn? He probably thinks I'm crazy."

She gave up on figuring herself out and hurried into the house. All in all, it had still been a wonderful day.

❦

This had to be some kind of record for the worst week ever. Kaleigh slipped into a chair at a back library table. She reached to the middle of the table and pulled a big book toward her. No one would disturb her if she was studying. Or reading—she flipped the book over to look at the title—Homer's *Odyssey* for pleasure. She slipped a tiny piece of paper out of her binder and focused on the little list. The goal for this week was circled. Look Totally Different.

The rest of the week she'd worn her hair up, but since this was the last day of the week, in a last-ditch effort to salvage her plan, she'd straightened it and worn it down. Not a feat for most people, but Kaleigh's hair was a mess of long, disorderly red curls that she knew gave the false impression she was wild and impulsive. Today, thanks to an hour of work with her CHI flatiron, the red strands lay sleek and shiny down her back.

In honor of the new her, she'd worn her most sedate black pants and a green and black top. To tone down the top, she'd borrowed a black sweater and a short string of pearls from her roommate. She'd forgone her lace-up-to-the-knee black Converse heels and gone with some black pumps with short heels instead. Her feet were killing her, but she looked every inch the sophisticated, calm, intelligent woman she knew she could be.

Several of her female teachers had complimented her on how great she looked. Even some of her classmates had mentioned it. But they were all girls. Not one guy, cute or otherwise, had even glanced at her. Her last class started in an hour, and she was hiding in the library, trying to regroup. So much for week one.

She heard footsteps behind her. She flipped a page in the big book and slid the list into her binder without looking. It wasn't that she didn't like people, but right now the last thing she wanted was to make conversation. Or hear another girl say how much she liked her hair.

"Did you know that many people think Homer wasn't the sole author of the *Odyssey?*" A deep voice behind her made her jump.

She turned to look at the speaker. She recognized him immediately. Carlton Weatherford III—or was it IV? Either way, his family was one of those that everyone on campus knew. But between his academic achievements and his football prowess, he was a star in his own right. And even though they'd attended the same university for three, going on four, years and he was in many of her classes, he'd never spoken to her until today.

His hazel eyes studied her. He had really long lashes.

She realized she hadn't answered him. "I've heard that." Probably in the same class he had.

"Most people don't realize that." He motioned to the chair next to her. "May I?"

She nodded.

He sat beside her and tilted his head. "Now you're. . . ?" His eyebrows drew together as if he was trying to place her.

"Kaleigh McCord. We're in a couple of classes together."

He nodded but still looked puzzled. "Nice to meet you."

Inwardly, she rolled her eyes at the fact that he hadn't bothered to give her his name. But outwardly, the new and improved Kaleigh just smiled sweetly. When Carlton asked her if she wanted to go get coffee after their next class, she happily agreed.

Week one of Operation New Me was definitely a success.

❧

Crystal looked across the church building at Jeremy.

Beka, next to him, turned around with her chin on the top of the pew and gave her a sad little wave.

Crystal smiled and waved at the little girl, but inside she was fuming. She couldn't believe he'd actually sit somewhere else. She glanced down at the ring on her finger. Last time she checked, they were still engaged.

Her Bible with its worn cover caught her eye, and she picked it up. She'd struggled too hard to get her relationship with God back in order. She wasn't going to let the hardheaded man in front of her distract her from worship. There'd be plenty of time after to deal with this craziness.

When the last amen was said, her thoughts went directly back to Jeremy. She didn't know whether to try again to talk to him or just let time pass. His mom and dad were two rows back from her, and she was ashamed to admit she felt like avoiding them. But when she turned around, Mrs. Buchanan was waiting for her.

"Hi, Crys." The older woman hugged her. "We missed you last Sunday at lunch."

To Crystal's humiliation, she felt tears welling up in her eyes. She blinked hard. "All my family was in. So I. . ." She looked away.

"I understand." Mrs. Buchanan squeezed her hand. "Is everything okay?"

Crystal pursed her lips and nodded. "I'm sure it will be." *Please let it be,* she prayed silently. She wanted to question Jeremy's mom, but if she and Jeremy had a communication problem that was that bad, they had no business getting married.

"I am, too."

She jerked her attention back to Mrs. Buchanan. In her eyes, she saw a calm assurance. "We're looking forward to the wedding, dear. And to having you as part of our family."

"Thanks. Me, too." She saw Jeremy almost to the back door. "I'm sorry, but I need to speak to Jeremy." She caught him just as he got outside. "Jeremy."

He turned, and when he saw her, his eyes lit up just like always. But just as quickly as it came, the fire was extinguished from the inside. Consciously. This made no sense. "Hi."

She stepped close to him. "We have to talk. Really talk. If it's over, it's over. But I deserve to understand."

Beka tugged on her dress.

Crystal looked down into those big eyes, and her heart melted. "Hey, sweetie."

"Daddy watched you on TV."

"What?"

Jeremy frowned and shook his head as if to say, "Five-year-olds."

He gently touched Crystal's arm and put his mouth close to her ear. "On Tuesday I'm going to Oklahoma for a couple of days to get some more cattle. I have some things to figure out. I'm so sorry. Can you give me a little time?"

"Okay." She couldn't say any more; her throat was already tight from holding back tears. She wanted to demand answers now. But not if it meant jeopardizing her future with the man she loved. "When will you be back?"

"Probably Thursday night." He disappeared into the crowd,

taking Beka with him. Crystal walked out to her car, numb and unsure what to think. How would she make it until he'd had enough time to think things through? And what then? If he came to a decision to end their engagement, how would she make it through the rest of her life without him?

❧

Over the weekend, Andrew had steered clear of the McCords. He figured with Jonathan and Elyse's brothers around, she had enough manpower to protect her.

Saturday, he'd gone into town and asked a few questions about Zeke. All he'd found out was what he'd already known—that Zeke was rotten to the core.

Sunday, after church, he'd headed straight to the river.

Monday, he'd been painting about an hour when he heard a movement behind him. He swung around.

Jonathan McCord grinned. "Quick reflexes for a painter."

Andrew returned his smile. "Years of karate and tae kwon do lessons."

"Lynda is cooking her world-famous pot roast tonight, and we'd love it if you'd eat with us."

"I appreciate the offer, sir. But just because I'm living here doesn't mean I have to be included in the family meals. I'm used to making it fine on my own. Tell her thank you, though."

Jonathan ran his hand over the top of a can of paint and sat down on one.

Out of politeness, Andrew did the same.

"My wife makes the best pot roast you've ever tasted. And it's enough to feed an army. We won't be begging you to come to every meal, but you'd be crazy to let this one go by."

"She found out you warned me last week about breaking Elyse's heart, didn't she?"

Jonathan's eyes widened, and he laughed. "Yes, as a matter of fact, she did. And she's decided that's why you made yourself so scarce this weekend. So are you going to help an old man stay out of the doghouse or not?"

Old man? Jonathan didn't look much older than his sons. Andrew guessed him to be fifty, maybe. "I'll make that sacrifice for you, I guess."

"In that case, supper is at six-thirty."

"Do Luke and Matthew know I'm coming?"

"Matthew has gone back to Tennessee. Escaped by the skin of his teeth. Lucas will be there, but you don't have to worry. I'm not the only one who got straightened out about trying to run guests off before they even get settled in."

Andrew raised an eyebrow. "Technically, I'm not really a guest. I'm a painter."

Jonathan stood and clapped Andrew on the shoulder. "Are you going to tell her that?"

"No sir. See you at six-thirty."

❦

When Elyse walked out the door to go to her parents' for supper, the sheriff's car was in her driveway.

Jack stood beside it talking to Andrew. He waved to her. "Good news. We found your Jeep."

"That's great!" Elyse dreaded asking the next question, but she had to. "What kind of shape is it in?"

Jack frowned. "The inside is fine. But the outside. . ."

"Oh no."

"Nothing permanent, but he wrote some stuff on it with spray paint."

"What kind of stuff?" Elyse asked, her stomach feeling sick.

Jack looked uncomfortable. "Oh, you know. Threats. We took pictures. I hope you didn't mind, but I sent it on down to the dealership to get them to buff those things out and repaint it."

Her mind raced as she imagined the threats Zeke would have written. She shivered. Jack's eyes met hers. "I don't want to scare you, but only a real sicko would stop while he was ditching a vehicle to paint a message to the owner. You definitely made an enemy. Be careful."

CHAPTER 10

She'll be careful." Andrew stepped up next to her, and she was glad he was there. "Any sign of him?" he asked.

Jack gave a slight shake of his head. "Nope."

Andrew frowned. "Where'd they find the Jeep?"

"About seven miles from here." Jack motioned with his hand. "Right outside of Hardy, down a little road off Bowman Hill." The radio on his belt crackled, and he put a finger on a button to silence it. "From all the signs, it looks like he ditched it the same day he stole it. But no one's been down there until this morning. A squirrel hunter found it and remembered the news report."

"So he could be anywhere," Andrew said, almost as if to himself.

She turned around to face him. "You think he's driving a little yellow truck now?"

"What are you talking about?" Jack asked.

Andrew quickly told him about the yellow Toyota.

Jack made notes in a small notebook. "I'll run a check and see if a truck matching that description has been stolen."

Elyse shivered. "Thanks."

"When can she get her Jeep back?" Andrew asked.

"The dealership said it should be ready by Thursday." Jack looked at Elyse. "If you want me to, I'll drive it out here and get one of the boys to pick me up."

"I'd appreciate it."

"I'll let y'all know if I find anything on that yellow truck," Jack said as he climbed into his patrol car. "Call me if you see it again."

They both nodded.

After Jack drove away, Andrew put his hand on Elyse's shoulder. "You okay?"

She shuddered. "I am. But it's weird. I almost don't even want to drive the Jeep again after knowing Zeke has been in it."

"That's normal." He slid his arm around her and gave her a side hug.

She put her arm around his waist and relaxed against him, taking comfort in his strength. "Thanks for that. Always nice to feel normal."

Just at the second that she started to feel really awkward, he stepped away from her. "Are you going to eat famous pot roast with your folks tonight?"

Her eyes widened. "Yep. Are you?"

He rubbed his stomach. "I can't wait."

"After you disappeared this weekend, I thought maybe you had a policy against fraternizing with clients."

"Even if I did, I'd make an exception for you."

"Thanks." She groaned inwardly. Thanks for what? Finally putting in an appearance?

As they walked down the pea gravel path, Andrew glanced over at

Elyse. "I want to ask you something, but it's kind of personal."

"Uh-oh." She chewed her bottom lip. "I guess you can ask. If I don't want to answer, I don't have to."

"You don't look like your sisters. And they don't look like each other. Same for your brothers. Well, except for Kaleigh and Chance."

She grinned at him. "Was that a question?"

He swallowed. "I was kind of hoping you'd fill in the blanks."

"Ohh," she exclaimed in mock enlightenment, "you wanted me to tell you that we're adopted." She paused. "Except Crystal. She's Mama and Daddy's biological child. And so was Cami. They were twins."

"Cami?"

"Our sister who was killed in a car accident several years ago."

He sucked in his breath. "The reason you're scared of reckless driving. I'm so sorry."

"It's okay. You didn't know."

"Thanks for telling me." He kicked a piece of white gravel. "About Cami, but mostly about all of you being adopted. You're all so much alike in mannerisms and so. . .brotherly and sisterly, that it didn't hit me until last night how much different you all look from each other."

"I forget sometimes." She looked over at him. "That we're adopted, I mean."

"Do you remember a time before you came to live here?"

"I try not to."

He took the hint. "How's Pal doing?"

The sadness disappeared from her expression. "So much better! You wouldn't believe he's the same dog. You'll have to come in and see him after supper." Her face reddened. "That wasn't an excuse to invite you in, by the way."

He chuckled. "I knew it wasn't. You don't strike me as a 'come on in and check out my DVD collection' kind of girl."

"I'm definitely not." Elyse ran ahead to the porch of the main house and waited at the door for Andrew.

He opened the door for her. "After you," he murmured.

"Manners. I like it," she said softly.

"I like you," he said even softer—soft enough that he could be sure she didn't hear it. But the fact that the words slipped out at all shook him to the core. What future could there possibly be with her? Or anyone else for that matter? None. He knew the answer, just as plainly as he knew that the police, though they'd officially let him go, still considered him a possible "person of interest" in Melanie's murder.

For the next few minutes, he let himself be absorbed into the buzz that was family. When they were settled at the table, he got his bearings enough to thank Lynda McCord for the supper invitation. "It would have been awful to miss this delicious roast." He grinned at Jonathan. "Your husband was right. It is the best I've ever tasted."

Lynda smiled at Jonathan. "Aww. . .that's sweet."

"But true," Jonathan said. He looked at Andrew. "That's the key to good flattery. It needs to be true."

"Doesn't that kind of make it not flattery?" Luke asked dryly. "I think they just call those compliments."

As the easy banter swirled around him, Andrew relaxed. Meals at the table in the Stone household had never been like this. His father had used the time to touch base with Andrew and make sure he was on track to the goal—to be just like his father and his grandfather, the best Texas Rangers there ever were. Andrew took a bite of roast. If only that had been his goal, too, instead of just one he inherited, his life might have been completely different. He pushed away the unpleasant memories and reached for a yeast roll.

After everyone had finished eating, he looked at Elyse next to him. "Want to help me do the dishes?"

Lynda McCord shook her head. "I've got all night to get these done." She glanced at her husband. "Besides, Jonathan's already volunteered to help me." She stood and gathered up an armload of plates. "You kids take the night off."

"I'm going to turn in early," Crystal said, her voice dull.

Lynda's eyes filled with concern as she looked at her oldest daughter. "You sure, honey?" She nodded toward the plates. "I can leave these for a while if you want to talk."

Crystal shook her head. "Not tonight."

Elyse hugged her and whispered something Andrew couldn't hear.

Crystal said something about "later," and Elyse nodded and released her. Crystal waved toward him and Luke. "Good night," she said as she headed up the stairs.

After they all said good night to Crystal, Jonathan and Lynda took the dishes into the kitchen.

Luke retrieved his cowboy hat by the hook at the front door. "I'm going to head on out to my apartment." He grinned at Andrew. "Some of us have to be at work early in the morning."

Obviously, the cowboy carpenter had noticed that Andrew wasn't up working when he left this morning. And Andrew wasn't about to tell him that he'd barely gotten in bed from keeping watch all night when he heard Luke's loud truck start up across the property. "Must be tough."

Elyse hugged Luke before he could answer. "Play nice," Andrew heard her whisper.

Luke nodded. "I am." With that, he let himself out the door and was gone.

Elyse turned to Andrew. "Sorry about that. My brothers can be a little overprotective."

"Really? I hadn't noticed." Andrew grinned.

She slapped him on the shoulder. "Sure you haven't. Now, be a gentleman and walk me home."

"Yes, ma'am." He held the door open for her.

"Did I mention I could get used to these good manners of yours?"

He chuckled. "You might have said something about it." A brisk wind almost pulled the screen door out of his hand. He shut it carefully behind them and turned back to her. "Looks like a storm's brewing." The porch swing swayed back and forth. In the sky, dark clouds rolled toward them so fast it looked like a video clip set on high speed.

"We'd better hurry," Elyse said over her shoulder.

Andrew came up beside her and grabbed her hand. It felt as natural as anything he'd ever done. Yet at the same time, touching her hand was like grabbing an electric current, and he could feel it to the center of his heart.

They jogged together past his camper. When they reached her walkway, they stopped.

"The thunder and lightning are still pretty far off, so it looks like we may have a few minutes before the front actually gets here."

Elyse nodded. "I haven't heard the weather, but I have a

basement. The dogs and I go down there when there's a bad storm." The wind whipped her hair across her face, but she didn't pull her hand away from his. "If you don't mind four dogs, you're welcome to join us."

He tugged her around to face him and looked into her brown eyes. "I like dogs."

A small smile teased at her lips. "That's good."

"It is convenient, isn't it?" If he leaned forward six inches, his lips would be touching that smile. And he would be dragging her into the mess he'd been involved in for the past three years. Yet he couldn't seem to look away.

❧

Elyse stared into his blue eyes. He was going to kiss her. And if she let him, her heart might not survive when he finished painting the barn and left. Before she had to make a decision, something over her shoulder caught his attention and his eyes narrowed.

She started to turn, but he pulled her into a tight embrace, nuzzling his face against her hair. "There's a man standing at this end of the lane, kind of behind a tree. He's watching us." His words were warm against her ear.

"Is it Zeke?" she breathed, not moving.

"No, he's a lot taller than Zeke. I'm guessing it's the driver of the yellow Toyota. I'm going to let you go, but don't look." He released her, and she could tell he was forcing himself to smile. "I'll walk you to the house," he said quietly. "I want you to go in and lock the door. Then I'll get him."

"No," she whispered. "What if it's just someone who's lost?"

"A lost person who is spying on you? When you get inside, call 911."

Suddenly Andrew let go of her and took off at a dead run.

She spun around to see the tall man sprinting down the lane. Andrew darted diagonally through the field, leaped the fence, and tackled him.

"Let me go," the man yelled as Elyse ran to them. "Let me go."

Andrew ignored his pleas and held him face down with his arm behind his back. "Call 911," he yelled to Elyse.

"No!" The man went wild, thrashing around and fighting to get loose.

Elyse pulled her phone out as she got close to them, but just then Andrew glanced back at her and the man broke loose. In that instant, his gaze locked with Elyse's. She sank to her knees and her phone tumbled out of her hand. This couldn't be right.

Andrew glanced back at her, and the man took advantage of his distraction and sprinted for the road. Andrew chased him, but Elyse heard a motor start up in just a few seconds. Even before Andrew came walking back up the lane alone, his hair whipping in the wind, she knew the man was gone.

Lightning flashed wildly across the sky, followed quickly by a loud clap of thunder, then more lightning. The storm had arrived.

CHAPTER 11

Crystal looked out the window of her upstairs bedroom at the darkening clouds. Jeremy's house didn't have a basement. She picked up her phone. Maybe she should call and just make sure he knew the weather was bad. She shook her head. His parents would call him. He didn't need her. He'd made that clear when she'd taken the brownies over. And even clearer after church yesterday.

Her phone sprang to life in her hand and her heart leapt. Jeremy.

"Hello?"

"Crystal, it's Jeremy."

Since when did he need to identify himself? "Hey."

"Listen, I don't know if you've been watching the weather, but there's a line of thunderstorms heading for Sharp County." He cleared his throat. "They mentioned Shady Grove specifically."

"Do you and Beka want to come down here? We can all camp out in the basement."

Silence.

"Jeremy?"

"We'd better just go to Mom and Dad's. It's closer. But you go on to the basement." He hesitated. "Please. Right now."

"Okay, I will." She couldn't wrap her mind around reality. He cared enough to beg her to go to the basement, but he didn't want to be around her.

"Crys?"

"Yes?"

"I love you."

Tears filled her eyes. "I love you, too, Jeremy." *And I'm not going to let you throw us away.*

"We've got to go get ready to drive down to Mom and Dad's."

"Y'all be careful."

"You, too." And with that he broke the connection.

She swiped the tears off her face and pulled on her sweat-pants and a sweatshirt. She didn't really care if she blew away in a storm right now, but she'd promised him she'd go to the base-ment. She'd promised him she'd love him forever. And she kept her promises.

❧

Andrew reached down and lifted Elyse to her feet. "What hap-pened?" He picked up her cell phone, dusted it off, and held it out to her. "Do you know that man?"

Her phone rang in his hand, and she stared at it as if afraid to answer it.

He looked down at the caller ID. "It's your mom."

Lightning flashed as she took the phone and slid it open. "Hello?" Thunder boomed. He kept his arm around Elyse and guided her to the house while she listened.

They were almost to the front door by the time she said,

"Okay. Thanks. Love you, too." She slid the phone shut and glanced up at him, her brown eyes huge in a pale face. "Mama said there's a severe thunderstorm heading this way. We have to get the dogs into the basement right now."

She unlocked the front door, and Andrew followed her inside. The dogs ran to greet them. "Do you have a weather radio down there?"

Elyse nodded and rubbed the dogs' heads absently. "I have a whole kit. Even food and water for the dogs. After the tornado hit Highland a few years ago, Daddy made us all get prepared." She slapped her leg with her palm. "Let's go, girls." She glanced at Pal. "And boy."

Andrew walked down the basement stairs behind her and the dogs. He was concerned about the storm, but most of all, he wanted to know what had happened outside awhile ago. Had Elyse just tripped in the storm? Or had she recognized the man he was struggling with? Something had changed in her eyes when she'd seen him.

By the time Andrew stepped off the bottom step, Elyse had already turned on the weather radio and cranked the volume up. They listened, in silence, to the computerized monotone voice repeating the local conditions. She plopped down on the tweed couch, and Andrew sat on a recliner next to it. She tucked the dogs around her, like a mother hen with her chicks. Her eyes met his, and she looked away.

The radio voice was talking about the storm now, naming the places in the path and the approximate arrival time. "Shady Grove at 9:45 p.m."

Andrew looked at the clock. Five minutes. He gave Elyse a tentative smile. "Are you scared of storms?"

She nodded. "One of my long list of fears."

He stood and gave Pal a gentle pat. "Scoot over, boy." He sank onto the couch beside her and put his arm around her shoulder. Pal plopped down in his lap. "Would it be okay if I prayed?"

Elyse looked at him, and for the first time, her eyes brimmed with tears. "I'd love that." She hit mute on the radio.

They bowed their heads, and he prayed from his heart, asking God to keep them all safe from the storm, to watch over those traveling in it, and to heal whatever brokenness tonight brought.

When he finished, Elyse laid her head on his shoulder. "Thanks." She closed her eyes.

He hated to bring his question up again, but if the answer was no, he needed to call Jack Westwood immediately. "Elyse?"

She opened her eyes. "What?"

"Did you know that man out there?"

She closed her eyes again.

The seconds ticked away, the storm a dull roar outside, while he waited for her to answer.

Finally, she sighed and opened her eyes. Tears sparkled in the brown depths. "I know who he is."

"Who?"

"His name is Luis Reynolds. He's my biological father."

Andrew stared at her.

"Biological father sounds like a term that ought to be used by people who were given up for adoption as babies, doesn't it?" Elyse said, almost as if to herself. "It doesn't sound right coming from someone who remembers when he brushed her hair and taught her to tie her shoes and answered to 'Dad.' "

Andrew's breath caught in his throat at the deep pain he heard beneath her words. "What happened?"

She shrugged and blinked hard. "A lot of things. But mostly prison."

"How old were you?"

"Eight when I went into foster care. Ten when the McCords adopted me."

"And you haven't seen him since?"

She shook her head. "I didn't even know he was out of prison." She shivered.

Andrew tightened his arm around her shoulders. "What about your biological mother?"

"Dead."

He read between the lines. Mother dead, father in prison. That had domestic violence written all over it. And now the man was out and after his daughter. "We need to call the sheriff."

She shook her head. "Absolutely not." All trace of tears disappeared from her eyes as they flashed. "You're not to tell a soul about him showing up. Or I'll never speak to you again."

He sat up straight. "Elyse. Use your head. He may intend to harm you."

"He would never"—she held his gaze, her expressive eyes telegraphing the certainty she had that she was right—"never physically hurt me. And emotionally, there's nothing he can do to me that he hasn't already done. We're not telling anyone."

Andrew could tell her mind was made up, and considering he had his own secrets from the local police, he felt he had no choice but to respect her decision. He didn't want to scare her, but he had to make sure she had all the information. "Your—Luis said something while we were struggling. I couldn't make out the whole sentence, but I did catch one word." He looked across at her. "It was 'Zeke.' "

Elyse shivered. "That doesn't make sense."

"I know. But I'm sure that's what he said."

Her phone rang. She answered it, talked for a minute, and then hung up. "That was Mama. Apparently the storm blew over without doing any damage. And she said that was the last front for tonight, according to the radar." She gave him a sheepish look. "Which we'd have known if I hadn't muted the radio and left it. Sorry." She pushed the dogs off gently and stood.

Andrew followed suit. "So if you're not going to tell the police, what are you going to do?"

"Pray. And keep my eyes open." She smiled at him. "And be thankful that you're around." Her expression grew serious. "Promise you won't tell anyone about him showing up here tonight, please."

Andrew couldn't refuse. "I promise."

She blew out her breath. "Thanks. Together we can figure this out." She hurried up the stairs with the dogs close at her heels. When Andrew got to the top of the stairs, she was looking out the window at the yard, lit up by an orange guard light. "I don't see any wind damage at all. But it does look like we got a lot of rain."

"Your dad will be glad." As soon as he said the words, it sounded awkward. Jonathan McCord was her dad, but after tonight. . .

He could see in her eyes that either she'd read his thoughts or it had sounded odd to her, too. "I only have one dad. So don't feel funny saying it."

He nodded. "I'd better get back over to the camper and try to catch up on the sleep I lost last night."

She gave him a tired grin. "Yep. You have to get an early start on the barn in the morning and impress Luke."

He chuckled. "You have my number, don't you?"

She walked him to the door. "I knew your pride wouldn't take his needling about sleeping late very well."

In the foyer, he stared into her eyes and wondered how she'd come to mean so much to him in such a short time. He'd known Melanie for years before they'd even dated. This wasn't like him. He knew there was no future here. Yet he couldn't stop himself from kissing her.

At the last minute, she turned her head and his kiss fell on her cheek. She stepped back and looked down at the floor. "I'm sorry, Andrew. But my life has been turned upside down lately. And when you get done with the barn in a couple of months, you'll leave. I'd rather not make that day any harder than it has to be." She looked up at him with a smile. "Friends?"

He nodded. At least one of them had good sense. It was a logical decision. But logic didn't stop the disappointment. "Good night then. . .friend."

"Good night."

He slipped outside and stood there until he heard the dead bolt engage; then he walked slowly back to his camper, all thoughts of sleep gone from his mind.

Kaleigh hit the snooze button on the alarm, and her hand came away with a sticky note attached. She squinted at it. Be Quiet. She rolled over. It was the second day of a new week with a new goal added to the first one: "Don't talk when silence will do." Since she was still in the privacy of her bed, she groaned. Her feet hurt, and she hadn't even gotten out of bed yet. And she had to get up an hour earlier to straighten her hair. Now, thanks to Operation New Me, she wasn't even going to be allowed to complain about it all day. This week was shaping up to be hard.

After her shower, she straightened her hair and slipped into the outfit her roommate had left on the bed for her. Ugh. Basic brown from head to toe. Same strand of pearls she'd borrowed last week. And brown shoes. She grunted with relief when she saw they were flats. "Happy feet," she whispered.

Her first class was Advanced Journalism, and Carlton was in it. When she walked in, he glanced up but continued talking to a girl with hair even straighter, wearing an even drabber outfit than Kaleigh had on. She wasn't all that surprised. Their coffee date after class last Friday had been kind of a bust. She'd been scared to talk, afraid he'd find out that even though she was a journalism major, she wasn't really a fan of Homer or the classics. She needn't have worried. He was nice, but most of his conversation subtly pointed out how smart he was.

It doesn't have to be him, Kaleigh reminded herself. A wedding date was a wedding date, whether he had numbers behind his name or not. She scanned the guys in the class and sighed. So many geeks, so little time. Not that she was opposed to a smart guy with glasses. But she drew the line at hands softer than hers.

She walked over to her normal seat and sat down.

"Kaleigh?"

She turned around to face Nathan Manchester, the guy she'd beat in the Ping-Pong tournament. "Yes?"

"You look different." He tilted his head. "You look good."

She bit back a sarcastic retort. *Be quiet*, she reminded herself. Not every word that came to her brain had to come out of her mouth. "Thank you, Nathan."

She turned back around and buried her face in the *Iliad*, which she'd actually checked out of the library this morning. Not that she was going to read it. But it made a good prop for being quiet.

"So what's so different about you? I can't put my finger on it," Nathan said from behind her.

Um, everything? Kaleigh sucked her bottom lip into her teeth and held it.

"I guess it's your hair."

Be quiet. That's all she had to do today. Just be quiet.

"Hi, Kaleigh."

She looked up. The *Iliad* was turning out to be better bait for a wedding date than a neon jig for a bigmouth bass. "Hi, Carlton."

"Would you like to go eat lunch after class?"

"To the cafeteria?" She had a meal plan card, so it was the cheapest choice.

He made a moue of distaste with his mouth. She'd never seen anyone actually make a moue before, but it was the only way she could describe what he did. She almost giggled, but she was pretty sure that would ruin today's goal.

"I was thinking more along the lines of Colton's Steakhouse."

"Are you buying?" the old Kaleigh would have said. The new Kaleigh just smiled. "That sounds good."

Carlton strode confidently back over to his seat. It was only Tuesday, and the second step of Operation New Me was already going well. To celebrate, Kaleigh turned around to smile at the guy behind her. "So, Nathan, played any Ping-Pong lately?"

CHAPTER 12

Elyse woke with a terrible sense of foreboding. She felt the weight of dogs all around her, which was unusual. In that moment between sleep and wakefulness, she remembered inviting them up there but couldn't quite recall the awful thing that made her need the comfort of having them close. When the full memory of last night came to her, she put her pillow over her face. For eighteen years, she'd been afraid that someday her biological father might find her. That was one thing she didn't have to worry about anymore.

She threw the pillow off, and the dogs stirred. Majesty and Missy leapt onto the floor, anxious to go outside. Nikki snuck in for a quick good morning kiss on Elyse's cheek then joined the other two. Pal, on the far corner of the bed, blinked several times as if wondering where he was.

"I'm right here with you, boy," Elyse murmured. "Some days it's hard to make sense of things." She sat up and looked at the clock. One hour until the first grooming appointment.

She slid her feet into her flip-flops. The dogs led her down the hall to the back door. She let them out, hurried into the kitchen, made coffee, snagged her Bible from the table, and went out to sit on the deck and read. Instead of starting in Proverbs where she'd been reading lately, she flipped over to the first chapter of 2 Timothy. She had verse 7 memorized, but today she needed to see the familiar words in black and white: "For God has not given us a spirit of fear, but of power and of love, and of a sound mind."

Elyse leaned back in her chair and closed her eyes. Why was it so hard to let go of her fears? Without opening her eyes, she made a noise of disgust. Maybe because she had so many. She ticked them off on her fingers, the rational as well as the irrational ones—fear of Luis coming back into her life, fear of cows, fear of people finding out that as a child she'd been a con artist, fear of storms, fear of speaking in front of people, fear of going too fast in a vehicle, and ultimately fear of being killed.

As she finished the list, she sat up and opened her eyes. Several of those she'd faced in the last few weeks. Luis was back, and sure, it was scary, but the world hadn't ended. She'd told Andrew about her childhood, and he hadn't shunned her. When they'd been in the basement last night and Andrew had prayed that God would keep them safe from the storm, Elyse had believed He would. She smiled. That was faith. Stronger than she used to have. She glanced out at the dogs, in her mind's eye seeing Zeke again raising that pistol to shoot Pal. And she'd thrown herself on top of him and the gun. The old Elyse couldn't have done that. God was giving her what she asked for.

She remembered a preacher saying not to pray for patience if you weren't ready to learn it through life experiences. For the past several years, if she had been pressed to describe her life in one word, she'd probably have said, "Boring." But since she'd made the decision to overcome her fears, her life had been filled with excitement and danger. And even though boring was. . .well, boring, it was a lot more relaxing than danger. Still, through danger she was facing her fears. And coming out alive. "Thank You, Lord, for Your protection," she whispered.

When she finished reading and praying, she hurried in to shower and dress and get ready for the day. Back to the routine was what she needed.

Five dogs later, Elyse wondered why she'd thought routine was so great. Her arms ached and her clothes were wet and sticky. But she was done for the day. She jumped in the shower again and had just finished dressing when the phone rang. Suddenly she regretted letting caller ID go on her home phone in an effort to economize. What if it was Luis?

She let it ring two more times. What if it was him? Wouldn't it be better to know what he wanted? What his angle was this time? "Hello?"

"Elyse, it's Jack. We're outside with your Jeep."

"Perfect timing. I'll be right out."

She pulled her damp hair up in a messy bun and slipped on her shoes. When she opened the door, she smiled. Her Jeep was back. She'd bought it a couple of months ago in an effort to be less afraid, and it had instantly become a part of the family. She felt like hugging it. The first thing she was going to do was clean out the interior. The thought of Zeke sitting in her seat and breathing the air inside the vehicle made her feel yucky. Crazy, but there it was. She waved at Jack. "Thanks for bringing it." She jogged down the walkway to him. "She looks as good as new."

"Smells as good as new, too, thanks to him," Jack said, nodding his head toward the pole barn.

"Thanks to Andrew?" she said as she stepped over and opened the Jeep door. The new car smell hit her in the face, and she saw paper mats on the floorboard.

"Yep. He called and asked me to have the dealership detail it inside before I brought it home. They said it's just like new."

Elyse laughed as she ran her hand over the clean, shiny seat. "This is awesome! Can you have them send me a bill?"

"No, ma'am. He drove into town awhile ago and paid them for doing the interior."

"That silly guy." Elyse couldn't believe how lighthearted she felt. What a nice thing to do.

After Jack left, she glanced at the barn. Andrew's truck was gone. She'd have to thank him later. She ran back to her Jeep and jumped in. Right now it was time to go for a ride. Somewhere neither Zeke nor Luis could find her. She called Crystal on the way up to the big house. "Whatcha' doin?"

Crystal groaned. "Working on my business plan for the drama studio."

Elyse wrinkled her nose. "Sounds like you need a break."

"You have no idea."

"Good. Let's go for a ride."

"When?" Crystal sounded interested but a little confused.

"Now."

"Where?"

"Wherever we feel like going."

Crystal hesitated then laughed. "That sounds perfect. Come on over. I'll be ready."

"I'm here."

"In that case, give me two secs to grab some shoes and brush my hair, and I'll be out."

A minute later, Crystal ran out and jumped in. "Let's blow this Popsicle stand."

Elyse shifted the Jeep into reverse and threw a little gravel as she accelerated out of the driveway.

"Wow," Crystal said. "What's gotten into you? You must have been going. . .like. . .twenty miles per hour."

"I know, right?" Elyse smiled at her sister and turned toward town. "I got my Jeep back, and I'm feeling wild and crazy."

"It smells brand-new again."

Elyse told Crystal about Andrew having it detailed.

"He really likes you already, doesn't he?"

Elyse shrugged. "Maybe. But we're just going to be friends."

"Been there, done that." Crystal held out her hand. "Got an engagement ring."

"You and Jeremy are different."

When Crystal didn't respond, Elyse glanced at her. "Crys? You okay?"

The smile Crystal gave her didn't quite reach her eyes. "I don't want to bring us down. Let's keep it light for now, okay?"

Elyse had heavy stuff she didn't want to talk about, too, so she could totally relate. "Hey, I have an idea."

"Uh-oh, what now?"

"Why don't you text Kaleigh and see if she's busy?"

"You want to drive all the way to Searcy?"

Elyse kept her eyes on the road, but she could feel Crystal looking at her as if she'd lost her mind for considering an hour and a half drive without planning it. "We could be there by the time she gets out of class and hang out for a couple of hours. Why not?"

Crystal pursed her lips then hit the dash with her hand. "It sure beats waiting around for Jeremy to call." She lifted her phone and punched some buttons. "Maybe I can catch her between classes."

Elyse turned right at the highway, just in case, and headed toward Batesville. They could always just go to a movie or something there.

In a few minutes, Crystal punched her fist in the air. "She's free. She's got something to talk to us about, so she's really excited that we're coming."

"Cool. Now would you do me a favor and text Luke and ask him to go over and let the dogs out when he gets home from work and again right before he goes to bed if we're not back by then?"

"Sure." In less than a minute, Crystal nodded. "He said he would. No problem. And I texted Mom, too, and told her neither of us would be around for supper."

"Thanks. So how's the business plan coming? Are you still planning on opening in January?"

Crystal sighed.

"Uh-oh, not light enough conversation?"

"Oh, it's fine. I always want to talk about the drama studio. At least I feel like I have some control of that situation. Yes, I'm still planning on opening in mid-January. I guess you know that Mama and Daddy are having Andrew paint the barn inside and out as a wedding present to me."

"Yes, he's really excited about it."

"Me, too. That's not an expense I have to figure in, but there are so many other things. The curtain, some basic props, insurance, and the list goes on."

"Anything worth having is worth working for," Elyse said.

"Okay, Daddy."

Elyse shrugged. "He's a smart man. What can I say? So are you going to advertise? Hand out flyers at the school? Or what?"

"Actually"—Crystal stared down at her lap—"I'm already filled to capacity for all the classes and have a waiting list."

Elyse glanced at her. "Wow. I guess I forgot you were a famous Broadway actress. Thankfully, everyone else remembered."

"Don't be silly. But having students lined up will definitely make things go better at the bank."

The family had always known that Crystal's move to New York after Cami's death was more about running away from her grief than about following a dream. And though Cami had been obsessed with going to Broadway, Crystal had always enjoyed working with kids. "I was proud of you for getting the lead in that play, but I'm so glad you're finally fulfilling your own dream."

"Me, too." A shift in Crystal's tone made Elyse nervous. "And even if Jeremy and I don't end up getting married, I'm not sorry I moved back home to open the school."

Not get married? Elyse clutched the steering wheel tightly, unsure what to say. "Is that a possibility?"

"I don't know. I went ahead and ordered invitations without him. We set a date, and if he doesn't want to get married, he's going to have to tell me. I deserve that much."

"Have you asked him?"

"Only over and over."

"What does he say?"

"He uses Beka's presence as an excuse not to answer. And when I ask on the phone, he always has to go. But the other night. . ."

Elyse listened quietly as Crystal told her about Jeremy calling the night of the storm. When she described the anguish in his voice when he told her he loved her, Elyse felt her eyes burning. "Something's not right."

Crystal nodded. "I know."

"Have you considered confronting him while Beka is at school? Just driving over there and asking him what's going on?"

"You don't think that would be sneaky? Like an ambush?"

Elyse shook her head. "You do deserve to know."

"Okay then. You convinced me. I'm going to do it tomorrow."

"Good." Elyse pulled up to a stoplight and looked over at her sister. "Call me after if you need me."

"I will. Now back to light subject matter. We're supposed to be having fun." She gave Elyse a mock-stern look. "Say something fun."

"Did you hear the joke about the three guy dogs who saw a pretty poodle go by?"

"Oh no, even your humor is going to the dogs."

"Fine. Lucky for you, we should be at Kaleigh's dorm soon. She'll have something fun to talk about. She always does."

Twenty minutes later they pulled up to the dorm. "There she is," Crystal said. She frowned. "At least, I think that's her."

"What is she wearing?" Elyse asked, puzzled. "Some kind of costume?"

Crystal shook her head. "It looks like a brown pantsuit."

Elyse squinted at the girl making her way across campus. "And pearls?"

"Yep. And her hair is straightened—all over."

Usually their impetuous sister only had the time or patience to straighten her side bangs. The rest of her hair was either swept up in a messy bun or it cascaded down her back in wild, beautiful red curls. Elyse loved it either way. Although with it straight, she looked more chic and stylish. "She looks like a model," Elyse whispered, even though Kaleigh couldn't hear her yet.

Crystal nodded. "But she doesn't look like herself. I guess this has something to do with what she wanted to talk to us about." She opened the door and got out.

Elyse joined her.

When Kaleigh got to them, she pulled them both into a hug at once. "I'm so glad y'all are here. Is everything okay?"

"Yep." Elyse grinned. "Just celebrating getting my Jeep back."

"Yea!" Kaleigh pirouetted. "So? Notice anything different?"

"Are you kidding?" Crystal asked. "We almost didn't recognize you. What gives?"

"I'll tell you about it at the park. I ordered pizza to be delivered there in"—she looked at her phone—"ten minutes. Is that okay?"

Elyse laughed. "What if we say no?" She glanced out the car window at the beautiful blue sky and still bright sunshine. Who could say no to being outside on a day like this?

"Then there will be one irritated delivery guy, won't there?" Kaleigh said as she shoved her corduroy Hollister bag into the backseat and climbed in after it. "I brought jeans to change into. But I wanted y'all to get the full effect so you'd know the sacrifice I'm making to get a date for your wedding."

CHAPTER 13

Elyse and Crystal exchanged a look. Kaleigh had never had trouble getting a date for anything. Elyse didn't question her. She had a feeling this explanation would probably go down better with pizza.

While Kaleigh went to change into jeans, the young delivery boy delivered a large pepperoni pizza. "Yum." Elyse breathed in the scent as she and Crystal split the cost, adding a generous tip.

Kaleigh ran across from the restroom toward them.

"She looks more like herself now, doesn't she?" Crystal murmured.

"Yes, why would she want to change that?"

"Hey! I didn't mean to skip out on paying." Kaleigh slowed to a walk and rummaged in her bag the last few steps. "What's my share of the bill?"

"Your share is telling us all the latest news." Elyse smiled at her. "It's on us today."

"When you're out of college and working next year, you can buy the pizza every time," Crystal said, grinning, as they claimed an empty picnic table. "Want me to say the blessing?"

Elyse and Kaleigh nodded and bowed their heads.

When Crystal finished, Kaleigh slid a slice of pizza from the box. "Actually, the future is what I've been thinking a lot about lately."

Crystal and Elyse ate pizza while Kaleigh told them about her plan to get a wedding date and how Chance had been honest with her, so she'd changed her plan from Operation Wedding Date to Operation New Me. When she finished her pizza, she pulled a black notebook from her bag and laid it on the table. "It just hit me when he was pointing out how guys never want to keep going out with me, that if I don't change, I'm going to end up like Chance's and my granddad before he died."

"Living on a houseboat on the Mississippi?" Crystal asked, her expression puzzled.

"No, silly. That's the same thing Chance said." Kaleigh rolled her eyes. "Old and alone before I die."

Crystal frowned. "He wasn't alone. You and Chance visited him for two weeks every summer until he. . ."

"Died three years ago," Kaleigh said flatly. "Old and alone."

"Honey," Elyse said softly. "You've got us. All of us. The chances of you ending up old and alone are very slim."

"Okay, I know that. But I also know that I can be difficult. And sometimes people don't like me."

Elyse couldn't believe her ears. "What's not to like? You're amazing." People who didn't know Kaleigh well sometimes equated her impetuousness with shallowness, but her family realized that her spirit ran as deep as the mighty Mississippi River she'd been raised on the first several years of her life.

Crystal's mouth dropped open. "Kaleigh, how can you say that? People love you."

"Not as much as they will if I become like everyone else."

"That would be such a waste," Elyse said. "I've always admired your spunk. And especially how you are you no matter what anyone thinks."

Kaleigh stared at her. "I thought you, of all people, would understand. What I'm doing isn't that much different than you buying the Jeep and trying to overcome your fears like you were talking about at the end of the summer."

Elyse didn't know what to say. It was very different. She'd wanted to deepen her faith in God and quit being so fearful. But she wasn't trying to change who she was as a person. Was she?

Kaleigh's chin lifted in that way that Elyse had come to recognize over the years. "Look. I'm going to change who I am, slowly but surely. First I'm going to get a respectable date to your wedding, Crys. Then who knows? Maybe even something more permanent, eventually."

Crystal shook her head. "But anyone worth having will love you just as you are."

Kaleigh sighed. "You have to say that—you're my sister. Besides, they *will* love me just as I am. I'll just be different."

Elyse laughed. "One thing hasn't changed. Your logic still makes my head spin."

"Mine, too," Crystal said. "Don't sacrifice too much for a date to my wedding. Who knows if there'll even be a wedding?"

Kaleigh frowned. "Why don't I call Jeremy and ask him exactly what his problem is?" She punched her fist in her palm and waggled her eyebrows. "I'll make him talk."

Crystal chuckled. "I'm going to talk to him tomorrow while Beka's at school. If that doesn't work out, I just might take you up on that offer." She waved her hand. "I just remembered.

Assuming there is a wedding, I need to get a list of your fishing guide schedule for between now and the wedding so we can plan things like fittings."

Another reason Elyse admired her youngest sister. Instead of denying their childhood as Elyse had, Kaleigh and Chance had put their river rat backgrounds to use by paying for a lot of their college with income from their own business, K & C Guided Fishing Tours.

"Okay. I know we've got one coming up in November for some medical group out of Memphis. Hmm. I guess if Carlton doesn't pan out as a date, I can do Operation New Me that day, and maybe I'll bring a doctor to the wedding." Kaleigh gave them an impish grin.

Elyse put her hand to her mouth at the thought. "I'm pretty sure if you try to be a 'whole new you' on the boat, Chance will have a heart attack and you'll need a doctor for more than a date."

"You're probably right." Kaleigh closed her notebook and slipped it back into her bag. "I'd better just stick to Plan A."

"I have a bad feeling about this," Crystal muttered.

Elyse set down her pizza. "Me, too, but what can we do?" One thing about it. Life with Kaleigh was never boring. Of course, Elyse thought her own life was suddenly far from boring. And all afternoon she'd found herself thinking that if she got home early enough, maybe Andrew wouldn't be asleep. She shook her head. That had to be nipped in the bud. *Friends, remember?* "So," she said, "who wants to go bowling before we go home?"

Kaleigh sighed. "Actually, I hate to break up a party, but I have a test in anatomy tomorrow."

"We really need to get home anyway," Crystal said. "I have to take my business plan to the bank tomorrow."

Elyse blew out her breath. At this rate, they'd get back to the farm by 9:00 p.m. And if Andrew's light was on, she'd have to go by and say thank you for getting the Jeep cleaned. She smiled. Poor her.

They gave Kaleigh the box of leftover pizza. "You're a college girl," Crystal said. "You need it worse. Besides," she said quietly as Kaleigh got out of the Jeep at the dorm, "it takes a lot of energy to be someone you're not. Believe me, I know."

Kaleigh turned back and looked at her, her green eyes wide. She nodded. "But maybe in my case it will be worth it. Love you guys."

"Love you, too," Elyse and Crystal chorused.

The trip home was quieter and more subdued, but Elyse wasn't sorry they'd gone to see Kaleigh. Not only had she found out about Kaleigh's crazy plan, but Crystal had opened up, too. It was good to know what was going on in her sisters' lives.

Guilt hit her in the heart. Funny how that didn't work both ways. She had no intention of them knowing about her visitor last night. Not yet anyway.

❦

The second time he saw Luke go over and let Elyse's dogs out, Andrew couldn't stand it anymore. He sauntered up the walkway and waited until Luke came out the front door. "Everything okay with Elyse?"

Luke glanced at him. "Yeah. Everything is fine."

"Okay then." Andrew turned to walk back to his camper.

"She and Crystal decided to take a girls' night out and go see Kaleigh."

Relieved, Andrew turned around to face him again, and Luke nodded. "She said after you got the Jeep all cleaned up, she wanted a road trip." He narrowed his eyes. "That was nice of you."

Andrew ducked his head. "It was nothing. I know how I'd feel if a lowlife like Zeke had been driving my truck."

"Speaking of that lowlife, you think he's still around here?"

If Andrew didn't believe that, he wasn't sure he would still be here himself. "Probably. But he could be anywhere." He couldn't tell Luke about Luis's visit last night, but he needed him to be vigilant in helping keep Elyse safe. "He made some pretty rough threats to Elyse. In person and written in paint on the Jeep."

"That's why you took the barn job, isn't it? So you could keep an eye on her?"

"The money's nice, too. But yeah, I want to be sure she's safe." *And be around if Zeke comes back.*

Luke tilted his head. "You're not so bad."

"Thanks."

A vehicle pulled out from behind the main house and headed down the pea gravel path toward them.

Andrew turned to look. He could tell from the headlights that it was a Jeep. "Looks like she made it back safely."

When Andrew turned back around, Luke was gone. In the distance, Andrew could see him walking back to his apartment at the barn across the property. Apparently his opinion of Andrew had risen enough that he wanted to give them some privacy.

The Jeep pulled up next to him and stopped. Elyse got out and walked around toward him. Her hair was pulled up in some kind of loose bun. It made her look like a teenager, but it was cute.

126

"Hey," he said softly. "Thought you skipped the country."

She laughed. "What's a girl to do with a Jeep that smells brand-new? Don't you know that particular aroma screams 'road trip'?"

"Ahh, I should have told them to turn the volume down a little on it. . .maybe to nice-short-drive-in-the-country." He stepped closer to her. "You scared me to death, disappearing like that, after last night."

"I'm sorry." She slipped her phone from her pocket. "What's your cell number?"

He called it out to her, and she punched it in.

"Okay, I saved it." She pushed a button and his phone rang. She grinned. "Now you can save mine to yours."

He did. "So if you'd had my number, you'd have called to let me know you were going?"

"And give you a chance to talk me out of it?" She shook her head. "Probably not. But I would have called you after I was on the way so you wouldn't worry."

"Did you have fun with your sisters?"

She hitched her thumbs in her jean belt loops. "It was great." She took a few steps toward the Jeep. "I'd better get in and check on the dogs."

"Luke let them out a couple of times."

"Good." She turned back to him. "Luke's really nice. He's just. . ."

"Protective of his sister," Andrew finished for her. "And that's definitely not a bad thing."

She looked relieved, and he couldn't help but be happy that his opinion of her family mattered to her. "Good night," she called as she climbed into the driver's seat.

"Good night." He stayed outside until she parked in her driveway and was safely in the house. Only when he was back in the camper did he admit to himself how tense he'd been with her gone tonight. What he'd told Luke was true—Zeke could be anywhere. But what he hadn't told Luke was what haunted Andrew. That the man who'd vowed revenge on Elyse might have already murdered once—and that he could have an accomplice who knew Elyse very well.

CHAPTER 14

In Jeremy's driveway, for the first time Crystal faltered. Just as she and Elyse had discussed, she'd chosen her time to coincide with five minutes after Beka got on the school bus. He'd be home, finishing off his last bit of coffee before starting work. But there'd be no buffer. If he wouldn't talk to her now, it was strictly because he didn't want to. Her heart squeezed. Maybe she'd been wrong to let herself love someone so much.

She knocked on the door and waited, suddenly remembering another time she'd stood here. Beka had still been missing, and Jeremy had just found out that her kidnapper, his ex-wife, Lindsey, had been found dead of an overdose, but there was no sign of Beka. When Jeremy had answered the door that day, he'd looked like all hope was gone. But Crystal had pulled together a community effort to find the little girl. If he'd lost hope in them now, in their future, was she up to making him find it again? She didn't know.

The door opened, and Jeremy's blue eyes widened. "Crys. . . what are you doing here?"

She gave him an uncertain smile. "We need to talk."

He nodded. "Okay." He stepped out onto the porch and sat down in one of the two chairs there.

She stared at him. He couldn't even stand to have her in his house. Her legs trembled as she sank into the other chair.

They didn't speak for a moment, until finally she said, "What have I done to make you act like this?" Her throat ached with the effort of speaking. She looked over at him and could see that his eyes were red-rimmed.

"The only thing you did was give up your dream to be with me. And I'm such a coward that I let you."

"What are you talking about?"

"I told myself that Broadway wasn't really your dream to begin with, that it was Cami's."

"That's true," Crystal said quietly. They'd settled this a few weeks ago when she'd first come back. Where was this coming from now?

He looked away from her. "Maybe, maybe not. But it became your dream. You fought like crazy to make it happen. And just as you got there, I pulled you away from it."

"Jeremy! Please tell me you're kidding."

He shook his head, still not looking at her.

"Why are you doing this?"

"I want you to go back to Broadway."

"No!" She couldn't imagine anything she'd like less. "I won't."

"Maybe we can make a long-distance relationship work." He finally turned to look at her. "I want you to be happy."

Tears trickled down her face, and she swiped them away, suddenly angry at his illogical decision. "You've got a funny way of showing it." She stood. "I was happy with you. Happier than I've ever been. Until you decided to throw it all away on a whim."

"No, wait." He stood, too, and reached for her hand. "I didn't decide this lightly. You sacrificed too much for this relationship. I begged Lindsey to give up her desire to travel, and you saw how disastrously that ended."

I'm not Lindsey, Crystal wanted to scream. Instead, she said, "Did you beg me to give up Broadway?" Crystal jerked her hand away from his, all emotion gone from her voice and from her heart. Her chest felt empty and cold.

He ran his fingers through his hair. "Maybe not in so many words. But you knew it was what I wanted."

"I have to go."

"Call your agent," he said. "Please."

Crystal shook her head and ran to her car. Jeremy had lost his mind if he thought she would willingly go back to Broadway. But she wouldn't stay here, on this property, where she obviously wasn't wanted.

❦

Somewhere in the bottom of her purse, Taylor Swift was singing "You Belong to Me." Kaleigh fished her cell phone out just before the last word died away. Squinting at the caller ID, she hit the answer button. "Hello."

"Kaleigh? This is Carlton."

"Carlton, how are you doing?" Kaleigh kept her voice evenly modulated, trying not to show her surprise. After their last date at Colton's Steakhouse, she hadn't expected to hear from Carlton again. Not that she would list the date in her top ten horrible dates, but she hadn't enjoyed it the way she had expected to. Or hoped to.

"Would you like to go to the Underground with me tonight?"

"To the Underground?" Kaleigh hoped Carlton wouldn't realize she was buying time while she tried to decide. The small restaurant was a favorite hangout of a lot of her friends, and she had been there several times. She loved the food, especially the chicken wraps. But did she really want to go with Carlton? "When did you want to go?"

"One of my friends is doing a poetry reading there tonight. I thought we'd listen to it and get something to eat. Can I pick you up at six thirty?"

Kaleigh pulled the phone away from her ear to check the time. Six. Not much time to get ready. Thankfully, the Underground was a casual place, so she could just wear the jeans and T-shirt she had on. "Sure. That sounds like fun." Fun? Maybe that was overstating. But in an effort to implement her plan, she wanted to give Carlton one more chance. Even if he did wait until the last minute to ask her. Bad manners as far as she was concerned.

"I apologize for asking you so late, but I just found out about the reading," Carlton explained. Almost as if he could read her mind. Or short notice was considered bad manners in his circle, too. "I'll pick you up in a few minutes, okay?"

After agreeing, she took a couple of minutes to brush her teeth. No time to straighten her hair; she'd just have to pull it back in a ponytail. Dabbing on some lip gloss, she headed out.

Carlton's red corvette was parked in front of her dorm when she opened the glass doors. He quickly jumped out of his car and ran around to the passenger side. With his hand on the door handle, he hesitated and glanced at her. "Um. . .we probably have a few minutes if you'd like to go back and change clothes." He looked at her jeans and Hollister T-shirt. "And"—she felt his glance run over her hair—"you know, get ready. I'm sorry I rushed you so much."

"No, it's okay." Kaleigh reached for the door handle. "I'm good. Let's go."

He dropped her at the door to get a table while he parked the car. The room was crowded; the sofas, chairs, and most of the tables were taken. She waved and smiled at people she knew as she snagged an empty table near the small stage. Carlton handed her a menu as he took the chair opposite hers. When they'd decided on chicken wraps, Carlton went up to the counter to place their orders. Kaleigh relaxed in her chair as the lights were dimmed and a guy she had seen a few times around campus took the stage.

Carlton returned and pulled his chair around beside hers so they could both face the stage.

"That's Bryan, the friend I told you about," Carlton whispered in her ear.

Kaleigh nodded, and the audience quieted as Bryan began his poem. It was something about dirt. Was this guy serious? Kaleigh glanced at Carlton. He looked entranced. Well, it was his friend, after all. She glanced around the room, trying to read expressions on other faces. Most looked as interested as Carlton, but a few looked as bored as she felt. She bit back a smile as she saw Nathan across the room rolling his eyes.

Kaleigh breathed a sigh of relief as she applauded along with the rest of the audience.

The lights came back on, and a waitress began making the rounds delivering food to tables. She placed a tray with their order on the table. "Wasn't that awesome?" She smiled at Carlton and Kaleigh. "Bryan is amazing, isn't he?"

"He certainly is." Carlton looked up at her. "His poetry reminds me of the early works of D. H. Lawrence."

"Yes, I agree. Hey, we're getting together Saturday afternoon around four at the Heritage Center for a poetry discussion." She unloaded the tray onto their table. "Would you guys like to come?"

"Yes," Carlton answered quickly. "What about you, Kaleigh?"

"Um. . ." Kaleigh cast around for a polite answer. She couldn't stand another second of this. But what about Operation New Me? She'd have to figure out another way. Her face brightened as she remembered that she *did* have plans. "Actually, I have to work this weekend." Too bad.

❧

Elyse sighed as she walked out of the store with a cart full of groceries. She hated when she stayed so long in the store that she forgot where she parked. Especially on a Friday night when normal people were on dates. And people like her were buying dog food by the ton. Okay, maybe that was an exaggeration. She finally spotted her Jeep, but a man was bent over the closed hood.

She froze. Had Zeke come to sabotage her vehicle? The man moved a little, and she recognized him. Anger shot through her. Why was her biological father doing this after all these years of no contact? She shoved her cart hard across the crosswalk and practically ran toward him.

He looked up from what he was doing and took off. Something fluttered to the ground behind him.

She stopped, out of breath and shaking. Why would he be stalking her? Unless Luis had changed drastically over the years, Zeke was way too crude to be his associate.

Two rows over, a yellow truck roared to life then shot out of the parking lot. A white piece of paper on the ground caught her eye. Had this been what she'd seen fall as Luis was running away? She picked it up and looked at it. It had only one word on it—Watch.

She shivered and walked around to throw her groceries into the back of the Jeep. She climbed into the driver's seat, laid the note on the console, and started her motor.

The truth was she didn't know how much her—how much Luis—had changed. Maybe he'd gone from con man to thug. But even if he had, he wouldn't join forces with someone to hurt his own daughter. Would he? What could be the reward?

She hated how in her thoughts he was "her dad" and she had to stop every time and mentally correct herself. How could two people be her dad? She remembered how glad she'd been that the McCords called Jonathan "Daddy." In the early years, it had given her a way to separate him from Luis in her mind. Luis had always been Dad, and Jonathan was Daddy. That had been an easy way to calm the ten-year-old's confusion. But the twenty-six-year-old needed more.

She drove home looking in her rearview mirror. Was Luis following her everywhere? If not, how had he known she'd be buying groceries? Had Zeke known where she was, too? She shivered as she pulled into the lane.

Andrew was outside his camper. She smiled, amazed by how her nervousness disappeared as soon as she saw him. At least she'd called him this time and told him that she was going to get groceries after eating supper at her parents'. Of course, he'd tried to convince her to wait until daylight. But she wasn't going to stop living just because there might be danger. She'd spent her whole life doing that, and now that she was finally breaking out of that mold, she wouldn't be forced back into it.

As soon as she parked the Jeep and grabbed the first bag of groceries, Andrew was there, helping her carry them in. The dogs pranced all around them. "They love grocery day," she told Andrew as they carried bags into the kitchen. "I always give them a treat when I get the new package."

He went out to get the last load while she gave each dog a treat.

In a minute, he came in with the last few bags and a small piece of paper. "Is this something important?" He held up the note.

She couldn't believe she'd forgotten it. "Luis was there."

"At the grocery store?" The alarm in his voice excited the dogs. Missy and Majesty both barked sharply.

"Okay, calm down. He was in the parking lot. When I ran toward him, he left."

"You ran toward him?"

"Yes, to see why he is following me. But he left and dropped something as he ran. When I got in the Jeep, I found this on the ground."

"We have to call Jack."

She started to remind him of his promise, but she could see concern etching his face. He wouldn't be easily dissuaded this time. "Let me get these groceries put away, and I'll tell you what I know about Luis Reynolds."

CHAPTER 15

Andrew sat on a bar stool in Elyse's compact kitchen and watched her put her groceries away. His dad used to say you could tell a lot by people's groceries. But he was in no mood to analyze hers.

Finally, she finished and turned to him. "I need some air. Would you like to go for a. . ." She glanced down at the dogs that were sprawled out around his feet. "W-A-L-K?"

"S-U-R-E." He stood and followed her to the foyer. He didn't know why, but he had a feeling she'd be more open away from her house.

"C-O-R-N-Y," she spelled back. She opened the closet, slipped on a red hoodie, and grabbed a blanket.

"I guess since I know what you think about my humor, I won't say a word about you being Little Red Riding Hood," he said as they walked out the door.

She glanced back at him and grinned. "That would probably be best." At the end of the walkway, she hesitated. "Is it okay if we go toward the river?" she called over her shoulder.

"If you're not afraid of the dark." Personally, he was so keyed up after reading that note, he thought he could take on Zeke and

Luis together, and at least five more.

She dropped back and let him walk beside her. "Why do you think I brought you?"

They left the gravel and took the cow path to the river. Andrew jumped across the cattle guard and held out his hand to help her over.

She waved it away and jumped by herself, landing neatly on the other side. "I don't want to get spoiled."

He looked out at the dark field. "What if a curious cow comes over to see what we're doing?"

She laughed. "You think I'd be here if there were cows anywhere in the vicinity? Daddy won't start using this pasture again until the next week or so."

"So this is your last hurrah?"

"Yep. My last midnight—give or take a few hours—river trek of the season." She sounded serious.

"You walk down here at night by yourself?" He'd tried to keep the concern out of his voice, but he could tell he hadn't completely succeeded.

"No."

"Oh good."

"Usually I take the dogs."

"Elyse!"

Her giggle sounded out of place in the dark night. "I do. But tonight I didn't want to be responsible for anyone else."

"Walking alone out here, with just the dogs, doesn't seem dangerous to you?"

"I haven't done it since Zeke. Before that I didn't have any enemies. . . ." She hesitated. "Or at least if I did, I didn't know it."

Andrew was sure she was talking about Luis Reynolds. Maybe

she was slowly coming to grips with the thought that he could be a danger to her.

They walked in silence for a while, and after a few minutes she took the lead.

He followed blindly since she obviously had a certain destination in mind. Sure enough, they came out to a small clearing in the trees along the river—a grassy bank, perfect for sitting and watching the current.

He helped her spread the heavy Navajo-style blanket on the damp grass and sat down beside her. The moon glinted off the water below and bounced back up to illuminate an old rope swing swaying in the mild breeze.

"This is where my childhood began." Her words sounded far away. She stared out at the water.

He waited for her to speak again.

"I'd never really been a kid until I came to live with the McCords when I was ten."

He nodded. "Did you grow up around here?"

She shrugged. "Here, there, everywhere. We always stayed in Arkansas, but we moved a lot." She looked over at him, and her expression was hidden by the shadow. "You can only raise money for a kid's kidney transplant once in the same town. Or trip in the grocery store parking lot over a small warped place in the asphalt. Or run behind a car when someone is backing out so that they bump you and pay you to keep quiet about it." She picked up a rock and threw it in the water.

Her words sunk in slowly. "Your parents were con artists?"

"I was, too. Well trained and profitable. Homeschooled." The bitter laugh that came from her mouth didn't sound like her. "Are you checking your wallet to be sure it's still there?"

"What?"

She pulled her knees up to her chest and hugged her legs with her arms. "I wouldn't blame you, now that you know what I came from."

He reached over and took her hand. "Elyse, what you came from is God. And He created you in His image. As far as I can see, you do a better job of living up to that than anyone I know." A far better job than he did, living with his half-truths and ulterior motives. He knew he should tell her the truth about his own past, but he couldn't stand to see doubt replace the trust he saw in her eyes.

She put her face down on her knees. Finally, she looked back up at him. "They were working some kind of con, and the people caught on and called the cops."

She didn't speak for a minute, and he thought maybe she'd told him all she was going to.

"My parents had guns. I didn't even know they owned guns. We prided ourselves on no violence. Ever. It was like an unwritten code. But my dad shot a cop in the leg, and the cops shot my mom. The cop was okay, but my mom died. Dad went to prison."

His stomach felt sick for the little, lost girl he heard behind the words. She hadn't even noticed that she'd called them her mom and dad. "I'm sorry."

She nodded and pulled her hand away to swipe at her eyes.

"So you came to the McCords?"

"First they put me in foster care. I didn't talk. . .so no one wanted me. Until the McCords brought me here." She motioned to the rope swing. "They gave me a puppy and a boatload of brothers and sisters and let me be a kid."

"I'm glad."

"Yeah, me, too." She stood and offered him a hand. "I guess we'd better start back."

He let her help him to his feet. "Yep. Your dogs are going to be wondering where you are."

They walked back hand in hand without talking. Andrew understood better why she didn't want to tell the police about Luis. But he couldn't help but think that if she hadn't realized when she was a kid that her dad was capable of violence, she might not realize it now either. Back at her door, he dropped her hand and smiled. "We've got to stop meeting like this."

"Like I said, c-o-r-n-y."

He gave a rueful laugh. "I never denied it."

She leaned up and dropped a kiss on his cheek. "Truthfully, I like it," she whispered. "Good night, Andrew. Thank you for everything." Before he could say a word, she slipped inside.

He stood with his hand to his cheek until she locked the door. As he walked back to his camper, a vehicle came up the main road. He froze in his tracks, waiting for it to stop. But it puttered on by, and he could hear it for a long time after it passed.

He peered into the darkness. Was someone out there? How could he ever know for sure she was safe? Even as he thought the question, he knew the answer. He couldn't.

He sat down in his lawn chair and looked up at the twinkling stars, too many to count. One thing he'd learned over the last few years: he wasn't in control. He sat there and prayed until he was too sleepy to pray anymore. Then he got up and went to bed.

❦

Andrew poured his second cup of coffee and stared at the phone in his hand. Was there another way to do this that would be easier? He still remembered a few buddies from his days in investigative journalism. But most of them had turned against him by the end, working to prove he was guilty rather than innocent. And at one time, he'd had plenty of law enforcement contacts. But he'd burned all those bridges while he was investigating Melanie's death.

In retrospect, he could see he'd gone a little crazy. No one seemed to care as much as he did that Melanie's murderer had walked away without a trace. Either that or they just thought he'd done it himself. No one else had to suffer through the first few hours of knowing she was dead while also enduring the knowledge that the husband was always the first suspect. He'd been obsessed for the first two years, determined to single-handedly bring her killer to justice and clear his own name.

A year earlier, he'd been down on the Texas coast following another useless lead when he barely stopped himself from getting violent with a guy who, as a prank, had answered his ad for information and pretended to know something about Melanie's murder. With his fist drawn back, inches from the guy's nose, he'd realized that he'd let this case own him. He'd gotten rid of his gun then and started back to church.

For the last year, he'd painted more houses and followed fewer leads. He could never have a future with a wife or a family as long as this shadow stayed over him, but at least he wasn't killing himself trying to get out from under it. Slowly but surely he'd found some peace just being with God and alone.

Then he'd gotten the call from the Shady Grove pawn shop dealer, and it had all started again.

But now there was more at stake than bringing a murderer

to justice and even clearing his name. Now it was about finding a murderer before he struck again. He pictured Elyse, so afraid and yet so brave at the same time. For that, it was worth calling anyone. Even his father.

He scrolled through his address book before he changed his mind. While it was ringing, he tried to think of exactly what to say.

"Andrew?"

He couldn't believe it. His dad had finally figured out caller ID. "Yes. Hi, Dad."

"My birthday's not for a couple more months. Did you lose your calendar?"

Andrew took a deep breath and held it in to the count of three. He let the air slowly escape through his nose. "Actually, I was hoping you could help me."

"The money finally ran out?"

Andrew looked down at the square tiles of his camper floor. *Just say what needs to be said.* "No, I need information."

"Son"—for the first time, the cocky arrogance faded from his dad's tone—"when are you going to give up on that wild goose chase? I know you didn't kill Melanie. Everyone who knows you does. Even the life insurance company paid you."

Yes, but the majority of people in their home county still thought he did it. The local newspaper had painted a dramatic picture of a huge fight between the newlyweds, a murder committed in anger, then an elaborate setup to make it look like a robbery. It had been a false picture, but that hadn't mattered to most of his colleagues. Only his closest friends had remained convinced of his innocence. And sometimes he was afraid even some of them wondered if he might have done it. "This is not directly related with Melanie's case. It's something different."

"What do you need?" His dad sounded tired.

"Information on two men. One has been in prison a long time until recently. The other one was in and out in the last three years."

"Names?"

"Zeke Moser and Luis Reynolds."

"What do you want to know?"

"If they ever served time in the same facility." It was the only thing that made sense.

"Okay, I'll call you back."

"Thanks."

As was his custom, his dad broke the connection without a good-bye. Andrew remembered, even as a teenager, thinking that his dad must just think he was too important and busy to waste time on things like ending a phone conversation politely. He flipped the phone shut and laid it on the table.

A few minutes later, it rang and he jerked it up and answered, half expecting to hear his father's voice. It was his preacher instead, telling him that one of the women at church had heard that Maxine was awake. "I knew you were concerned about her, so I thought I'd let you know."

Andrew thanked him and hung up, his stomach clenched. He was concerned about her. But he was more anxious to find out what she knew. Even though he felt bad about his motives, now that Elyse was in danger, it was more important than ever to question Zeke's sister.

CHAPTER 16

Elyse stayed behind Andrew as he tapped on the hospital room door. She was thrilled that Maxine was awake.

"Come in," a man's voice called from inside.

"Oh." Elyse grabbed Andrew's shirt from the back. "Someone else is already here visiting."

He gave her a puzzled look. "Then we won't stay long."

She unclenched her fingers from his shirt and smoothed it out. "Okay."

Andrew pushed the door open and led the way into the room. Beside the bed, a man who appeared to be about the same age as Elyse smiled at them then at the woman in the bed. "Look, Aunt Maxine, you have visitors."

Andrew stepped back to let Elyse go first, but she side-stepped and slipped back behind him. He glanced back at her, his eyebrows drawn together. Then he turned back to the bed. "Hello." He leaned toward Maxine. "We're the ones who found you."

They'd discussed on the way over about keeping details to a minimum, just in case she didn't know about Zeke and the gun.

"Thank you." Maxine's voice was feeble, but her eyes were sharp.

"And you must be Miss Maxine's nephew," Andrew said to the man.

He nodded and stuck out his hand. "I'm Doug."

Andrew shook his hand. "Andrew Stone. This is Elyse McCord." He smiled. "You look familiar."

Elyse had thought the same thing. And now she realized why. Zeke looked like an inflated caricature of this man.

Doug had a stricken look on his face as if he hated for them to know why he looked familiar.

"He's Zeke's son," Maxine said, her raspy voice bringing all eyes back to the bed. "But take my word for it, even though he favors his father in looks, in this case, the apple fell far from the tree."

So she did know.

"No worries." Andrew smiled at Doug. "I don't think we ought to be held responsible for who fathered us."

Elyse didn't say anything, but she couldn't have agreed more.

"Thanks." Doug leaned over and kissed his aunt's forehead. "I'm going to go get something to eat and let you visit with your good Samaritans."

Elyse cringed at his inadvertent use of the same words Zeke had used.

When the door swooshed shut behind Doug, Andrew tried again to step behind her, and this time she let him.

"Elyse has been taking good care of Pal." Andrew looked at Elyse expectantly.

"Oh? I'm so glad." Maxine smiled. "How is he?"

"Fine." She looked over her shoulder at Andrew. Maybe he'd fill in the blanks.

Andrew's eyes widened. "Elyse has three other dogs, and Pal loves them. I know he misses you, but right now he's having the time of his life."

Maxine's eyes filled with tears, and she reached toward Elyse. Elyse took her veined hand and patted it.

"Thank you," Maxine whispered.

"I'm enjoying having him." Maxine's obvious emotion pushed the words out of Elyse, in spite of her shyness. "I promise to take good care of him until you're ready for him back."

"You're an angel."

Elyse's face burned, and she shook her head.

A few moments later, Maxine started to cough. When she finally quit, she collapsed backward on the bed and closed her eyes.

Elyse stood quietly by her bed, uncertain what to do. She turned and raised her eyebrows at Andrew.

He stepped forward. "We're going to go and let you rest."

Maxine opened her eyes and smiled. "Okay. Come back soon." She patted Elyse's hand. "Keep me posted on my baby."

"We will," Elyse promised. Her eyes were moist as she followed Andrew out of the room.

⁂

Andrew didn't speak when they first left the room. How many times had Elyse said she was shy and he'd just brushed it off? But seeing her in front of strangers gave new meaning to the term *painfully shy*. He looked over at her. She looked like she'd been through an ordeal. "Elyse?"

She jerked her gaze up to meet his. "Yes?"

"Want to get some lunch?"

"Sure." She sounded like she couldn't care less.

"Maxine seemed really glad to hear about Pal."

Elyse's face flamed almost as red as it had in the room. "Yeah," she said wryly. "Thanks for telling her."

Andrew glanced in the glass windows of the cafeteria as they passed. Doug was sitting at a table alone. Elyse obviously wouldn't want to sit with Maxine's nephew, but after they got settled in at their table, Andrew could casually drop by to say a word to Doug. It might be the perfect time to find out what he knew about Zeke. "Hey, how do you feel about hospital cafeteria food?"

"Actually, I've heard it's excellent. Some of my grooming customers come here to eat, even when they're not visiting someone in the hospital."

"In that case, let's give it a try." He guided her in, and they went through the line. She started to dig in her purse. "My treat," he said. "I asked you."

She frowned. "That's silly. It's lunchtime and I had to eat."

"Please. . ."

"Fine. But next time, I'm getting it."

"Next time?" He grinned at her. "I'm glad to know you see a future for us."

The cashier handed him his change, and he turned around with his tray just in time to see Doug going out the door. Andrew would have to get back to see Maxine soon and ask her his questions directly.

The sunny cafeteria was about half full, but there were plenty of available tables. They set their plates on a table for two, and Andrew stacked their trays together and set them on an empty table next to them. Several muted conversations swirled around them.

After Andrew had quietly offered thanks for the food, Elyse looked up at him. "So I guess now you see what I mean."

He started to pretend he didn't know what she was talking about, but he respected her too much to do that. "It's really hard for you to talk to strangers."

She grimaced. "That's an understatement."

"Can we talk about it?"

"Me and you? Sure. I have no trouble talking to you."

He grinned. "I have to admit I'm very flattered by that."

"It's not something I chose," she said then put her hand to her mouth. "Wait, that didn't come out right."

He started laughing. "Okay, my ego is properly deflated now. You can quit."

They ate in silence for a minute.

"Does your shyness make it hard for you to do business?"

She finished chewing and swallowed. "Groom dogs? No, not really. I just give them back to their owners, tell them an amount, take the money, and shut the door."

He nodded. "Makes sense." From the look on her face, he was pretty sure there was more. "But what if you wanted to do something else?"

A rueful smile played across her lips. "That's the problem." She leaned forward slightly. "I'm a dog trainer. It's what I love to do. I wanted to do something with the gift God gave me, so I pushed myself to take classes." She peered up at him. "Since that involved lots of listening, not much talking, and mostly working with the dogs, I got my certification."

"But now you can't use it."

"Exactly." She set her fork down and took a sip of her tea. "Matthew made me an offer last time he was home. He wants me to share an office space with him here in Shady Grove."

"As a dog trainer?"

She nodded. "I'd probably still do a little grooming while I was building up my clientele, but yes, my ultimate goal would be to concentrate on dog training and working with troubled dogs." She waved her hand as if pushing away her words. "What am I saying? I can't do it. He asked me to wait until Thanksgiving to give him an answer, but I already know. I can't do it."

"You're awfully quick to be defeated, aren't you?"

She frowned. "Hello? Did you see me in there? Maxine's bedfast, and I couldn't even talk to her about her dog."

He nodded. "I was there." It had been hard to watch a woman he knew was so strong unable to do something so seemingly simple.

"Well then, you know. . ." She made a crash and burn noise with her mouth and motion with her hand.

He chuckled. "Okay, maybe not that bad. But there ought to be a way you could get around that and still be able to do what you need to with Matthew."

"Like what?"

"I don't know yet, but maybe we can figure it out." He put his fork down. "Matthew's offer is an opportunity of a lifetime for you. If you don't at least try to make it work out, you'll be sorry."

Her eyes widened. "Is that the voice of experience talking?"

He was caught off guard by her insight. Was he concerned because he recognized the same passion in her for dog training that he'd once had for his art? "Maybe. But my window of opportunity closed. I'd hate to see the same thing happen to yours." He pulled out his phone and flipped it to his calendar. "Thanksgiving is four weeks away. If I can prove that you're able to comfortably talk to strangers about their dogs by then, will you tell Matthew yes?"

Her eyebrows drew together. "Andrew, that's impossible."

He held up his hand. "No negative thoughts allowed." He looked at his calendar again. "Do you have Monday night open?"

She nodded. "I have 4-H on Thursday, but other than that I'm free every night." She blushed. "Boy, that made me sound desperate, didn't it?"

He grinned. "Not at all. Let's get together for supper after work Monday night and throw around some ideas. Okay?"

A wide smile spread across her face. "I guess. But why are you doing this?"

"I'm your friend, remember?" It was good to remind himself that was all they could be.

She shook her head. "You're crazy."

"Maybe, but I still think this will work." He held out his hand. "Are you committed to giving it your best shot?"

She returned his handshake. "I should probably *be* committed for going along with it," she teased. "But sure. Count me in."

❧

A deep growl woke Elyse in the wee hours Monday morning. She opened her eyes and lay still, letting her vision adjust to the darkness.

Missy was straddling her, and even though Elyse couldn't see her face, she could tell the dog's teeth were bared by the sound of her growl. Somewhere in the darkness, Majesty growled, too. Even though she didn't move, the hair on the back of Elyse's neck stood on end. Was someone in the house?

Suddenly, Pal came awake on the floor at the foot of the bed and took off down the hall toward the back door. The other dogs followed, all barking madly.

Elyse got slowly out of bed and picked up her cell phone. 4:40 a.m. Should she call her dad? Or Andrew? Or even 911? The dogs were still going wild, so if someone was in the house, she wouldn't be able to hear him.

She tiptoed down the dark hallway and scooped a small brass clock off the hall table as she went by. If she had to smash it on someone's head, she could at least give him a serious headache.

The dogs clamored against the back door. Elyse turned on the porch light and peeked out the blind. No movement at all. She stood and watched for a few minutes. One at a time, the dogs deserted her, as if once they'd gotten her up, they'd lost interest.

She stayed there for another minute alone, still considering calling someone. But what would she say? *My dogs growled and I'm scared?* Using her phone as a flashlight, she made her way back to her room. She set the clock back on the hall table as she walked by.

In her room, she blew out her breath. All four dogs were asleep on her bed. She felt better with them there, so she made room for herself and climbed under the covers. She wished the police would find Zeke. Danger was not her game.

She woke up late the next morning. "Silly pups, keeping me up half the night," she muttered as she walked down the hall to let them out. "Now I'll be draggy all day."

At the back door, she watched them all run to their favorite places. Something odd caught her eye in her peripheral vision, and she gasped. The gate stood wide open. Nikki wasn't far from it. "Come."

Majesty and Missy bounded back to her with Pal right on their heels. She gave a hand motion, and they went in the house. "Nikki!" The little white dog had discovered the open gate and lost her hearing at the same time. She bolted for it like a prisoner who'd been suddenly set free.

CHAPTER 17

Elyse slammed the house door with the other dogs inside and took off after Nikki, praying as she walked quickly. *Never chase a running dog*, she reminded herself.

"Nikki, come!" She followed the streak of white across the grass. The morning dew made her feet slick inside her flip-flops. And the little bichon frise still hadn't slowed. "Not the pasture, not the pasture," she begged under her breath.

Nikki, so short she cleared the fence without even touching the first row of wire, took off through the pasture. She looked like a tiny white lamb hopping through the clover. By the time Elyse got to the fence, the dog was halfway between her and the cows milling next to a big oak tree.

"Nikki! Come!" She slipped between the wires as she shouted.

Nikki stopped and glanced back at Elyse. The big cow nearest the fence gave Elyse the evil eye. She froze and kept her gaze locked on Nikki. A curious calf stepped cautiously over to Nikki and snorted.

The dog went wild. She ran toward the calf, barking. It scurried back to its mama. Elyse watched in horror as some ancient herding instinct apparently kicked in and Nikki went after both cows, nipping at their heels.

Elyse gave up on being still and dashed toward the pandemonium. Her flip-flops were causing her to trip, so she just left them behind. The closer she got, the bigger the cows looked.

Nikki apparently wasn't worried. The dog had added a few more cows to her herd and was running them in a large circle, biting at their heels. Her brothers thought she didn't know they called Nikki that little "ankle biter." If only they could see her now.

"Why cows?" she moaned. "Why couldn't you chase bunny rabbits?"

Any second now, one of the huge cows would get fed up with being run in a circle like a carnival pony ride and step on the white fluff that was causing it. Elyse suddenly remembered a thread she'd read on an online bulletin board about unconventional ways to catch a runaway dog. She glanced at the trampled muddy ground and shook her head. She had to try it.

She threw herself down. "Ow!" she yelled in her best hurt voice, which wasn't hard since there were a few stray rocks in the mud. Then she waited.

Nikki hesitated for a second, but instead of coming alone, she turned and guided her cows directly toward Elyse.

"Oh no!" Elyse jumped up, mud dripping off her, and gaped at the angry cows coming toward her. Her brothers had always said that she shouldn't be scared of cows. "All you have to do is wave your arms and they'll run away," Matthew had told her more than once.

She waved her arms and screamed, jumping up and down like a mad woman. The cows, apparently deciding she was more of a threat than Nikki, turned and ran away. Nikki stopped in front of Elyse and tilted her head. Elyse picked the little brown and green ball of fluff up in her arms and half cried, half laughed. "You scared me to death."

"You scared us to death," a voice behind her said. She turned around to see Andrew standing a few feet away and her daddy beside him.

Elyse pushed a muddy strand of hair out of her face. "Now you come to help."

"We didn't know anything about it until we looked out here and saw you doing some kind of crazy mud dance in the pasture," her daddy said, but he was fighting back laughter.

Elyse looked down at her flannel pajamas, dripping mud and who knew what else.

"We hurried to get to you, but sadly the ritual was over about the time we got here." Andrew's eyes twinkled.

Elyse stepped toward them with one arm out. "I think you both deserve hugs for your heroic attempt at rescuing me."

"Oh no, that's okay," Andrew said.

"Gotta run." Her daddy held his cowboy hat on his head and took off toward the house in a literal run.

She took another step toward Andrew, and he soon caught up with her daddy.

Elyse almost didn't see the bottle beside the big tree before she stepped on it. Clutching Nikki, she bent over and fished it out of the mud. 90 Proof Whiskey. The label was still intact and very readable. It couldn't have been out here more than a day or two. She looked toward her house, plainly visible from here. This was the perfect lookout. She held the bottle up to her nose. Or the perfect place for a man to drink enough to get up his nerve to go closer.

Elyse put Nikki in her crate. "Sorry, baby. I'd bathe you first, but I'm dirtier than you are." She took a long hot shower and scrubbed the mud out of her hair. After she dressed, she wrapped a towel around her damp curls and groomed Nikki. She carried the crate outside on the back deck to wash out the remaining mud.

When she was finished, she decided to solve the mystery of the open gate. The sturdy latch on it had never given her any trouble, and she was fanatical about keeping it closed. Everything appeared to be in working order.

She turned to go back in and stopped. Footprints in the soft dirt went around the deck and up to the den window. She walked over to get a closer look. Her pansies were broken and bruised. In the mud around them were several big boot prints. Her heart caught in her throat as she remembered the whiskey bottle.

She swung around and looked at the yard. Was Zeke here? She hadn't locked the back door when she'd taken off after Nikki. What if he was hiding in the house? A chill ran up her spine. She pulled her phone out of her pocket and called Andrew. When he answered, she quickly explained the situation.

"I'll be right there." In less than a minute, he came in the back gate.

She told him about the dogs going wild in the wee hours of the morning.

When he saw the bottle and the footprints, his expression grew serious. "We have to call the sheriff. No arguments." He looked at her. "Please."

A hysterical laugh bubbled up in her throat. "You aren't getting any arguments from me."

Jack said he'd be right out. When Andrew hung up, he put his hand on Elyse's shoulder. "Let's go in and get you some coffee."

"What if he's in there?"

"How did the dogs act when you got back with Nikki?"

"Perfectly normal." She slapped her palm against her forehead. "Silly me. I'm so jumpy I didn't even think about that." She followed him onto the deck and into the house.

"Are you going to tell the sheriff about Luis?"

She shook her head. "This wasn't Luis."

"How do you know?"

"Whoever did this wore work boots. Big work boots." She looked down at her feet. "Luis's feet are small. . .like mine. Small and narrow."

"Maybe you should just tell Jack anyway and let him decide."

She shook her head. "I despise my biological father for everything he did. As far as I'm concerned, he killed my childhood, my mother, and my future. But he paid his debt to society. If I drag him into something like this and he ends up back in trouble. . ." It was hard to explain, but she wanted him to be okay. Just somewhere far away where she couldn't get sucked into his latest con. "I can't do it. Not when I know this wasn't him."

"I'm pretty sure this was Zeke."

She shivered. "Me, too. And that thought scares me to death. He knows where I live."

"Maybe he doesn't know where I live," Andrew said menacingly. "But if he shows up here again, he's going to find out."

"Thank you."

The doorbell rang and the dogs all started barking.

"Quiet," Elyse said. They all shut up.

Andrew followed her to the door. "That's amazing."

"What?"

"How well you control them with just your voice."

"Oh yeah, look at how well I controlled Nikki this morning."

"There are exceptions to everything." He chuckled.

"It wasn't that funny."

"Oh yeah, you should have seen you waving your arms, all covered in mud."

She gave him a mock glare.

He bit his lip and ducked his head. "Okay, not funny at all."

She was smiling when she opened the door and let Jack in. She gave him the bottle in a gallon ziplock bag and let Andrew take him out to show him the boot prints while she called her parents to fill them in on the situation. Her mama answered, but her daddy got on the extension.

"Do you want me to come over there?" her daddy asked.

"Andrew's here. He's showing Jack the prints."

"That boy's making himself indispensable, isn't he?"

Elyse felt herself blush even though she was alone.

"Jonathan," her mama admonished, "he's just trying to help."

"I know, I know. I'm just saying he's awful handy to have around sometimes."

A smile tugged at Elyse's lips as she hung up the phone and looked at Andrew out in the backyard. He really was handy to have around. She could easily get used to it. And that might end up being the biggest danger of all.

❦

Andrew ran a towel over his damp hair. He'd worked extra hard painting today after getting a late start, so he was tired, but a shower had given him fresh energy. The thought of seeing Elyse tonight hadn't hurt either. He flung the towel across the metal bar. He'd have to remember that they were getting together to brainstorm ways she could achieve a goal. Being with her was just an added bonus. Just as he was about to walk out the door, his phone rang.

"Got your answer," his dad barked. "Eight years ago, Zeke Moser and Luis Reynolds were in the same maximum security prison in Arkansas. Actually on the same block."

Andrew had strongly suspected that was the connection, but he'd been hoping that he wasn't right. That maybe Elyse's biological father had heard Zeke's name on TV.

"Is that all you wanted to know?"

"Eight years ago? Do you know what Zeke was in for?"

"He served four years for two counts of stalking and one of assault."

Andrew put his hand to his forehead. There was some news he dreaded telling Elyse. As if it weren't bad enough that Zeke and Luis were prison mates. "Wasn't he in again recently? What was that for?"

"Went in a little over two years ago. Spousal abuse and hot checks. He's only been out for a couple of months."

That would explain why he was just now pawning Melanie's jewelry. "But he didn't serve in the same facility as Luis Reynolds that time?"

"I never said that. He was at the same prison, but Reynolds got out about a week after Zeke started his second stint."

So Luis had been out of prison for two years. And had made no attempt to contact Elyse until now.

"Thanks, Dad."

"When are you coming home?"

Andrew had no answer for that question. He didn't even know where home was, but he hated to say that, especially after his dad had just helped him. "I don't know. But thanks again."

But his dad was already gone.

❧

"Your goal this week is to be more refined?" Kaleigh's roommate, Candice, narrowed her eyes. "Who uses words like *refined*, anyway?"

Kaleigh yanked the notepad away from her. "Carlton does, for one. And it's an area I'm seriously lacking in, and I know it. My granddad taught me that being refined meant not spitting into the wind. Or putting on my least holey jeans when we had to go into town for something."

Candice sighed. "I want to go on the record stating I think this is crazy."

Kaleigh glanced toward the corner. "Did you get that, Miss Imaginary Court Recorder? She wants to go on record stating I'm crazy."

Candice rolled her eyes. "Very funny. Even if you manage to catch this Carlton guy, what are you going to do with him?"

"Take him to my sister's wedding, for one thing."

"There are twenty guys I know who would jump at the chance to take you to Crystal's wedding."

Kaleigh shook her head. "You're delusional."

Candice grabbed a towel from the shelf and headed into the bathroom. "One of us is delusional. But it's not me." She shut the door with a loud click.

Kaleigh stuck her tongue out at the door. She caught a glimpse

161

of herself in the mirror and stopped. "See? That's not refined. I'm right," she said to the empty room.

She had to admit she was getting tired of Operation New Me. But Carlton had never even noticed her before. So she must be doing something right. She plopped down on the bed. Not that she'd been sitting around waiting for him to notice her. But that was beside the point.

CHAPTER 18

Elyse stood in the middle of her closet and did one more slow turn. Finally, she grabbed a turquoise broomstick skirt and held it up in front of her. All four dogs sat on their haunches watching her every move. "What do you think about this with my white shirt and denim vest?"

None of them nodded. Or even barked.

"A lot of help y'all are. It'll have to do."

She ran her hand over her stomach, trying to calm the butterflies there. For some reason, this crazy meeting had started to feel like a date. And she hadn't had one of those in so long she'd forgotten how to act. Not that she'd ever been good at it. Inevitably, she'd stammer and turn red every time her date spoke to her.

She quickly dressed and slipped in her silver hoop earrings. Suddenly she panicked. She usually wore this outfit with a pair of brown leather sandals, but it was October, and even though it was unseasonably warm, it was too late in the season for open toes. Her eyes lit on the short boots her parents had gotten her for Christmas last year. Soft and comfortable with tiny turquoise and silver accents. Perfect.

When she was finally finished, she walked to the back door to let the dogs out one more time. It was still dusk, but she turned the porch light on anyway and leaned out until she could see the gate was closed. Then she let the dogs out and watched them. Within a minute, they were ready to come back in. Could they smell that a stranger had been in their haven? A flash of irritation poked at her good mood. She'd always felt safe here, but those boot prints she'd found this morning proved she wasn't as safe as she'd thought.

Back inside, she stood nervously by the front door. Should she wait until Andrew came and rang the doorbell? Or just meet him outside? When she'd seen him right before he'd gone to work this morning, he'd mentioned eating at the Fisherman's Wharf, a local fish place that had seating out over the river. He said he'd been wanting to try it, but not alone, so it was his treat. She'd argued, but he'd been adamant, and finally she'd agreed. She hadn't seen him since.

The doorbell rang, and she couldn't move. What if she was dressed wrong? What if he still had on his painting clothes? She blew out her breath. Well, then he'd be silly, wouldn't he? She wasn't going to be like this. She was happy with how she looked, and that's what mattered. Sometimes it was nice to dress up a little.

She opened the door and realized immediately that she needn't have worried. Andrew looked gorgeous tonight in black slacks, black boots, and a crisp red shirt with his damp hair curling slightly around his collar. Her heart hammered against her ribs. On second thought, maybe she should be worried. "Hi." The word came out breathy, and she cringed.

"Hi." His eyes twinkled with obvious appreciation. "You look beautiful."

"Thanks." *So do you?* She didn't think that would be exactly appropriate. "You look nice, too." *Much better.*

As they walked to the truck, he veered to the left and opened her door for her. She considered saying something teasing about how this wasn't a date, but instead, she got in and smiled graciously. "Thank you."

He grinned. "You're welcome."

She watched him walk around, and a sudden realization hit her. Even though this wasn't technically a date, this was what a date was supposed to feel like. The underlying tones of attraction and curiosity. Will he like me? Will I like him? What did he mean by that? She'd never had this kind of interaction before because she'd always been too shy to have any playful conversation. She smiled. This was fun.

"What are you smiling about?" he asked as he slid into the driver's seat.

"Nothing, really. Just figuring some things out."

"See? We haven't even started brainstorming yet and you're already figuring things out." He hit his hand on the steering wheel. "This is going to work. At Thanksgiving, you're going to tell Matthew yes."

She thudded back to earth with a bang. Andrew was here to help her overcome her shyness. She needed to keep her head out of the clouds and give that her full attention. "I hope you're right. But I can't imagine it being true."

She stared out the window at the familiar scenery. It wasn't as if she'd never tried to quit being shy. But when she was around strangers, she didn't seem to have any control over it.

Andrew cleared his throat. "I have some news."

She turned to look at him. "Let's hear it."

"It turns out that Zeke was in prison with Luis Reynolds."

She clasped her hand around the leather door handle. "How do you know?"

"I had a law enforcement contact check on it."

"Jack?" He'd known she hadn't wanted to bring Luis into it. He shook his head. "Someone in Texas. I figured you wouldn't want me trying to research it around here."

She blew out her breath. "Thanks. So were they. . .friends?"

"It's not exactly summer camp. And the records won't show whether they hung around together. They were on the same block."

She listened as he went into more detail about Zeke's two stays. "He was in for stalking?" She shivered. "Comforting." She pushed the thought away and stared at her knuckles turning white from clenching the door handle so hard. She forced her fingers to relax. "So Luis has been out of prison over two years?"

"Looks that way."

"Why would he contact me after all this time?"

"I'd say it definitely has something to do with Zeke."

"Yeah." She tried to make sense of this news. "So either he's trying to warn me about Zeke or he's in cahoots with him."

Andrew nodded. "Those seem like the most likely choices."

"I guess I should assume the worst."

Andrew glanced at her, sympathy shining in his eyes. "I think that would be wise."

They passed Maxine's house, and Elyse tensed.

"Pal seems to be liking it so well at your house, he may never want to come home," Andrew said.

She appreciated his trying to make her relax, but she wasn't sure it was possible. "I didn't think about us having to drive by here."

"I'm sorry. I really didn't either. But this is the last place Zeke will be if he's got any brains."

She gave him a halfhearted smile. "Who says he does?"

"Good point. But we're past it now."

A few seconds later, they passed the River Road Campground.

"Do you miss staying there?"

He shrugged. "It was nice being able to fish out the back door." A slow grin spread across his face. "But there are advantages to my new location, too."

She bit her lip to keep from smiling. "Oh really. Like what?"

"The scenery is really nice." The glance he gave her left little doubt that was a compliment. "And the neighbors."

"Neighbors are friendly, huh?"

He chuckled. "Entertaining anyway. Doing all kinds of crazy mud dances at dawn. . .that kind of thing. Never a dull moment."

She burst out laughing. "I guess you'll never let me forget that."

He pulled into the parking lot of the Fisherman's Wharf and killed the motor. "Sure I will. Maybe when you're a hundred."

She was too flustered to reply. They both knew he wasn't going to be around that long.

He saved her from embarrassment by getting out and walking around to open her door.

"Thank you. I'm impressed."

As he tucked her arm into the crook of his elbow, she was almost positive he murmured, "So am I."

Or maybe that was just wishful thinking.

❧

Andrew couldn't remember the last time he'd truly been nervous.

But as soon as they walked into the restaurant, he couldn't say that anymore. As if his feelings for her weren't complicated enough, he'd inadvertently brought Elyse to a date place. The interior lighting was muted, but tiny white lights twinkled in silk trees in every corner, and the walkway to the deck was lighted as well. A young woman stepped up to greet them. "Reservations?"

Andrew shook his head. He'd heard the fish was delicious, but not a word about reservations.

The hostess smiled and leaned toward them conspiratorially. "We have plenty of room tonight. The boss just likes me to say that so people will know it's a nice place." She stepped back. "Do you prefer the dining room or the deck?" she said in a louder voice.

Andrew turned to Elyse.

She smiled. "I brought a jacket. Is outside okay with you?"

"Perfect." He would take the breeze blowing off the river any day over a stuffy dining room. Plus, out there it might not be quite so. . .intimate.

He realized how wrong he was as soon as the hostess led them out onto the deck. White lights twinkled everywhere. Silk trees divided the area into individual rooms. An outdoor fire pit burned softly beside each table. The reflection of the moonlight bounced off the river down below. The hostess motioned to a table next to the deck rail.

When they sat down, he shrugged. "So, shoot me. Fisherman's Wharf?" He waved his hand. "Does this look like a place that would be called Fisherman's Wharf?"

She giggled softly. "Probably not. But I like it."

They studied their menus for a minute, and when the blond waitress came over, they both ordered the fried catfish special and sweet tea.

After she was gone, Elyse looked around again. "I can't get over how magical it feels here. Like dreams can come true."

He smiled at the wonder on her face. "Seeing that look on your face almost makes me believe that dreams can come true."

She wrinkled her nose. "Are you saying I'm naive?"

"No. Just that I think the world looks better and more hopeful through your eyes than mine."

The waitress came back with their glasses of tea.

When she was gone again, Elyse met his gaze. "Why do you have such a bleak outlook on life?"

He flinched. "I wouldn't say it's bleak. Just that I'm more of a realist. Life throws curve balls."

Elyse grinned. "Sometimes you hit the sweet spot and knock it out of the park."

"And sometimes you strike out."

"Hey, I thought you were here to give me a 'you can do it' pep talk." She gave a mock pout. "Now I'm ready to give up for sure."

He knew she was teasing, but in a way she was right. She was the first woman he'd been interested in since Melanie, and knowing there was no possibility of a future with her bothered him.

CHAPTER 19

Andrew needed to focus on the matter at hand and quit acting like a moonstruck schoolboy. "You really can do it." He took a sip of his tea to gather his thoughts. "Were you shy before your—before you ended up in foster care?"

She shook her head. "No. I might have had a tendency to be a little introverted, but I didn't have a problem talking to people."

"So do you think your problem with talking to people now may stem from being afraid they'll find out about your childhood?"

"No!" She shook her head. "Not at all."

"So you don't care if people know about your biological parents?"

She took a long sip of her tea and picked a leaf off the table-cloth. She tossed it carefully toward the river below. When she looked up at him, her brown eyes were wide. "Okay, I do care. I definitely don't want anyone to know about them. About my life before becoming a McCord. So maybe it could come from that some, I guess."

He admired her honesty. It was hard to look inside one's heart and see the truth. And even harder to say it out loud. "At the risk of sounding like an amateur psychologist, what do you think would happen if people found out about your past? Worst case scenario?" He hoped this didn't backfire. In his case, the answer would be disaster. The McCords, for example, certainly wouldn't want a man who'd been suspected of murdering his wife painting their barn. Or taking their daughter to dinner.

She shrugged. "They wouldn't want anything to do with me?"

"I know all about it, and I still want to be around you."

She gave a half laugh. "You're different."

He couldn't help but be glad she thought so. But this wasn't about him. "Really, I'm not."

The waitress walked out to their table, her arms weighed down with two big fish plates. She smiled at them. "Enjoy," she said as she walked away.

Andrew said a prayer of thanksgiving for the food and decided it was time for a subject change. "That was brave of you following Nikki out to the cows."

Elyse chuckled as she dipped a hush puppy in tartar sauce. "I didn't exactly stop to think."

"Sometimes that's the best way."

"Yeah." Her voice faltered. "For example, if I think too much about Zeke being outside my house last night, I might decide not to go home."

"I'm sorry that happened." He felt as if he'd fallen down on his self-appointed job of protecting her.

She shivered and pulled her jacket a little tighter around her. "Me, too. But it's not your fault. I should have called someone when the dogs woke me up barking."

"Next time, call me."

She met his gaze. "I will." She ate for a few minutes then put her fork down. "Why would Luis want to join in with Zeke against me?"

Andrew wiped his mouth. "I can't think of a reason."

"Unless he wants to con my family or me. Make us trust him by playing at being a hero."

Andrew didn't know what to say. He really couldn't figure out why Elyse's biological dad had come back into the picture.

She leaned forward. "So do you have a lot of brothers and sisters?"

Andrew sat up straighter in his chair. "No. Just me."

"And your parents live in Texas?"

"My dad does. My mom died when I was five."

"I'm sorry," she said softly.

He nodded. He knew she could relate. "Thanks."

"I guess you and your dad are really close?"

He blurted out a nervous laugh. "Not so much. To be honest, we never have been, but since my wife died, we don't see eye to eye on anything."

Elyse picked at her fish with her fork. "I'm sorry. And sorry if I was being nosy. I just needed to think about someone else's family tonight."

"I don't mind talking about it with you," he said, surprised to find it was true. "My dad is a Texas Ranger. Just like my grand-dad before him." He forced a grin. "I'm not."

"But he wanted you to be. . ."

"He raised me to be. Put me in every class, gave me every training available to prepare me for a career in law enforcement." He was amazed that after all he'd been through the past few years, it still hurt to talk about what a disappointment he was to his dad. "I went to college instead. Determined to make him proud some other way."

"Your art?"

"I remember one time in high school my teacher entered several of my paintings in a local art show. I tried to get Dad to go." He ran his finger around the rim of his tea glass and considered the amber liquid. "He said, 'I wouldn't walk across the road to look at a bunch of sissy paintings.' "

She reached across the table and covered his hand with hers. His heart warmed at her touch.

"Thanks." He tried for a silly grin. "Between you and me, I think I always thought I might get famous someday and he'd have no choice but to at least look at my paintings. But in the meantime, I got a double major—art and journalism."

"You're a writer?"

"I was an investigative journalist." He gave her a sideways glance. "Which seems kind of close to being in law enforcement, doesn't it?"

She nodded. "But not close enough for your dad?" She was sharp.

"Nope. Not even close to close enough."

"You didn't like being a journalist?"

He shrugged, pushing back all the painful memories. "I'd rather paint houses."

"So here you are."

He paused. It wasn't that simple. But tonight was about her. When the time was right, he'd fill in some of the gaps in his life story. "Yep. Here I am."

After the waitress brought the check, Andrew paid, and they walked over to lean on the deck rail and look down at the river.

A few strands of Elyse's hair blew across her face. She laughed as she pushed it away. "Thanks for finding this amazing place. I guess our brainstorming session didn't accomplish much, but I had fun."

"I had fun, too," Andrew said, glancing over at her, measuring his next words. "And I actually had an idea for you."

"Let's hear it."

He kept his gaze on the river. "How many people in Shady Grove know about your childhood?"

She frowned. "My family. And you."

"None of your friends?"

She shook her head. "No."

"What if. . .you chose one friend to tell about it? Someone you could trust? And then you report back and tell me what telling did to your friendship?"

She didn't say anything for a moment; then she gave a soft, strangled laugh. "You want me to experiment with one of my friendships and see if it self-destructs?"

He shrugged. "If it does, it wasn't much to begin with, was it?"

"I don't know." She sighed. "I'm not trying to be uncooperative, but I just don't know if this would even help at all."

He touched her arm. "You'll never know until you try."

She kept her face turned away. "I'll think about it."

"That's all I'm asking."

⸎

As they walked to the truck, Elyse silently considered and rejected Andrew's idea at least five times. She couldn't possibly tell one of her friends. For one thing, how would she even do that? Just corner one of them and say, "Let me tell you the real truth about how I came to be in the McCord family?"

He opened her door for her.

"Thanks." She climbed in, still thinking.

"You think I'm crazy?" He slid into the driver's seat and buckled up.

Not crazy, maybe. But close. "I think you're desperate to help me. And that's really sweet."

As he pulled out onto River Road, in the distance, bright flashing blue lights illuminated the treetops.

"Looks like somebody was having a little too much 'fun' down on the river," Andrew said.

Elyse nodded. They passed the campground, and the lights were still in the distance. She realized exactly where they were and sat up straighter.

Andrew tapped his brakes as they rounded the curve. Up ahead, four police cars lined Maxine's driveway, blue lights flashing.

Elyse gasped.

He looked at her. "You okay?"

"Yeah. Can we stop and see what's going on?"

"I was hoping you'd say that." He yanked the steering wheel and pulled the truck in next to the back cop car.

Jack, in the front yard, was talking to two of his deputies, but he waved when he saw Andrew's truck. Andrew rolled his window down, and in less than a minute, the sheriff walked over to them. "Attempted break-in," he said tersely. "From the description, we're 90 percent sure it was Zeke, trying to jimmy a window open. A neighbor was out walking his dog and called 911 from his cell phone. By the time we got here, he was gone."

Elyse's shoulders tightened, and she frowned. "If he's Maxine's brother, wouldn't he have a key?"

Jack, leaning in Andrew's window, raised his eyebrows. "If Zeke were your brother, would you give him a key?"

"Good point."

"Besides, if he had a key, he probably left it behind when he ran off that day, and we locked the house up tight that evening after y'all got the dog." Jack's radio crackled. "I'd better get back. I'm going to have a deputy patrol your place tonight. Don't be surprised if he drives up the lane a few times."

Elyse nodded, still on edge. "That would be great."

"Thanks," Andrew said and shook Jack's hand.

When Jack walked away, Andrew looked over at her. "You want to sleep at your parents' tonight?"

"Daddy and I have already been through this discussion." The idea was tempting, but her dogs needed her, and moving them was way too much trouble. "I'll be fine."

"I'll sleep with one eye open."

She shook her head. "Don't worry about me. The deputy will be patrolling."

He put the truck in reverse and pulled back out onto the gravel road. "And I'll be watching. If Zeke comes around, he should be the one who worries."

She grinned in the darkness, some of the tension leaving her. "I love it when you say things like that."

"Like what?"

"Never mind." She leaned her head against the seat. She was just glad he was here.

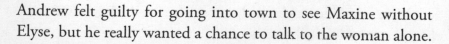

Andrew felt guilty for going into town to see Maxine without Elyse, but he really wanted a chance to talk to the woman alone.

He hadn't brought flowers this time. That just seemed too hypocritical. The sad part was he really did care about how she was doing. But he needed to know if she knew anything about the necklace Zeke pawned. He couldn't help but wonder if the rest of Melanie's jewelry was in Maxine's house. Maybe that was why Zeke had tried to break in at his sister's last night.

As Andrew walked into the hospital, he silently reminded himself not to mention the break-in. And he'd need to be really subtle in his questioning about the jewelry.

The nurses' station on the left was a flurry of activity, but Miss No-Nonsense looked up when he walked by. "Hold it."

He turned around, his eyebrows raised. Had she discovered that he was a fraud?

She walked over to him, and her eyes softened. "Maxine isn't able to have visitors."

"What do you mean? Is she worse?"

She glanced around as if to be sure no one was listening and half nodded. "Her nephew is on his way."

"Can I just peek in? Maybe say a word to her?"

"She's in ICU."

"Did her pneumonia come back?"

"I really can't answer that. Sorry."

He could see the answer in her eyes. No, it was something worse.

CHAPTER 20

The chapel door was on the right, and when Miss No-Nonsense had gone back to the nurses' station, he slipped into the quiet room. To his relief, it was empty. Whatever was wrong, Maxine needed prayer. The woman had been through so much already. He sank onto the cushioned pew. Resting his hands on the back of the pew in front of him, he linked his fingers together and bowed his head. For the next several minutes, he pleaded with God on Maxine's behalf.

When he finished, he kept his head bowed. *Lord, You know my struggles and my needs. I'm frustrated and my faith is weak. I'm sorry. Please forgive me and make me stronger. . . .*

A few minutes later, he left the chapel and made his way out to his truck. He'd counted on Maxine giving him some information about the necklace. Or at least about Zeke and whether he'd ever spent time in Texas before his last prison stint. For now, he'd have to figure it out himself, some other way. Still thinking hard, he eased his truck out of the hospital parking lot and headed toward the McCords. The necklace he'd redeemed from the pawn shop looked like Melanie's. But it wasn't a one-of-a-kind piece. What if he wasn't even in the right state?

He considered that for a moment. What if he was after the wrong person? What if Zeke wasn't Melanie's murderer and was just a crazy man after Elyse? If Andrew knew that for sure, could he leave and not look back? He caught sight of himself in the rearview mirror, shaking his head. He couldn't leave. He'd committed to painting the barn for Jonathan McCord, and right now he had no place better to go. He looked away from his reflection and kept his gaze on the road.

His reluctance to leave Shady Grove was purely practical. Not in the least influenced by the presence of a certain brown-eyed brunette. And if he believed that, he scoffed to himself, he might as well believe that the necklace from the pawn shop was poor innocent Zeke's only inheritance from his mother.

❦

It was three thirty, and Andrew had been painting the barn without stopping since midmorning. He hadn't even taken a lunch break. Elyse was embarrassed that she knew this, but she did. Because in between each grooming appointment, she'd peeked out the window. And he was always there.

Her mama had called and said she'd heard that Maxine had had a stroke early this morning. Andrew would want to know. If she was going out there to tell him, she might as well take him something to eat.

She used the tuna salad left over from lunch and made him a sandwich. Then, just in case, she made a ham and cheese sandwich, too, and stuffed it into the insulated lunch box with a cold bottle of water. By the time she finished stirring up some homemade hot chocolate and poured it into a thermos, she was completely aggravated at herself. What was she doing? This wasn't a Janette Oke book, and Andrew wasn't her homesteader husband trying to raise a barn by himself. She seriously needed to get a grip on reality. She slapped the lunch box on the bar and poured herself a mug of hot chocolate. That was a grown man out there, and he surely had sense enough to eat lunch.

She sank onto the bar stool and sipped her hot chocolate. And tapped her fingers on the counter. It was crazy to waste two sandwiches. She might as well offer them to him. If he didn't want them, he could just tell her so. And she'd understand. Really.

The first thing she noticed when she stepped outside was that he wasn't painting the barn anymore. The second thing was that he was sitting outside his camper in one of the lawn chairs looking at his laptop. He waved as she approached and lowered his laptop screen.

She waved the thermos, feeling increasingly foolish. "Hi."

"Elyse, good to see you."

"Thanks. Mama called awhile ago. She heard Maxine had a stroke. I don't know how bad she is, but I think they moved her to ICU."

"Oh no." He squinted into the sun as if processing the information. "I was in town this morning and stopped by to see her. I knew they'd moved her to ICU, but I didn't know what had happened."

She stared at him. He'd gone to see Maxine without her? And he knew Maxine was worse but hadn't stopped to tell her?

He looked down at the ground. "I'm sorry. I should have told you."

"Oh, that's okay." As she'd reminded herself earlier, it wasn't as if they were married. She held up the soft-sided lunch box. "I brought you a couple of sandwiches."

His eyebrows raised. "How did you know I was about to starve to death?"

She shrugged, feeling better. "Just a guess." She set the thermos down on the plastic table beside him. "Hot chocolate. For dessert."

He grinned at her. "Thanks a million. I was just trying to convince myself I could wait until supper to eat. It wasn't working."

He opened the lunch box and pulled out a sandwich.

"It's tuna," she said helpfully, as if he couldn't figure that out.

"Oh." His grin froze in place. "Thanks."

"You don't like tuna?"

"Well. . .aw. . ."

She smiled. "It's okay. The other sandwich is ham and cheese."

Relief was so evident on his face that she laughed.

"I'm sorry. There aren't many things in this world I won't eat."

"But tuna salad is one of them?"

"Yep."

That figured. She was glad she'd fixed a ham and cheese as an afterthought. "I'm going to go look at how the barn is coming while you eat."

"Okay. Thanks again."

She was about five steps away when he called her name. She turned. "Yes?"

"You will come back and drink hot chocolate with me, won't you?"

She thought of the mug she'd left on the warmer on her stove. She could always drink it later. "Sure. I'll be back in a few."

Five minutes later, she walked back around to join him. He was done with the sandwich. He grinned. "I told you I was starving. It was delicious. Thanks."

"Sure you don't want this tuna?" she teased, slipping the other sandwich back in the lunch box.

He chuckled. "You're mean."

She poured them both Styrofoam cups of hot chocolate and passed him his.

He took a sip. "That's good." He opened his laptop back up and carefully set the hot chocolate on the tiny plastic table beside his lawn chair. "One reason I took a break is because I had an idea while I was painting."

"What about?"

"You've probably already done this, but I thought if we did an online search for Luis's name, we might get a better idea of what he's up to."

Elyse shook her head. She, who googled everything she wanted to know, had not looked up Luis. She used to consider trying to find information on him when she was younger, but she'd always decided against it. But now that he was back in her life, she hadn't even thought of using the Internet to find him. "So did you do it?"

"No, I was just searching for information on Zeke. I didn't find anything significant. I wanted to wait until you were here to look up Luis." He patted the chair next to his.

She sank onto it. He scooted closer so she could see the laptop screen better. In the search engine box at the top of the screen, he typed "Luis Reynolds" and "Arkansas." Hundreds of hits came up, and he scrolled down slowly.

"Here's one from a church down in Jackson County."

"A church?" The hot chocolate set a little less easily in her stomach.

Andrew clicked on it. "This says Luis Reynolds is one of the teachers in their prison ministry." He turned it so she could see the picture. It was obviously him.

"Does it say how long?"

He scrolled then stopped. "Yes, it has a whole story here about him. Do you want me to read it to you?"

She closed her eyes and shook her head. "Just tell me what it says."

"Basically, he became a Christian in prison ten years ago and has been working in the prison ministry ever since. First from the inside and then, since his release from prison two years ago, from the outside, under the oversight of this church."

She snorted. "If he found Jesus in prison, it was a con. And now he's conning all those people at that church. There's no telling what they're paying him."

"It doesn't say it outright, but it infers that he's volunteering."

Anger—at Andrew for not understanding and at Luis for not changing—welled up inside her. "It's a con," she said through gritted teeth.

"Okay. Maybe it is a con. But this still doesn't explain what he's doing here in Shady Grove."

She stood. "You know what? I don't want to know any more."

He looked upset. "I'm sorry."

She shook her head and picked up the lunch box. "It's not you. I'm sorry for overreacting. This is just so hard, dredging this all up now."

"I understand. Sometimes we wish the past could just stay buried. But it rarely does."

She nodded toward the thermos. "Keep the hot chocolate."

He stepped toward her and put his arms around her. She leaned against him for a minute, drawing strength. "I guess this was a bad idea," he whispered.

She shook her head again. "No, it wasn't. I'm just not ready to know more. You have my permission to find out whatever you can, but I can't do it." She looked up at him and realized how close she was to him.

She saw the realization dawn on him at the same time, and he stepped back. Not flattering but helpful. She needed to figure out how to keep him at a distance. If only it wasn't so hard to want to.

CHAPTER 21

Crystal was finalizing her curriculum for the drama classes when her phone buzzed. She glanced at the caller ID, and her heart sank. Mia. . .again. Her agent had called several times over the last couple of weeks. Crystal hated not to answer it, but she could tell by the messages—"Call me immediately, darling; I have something important to talk to you about"—that Mia wasn't RSVP'ing to the wedding. Especially now that she knew that Jeremy's weirdness had to do with wanting her to go back to Broadway, Crystal didn't want to talk to Mia. One of them was bad enough without them ganging up. As soon as the thought settled into her brain, she jumped straight up and threw her pen down.

Of course. Mia had called Jeremy. That's why he'd said, "Call your agent." Mia had, no doubt, tried to make him feel guilty for letting Crystal give up her Broadway career. Crystal's hands shook as she pulled up Mia's number on her phone and hit SEND.

"It's about time you called me. I have wonderful news!" Mia's voice bubbled through the phone line.

"Did you talk to Jeremy?"

"Just wait until you hear. Jon wants you back. Melissa is

moving on to a bigger play next month, and Jon called me and specifically asked if you'd be interested in reprising your role in *Sisters*."

Crystal didn't care at all, and in that moment, she knew for sure she'd made the right decision. Not that she'd ever really doubted it. "Mia, I'm not interested. What can I say to convince you of that?"

"Say yes. Think about it and give me an answer next week."

"No. My answer is no, and it will be no next week. I'm sorry. But now I need an answer. Did you call Jeremy?"

Mia's voice grew three shades cooler. "No. No, I didn't call Jeremy."

Crystal couldn't believe Mia would lie to her. "Okay then. I'll talk to you later. I'm really sorry."

Mia broke the connection without another word.

Crystal cradled the phone against her chest. She'd just severed her final tie to Broadway. She should be devastated. But it meant nothing to her. Less than nothing compared to convincing Jeremy that her biggest dream right now was to be his wife.

❧

"Mom, can we hang around thirty minutes while Katie helps me with my algebra?"

Elyse and Victoria looked up from where they were sorting out paperwork for the upcoming dog show.

Victoria's eyebrows drew together. "Okay, but it's a school night, so no goofing off."

Elyse watched Dylan walk across Coffee Central to a quiet table in the corner near one of the bookshelves that surrounded the coffee shop area. "He's a good kid."

Victoria smiled. "Yes, he is. Oh, I mean. . .thank you." She slid a stack of flyers into a folder. "I've been meaning to apologize to you for what I said last week when I came to pick up Sweetie."

Elyse glanced at her. "Apologize? For what?"

"You know, when I said you'd wasted three years on 4-H meetings. Nothing could be further from the truth."

Elyse waved her hand. "It's fine. And in a way you might be right."

Victoria shook her head. "No, I'm not right. If Dylan is a good kid, it's partly because of you. Because of all the hours you spent helping him and a lot of the other kids in the group get their dogs certified as therapy dogs and lining up places for them to go to volunteer. Taking his dog to the nursing home and the hospital changed him from a boy who cried if someone said 'boo' to him to a young man who helps others on a regular basis and is filled with self-confidence."

"Charlie was a natural for a therapy dog, and Dylan has a way with people, too."

"Still, if you hadn't started the foundation and gotten these kids interested in volunteering, it never would have happened." Victoria frowned. "I just wish you'd take the credit. Everyone in town suspects that you're behind it, but you're like the Howard Hughes of Shady Grove philanthropy." She raised her eyebrows at Elyse. "Frankly, I'm tired of being your cover."

"You've done a lot yourself. All the corporate-level fund-raising, for example. And we both know that's where most of the money comes from."

Victoria blushed. "It's easy to raise money for a good cause when you're a Worthington."

Elyse stared blindly at the papers in her hand. Born into the wealthiest family in town, Victoria had a family heritage she could be proud of. And since the McCords adopted Elyse, she did, too. But she couldn't help but wonder what her friend would think of her if she knew the truth about her childhood. She turned her back and shoved all the papers into her bag. Andrew's suggestion niggled at her, but she didn't think she could do it.

"Want to get decaf while Dylan's working on homework?"

Elyse spun around to look at Victoria. What went better with a confession than a cup of coffee? "Okay. Let me run this stuff out to the Jeep first. I'll be right back."

"I'll get us a table."

As Elyse stepped outside, she was grateful for the cool air on her warm face. If she was this flustered just thinking about telling Victoria the truth, how could she go through with it? She unlocked the Jeep and put the bag inside then locked it back up.

Turning, she saw something at the other end of the parking lot. A little yellow truck was parked in the shadow of a tree. She was almost positive it was the same one she'd seen at Walmart. Her heart thudded against her ribs and she quickly looked away. Should she call Andrew? Was Luis following her everywhere? Why? If he was working for Zeke, filling him in on her whereabouts, wouldn't Zeke have grabbed her already?

She forced herself to take a deep breath. The best thing she could do right now was to go have coffee with Victoria then walk out with her and Dylan when it was time to leave. A rustling noise in the tall evergreen shrubs next to her decided it for her. Elyse jumped and ran inside without looking back.

Victoria looked up as she approached the table. "I got you a cup of coffee, too." She frowned. "You okay?"

Elyse slipped into a chair across from her friend. "I will be."

"What's wrong?"

"I've got something to tell you."

"Uh-oh. You're quitting 4-H and the foundation because of what I said the other day."

Elyse laughed softly. "Don't be silly, Vic. I promise that didn't offend me. I know you were just trying to motivate me to do more with my life."

"I really was."

Elyse blew out her breath and tried to think of how to even start. She opened a couple of sugar packets and stirred them into her coffee. Why had it been so relatively easy to tell Andrew the whole story? Partly because she'd been forced into it, but there was something about Andrew that made Elyse react differently than she did with anyone else. And she didn't want to delve too deeply into the reason for that. She poured some creamer in and stirred again.

"You're really making me nervous." Victoria took a sip of her coffee.

Elyse forced a smile and set the spoon down on the table. "Don't be nervous. This is really nothing to do with you. I just promised someone that I'd to try to tell a friend about my past, and you got elected."

"It can't be that hard. Just tell me."

"You know I'm adopted?"

Victoria nodded, cupping her coffee mug with both hands.

"But here's what you don't know." She looked down at the table instead of at Victoria as she spelled out the whole story of being raised by con artists, ending with her mother being shot and her dad being arrested.

A warm hand clasped hers, and she looked up.

Victoria's eyes were brimming with unshed tears. "You are so brave."

"To tell you about what an awful person I was?"

A burst of disbelieving laughter escaped Victoria's lips, and she shook her head. "To have coped with all of that and come out of it. And not just survived it, but you. . ." She waved her hand. "Look at you. You came through that terrible unfair experience, and instead of being bitter and angry, you're the most loving, kind, caring person I know."

Elyse felt tears edge her own eyes. She took a drink of coffee in an attempt to distract herself. "Vic, you don't have to be so nice. I know it can't help but change how you feel about me. What if I'm conning you right now?"

Victoria set her coffee mug down with a thud on the table. "Are you kidding? You really don't know how crazy that is that you could even say that?"

Elyse took another gulp of coffee and stared into the creamy liquid.

"You're right." Victoria thrust her head forward to look up into Elyse's face. "Knowing this does change how I feel about you."

Elyse stared at her, holding her breath.

"It makes me admire you even more. And if you think you still have the ability to con someone, then you are conning yourself. If I had a daughter, I'd want her to be just like you."

Elyse didn't know what to say. She shook her head.

"Not that I'm saying that I'm old enough to be your mother." Victoria gave a shaky laugh and swiped at her eyes with her hand. "Maybe I should have said, 'If I had a sister.' "

Elyse laughed with her and felt her stomach unclench more

than it had in a long time. "Thanks."

They chatted about the 4-H plans until Dylan was done with his homework. When they split up in the parking lot, Elyse hurried to the Jeep, climbed in, and relocked the door. Then she allowed herself to look.

The yellow truck was still parked by the tree. He'd probably just run, but she'd learned tonight that sometimes facing things head-on made life much easier. She started the motor and drove slowly down to the other end of the paved area. A shadowy figure sat in the driver's seat.

She eased the Jeep closer to the Toyota, and her heart slammed against her ribs. No doubt Luis recognized her vehicle, but he hadn't started the motor or turned his lights on.

Was he going to let her catch him? She shivered in spite of her coat. Or was this a con so he could catch her?

Her headlights shone in the cab of the truck, and she gasped. The driver was slumped over the steering wheel, unmoving. She slammed on her brakes and jumped out. As soon as her feet hit the pavement, she realized what she'd done. If this was a trap, she'd fallen right into it. She stood, frozen, staring at the unmoving body.

CHAPTER 22

Quickly, Elyse glanced all around. No one was in sight. Her hands trembled as she pulled out her cell phone and punched in 911.

She quickly gave the operator her location. "There's a man in a truck, slumped over the wheel."

"Did you try to wake him?"

"No. But my headlights are shining on him and he's not moving."

"Okay, ma'am, stay calm. We have an officer in the vicinity. He'll be right there. Can you tell if the man is breathing?"

The thought that he might not be made her sick all over again. "I can't see. Should I go see if he's okay?" A car pulled up behind her, and she stepped closer to the Jeep as she turned to look. "Oh. The officer is here." She broke the connection.

A tall dark-haired man with a crew cut climbed out of the Shady Grove police car. He nodded to her and rushed over to the door of the Toyota. It was unlocked, and he opened it. His body blocked her view of the man behind the wheel, but he yanked his radio from his belt.

Elyse felt a sob well up inside her. In spite of the police jargon, she got the message. The man in the yellow truck had been badly beaten. He was breathing, and an ambulance was now on its way.

She edged closer until she could see around the officer. Nausea welled up inside her, and she felt hot tears slip down her cold cheeks. It was him. And he looked bad. His nose was broken and blood trickled from his lip. His right eye was swollen and purple. "Is there anything we can do?"

The officer looked back at her and shook his head. He looked again. "Do you know him?"

She nodded.

"Is he related to you?"

She stared at him, uncertain what to say. Life wasn't as cut and dried as she'd like to believe. Jonathan McCord was her daddy, and she wouldn't change that for anything in the world. But this bruised and broken man in the yellow truck was definitely related to her. An ambulance siren wailed in the distance. She nodded. "Yes. Yes, he is."

"It looks like he suffered a concussion, but his pulse is strong and his breathing doesn't seem that labored." Just as he said that, Luis moaned.

Involuntarily, Elyse stepped closer so she could clearly see his face. In her darkest hours, she'd daydreamed of seeing him suffer. But now that it was real, she hated it.

His swollen right eye twitched, and his left eye opened. He blinked as if he was having a hard time focusing, but then his one-eyed gaze locked onto her face. "Elyse," he mumbled.

She nodded.

"Be careful—" He winced. "Zeke."

She gasped. "Zeke was here? He did this to you?"

But he was out again. The ambulance siren grew louder, and the policeman looked at her. "Ma'am, I'm going to need you to go down to the station with me."

❦

Andrew paced impatiently in front of the camper. Ever since he'd heard from his dad earlier, he'd wanted to call Elyse and tell her about the conversation, but since she was in a meeting, he hated to. He checked the time on his phone. Where was she?

He should have gone with her or at least followed her. But she'd assured him that she'd stay alert and watch out for anything suspicious. If she wasn't here in ten minutes, he was going to look for her. His phone vibrated and lit up in his hand. Elyse. He punched TALK. "Hello?"

"Andrew?"

His gut tensed. "What's wrong?"

"It's. . .Luis. He's in the hospital."

Luis? Andrew had to mentally shift gears. "Is he sick? Are you with him?"

"No. He's been beaten. And I'm at the police station downtown."

He clenched the phone so hard he was afraid he'd break it. "What's going on?"

He listened as she gave him a quick rundown on the night's events.

"Are you okay?"

"I'm fine. I'm waiting for Jack to get here so I can fill him in. But right now I need a favor."

"I'll be right there." With his free hand, he pulled his keys from his jeans pocket.

"Wait." Her voice softened. "I'd love for you to be here with me. But I was really hoping that you'd let the dogs out for a minute then go to the hospital and check on Luis."

He fought to keep the frustration out of his tone. "Elyse, I don't want you there alone. Let me come to the station; then when you're done, we'll go to the hospital together."

She hesitated. "The thing is. . .I'm not ready to see him yet. But I also hate to think of him being there with no one to care what happens." She lowered her voice. "I wouldn't wish that on anyone."

Andrew walked slowly to his truck, sure he was losing this argument but not ready to give it up. "What about you being out alone? If Zeke beat up Luis, it has to be because he thought Luis was standing between you and him. Now he's not anymore."

"Andrew, I'm at a police station. There are men in uniform milling all around. I'm fine. Besides, I'm going to call Mama and Daddy."

"And tell them about Luis?"

"Yes. I should have been honest with them in the first place. They're not wimps. They've never given me any reason to think I couldn't trust them with the whole truth. I hid behind the thought that I was protecting them."

He stopped with his hand on the truck door. Her words pierced him. But his circumstances were different. He really was protecting her by not telling her about his past. If she'd known, she'd never have been able to get past her suspicions enough to let him help her. Was that a matter of his not trusting her with the truth? He hoped not.

"Anyway, some of my family will come down here if I need them to." She laughed softly. "And probably even if I don't."

Andrew blew out his breath and climbed into the truck. She was right. Her family would be there for her. "I'll stop by and let the dogs out on my way to the hospital."

"Call me after you see him, okay?"

"Will do." He wanted to say something else, but he didn't know what. Something to let her know how important she was to him. "Take care." That was inadequate, but it would have to do.

"You, too."

❦

It was hard to quit being a coward overnight. While the phone was ringing, Elyse flip-flopped about which one she hoped would answer.

"Hello." Her daddy's deep voice always made her smile.

"Hey, Daddy, it's Elyse."

"You sound funny. Everything okay?"

Tears burned her eyes again, and she nodded then kind of laughed when she realized he couldn't see her. "Mostly." She reconfigured the words several times in her mind before she finally spit them out. "I'm fine and I'm not in any trouble with the law, but I'm at the police station downtown."

He echoed her words, and she heard her mama pick up on the extension. "Honey, what happened?"

"Zeke apparently was outside Coffee Central tonight and. . ."

Her mother gasped.

"Did they catch him?"

She just wanted to calm the concern in her daddy's voice, but she knew what she had to say next would only upset them both more. "No, they didn't. But I'm pretty sure he beat a man up."

"A man? What man?"

"I should have told you this a couple of weeks ago, and I'm sorry, but there was a little yellow truck lurking around at the end of the lane several nights in a row. The night of the storm, Andrew tackled the man who was driving it."

"Andrew tackled him here? And Zeke beat the same man up at Coffee Central?" Her mom sounded near hysteria, something Elyse had heard only once before in her voice—the night Cami died.

Shame mixed with tears trickled down her face. "Yes."

"Do you know who he is?" her dad asked.

"I just got a glimpse of him that night of the storm, but I recognized him."

"Who was it?" Her dad was obviously impatient with her hesitant answers.

"My biological father."

Another gasp. Her mom, she thought. Then silence.

She started to tremble. What if they were upset that she'd allowed her past to drag itself into their family life?

"Is he okay?" her mama asked quietly.

"I think so."

"Why are you at the police station?" Daddy just sounded concerned about her and nothing else.

"I'm waiting to answer some questions for Jack. About Zeke. And about Luis."

"I'll be right there, honey," her dad assured her quietly. "Just sit tight."

Jack Westwood came in the door, and the desk sergeant pointed to her. He waved and walked toward her.

"Okay, Daddy. Jack's here. I'll see you in a few minutes. And. . .I'm really sorry."

"Don't worry about anything." Mama's voice sounded so much calmer than it had.

Elyse said good-bye and flipped her phone shut then turned to Jack. "Let me just say up front that I'm sorry for not telling you sooner. I didn't want the world to know that besides the fact that Zeke is apparently out to get me, my biological father, Luis Reynolds, who was in prison with Zeke, is also stalking me." She was getting better at this.

Jack's eyebrows raised. "Whoa. Slow down. So the man who was beaten is your father?"

"Was my father. Until I was eight. He went to prison for armed robbery and wounding a cop. Or technically until I was ten and the McCords adopted me. Either way he *was* my father."

He put his hand on her elbow. "Let's go sit down. Are you okay? You seem a little wired up."

"Stress."

He nodded. "Let's just de-stress for a second and start at the beginning." He pulled a pen and a tiny black notebook from his pocket.

For the next fifteen minutes, he picked her brain and made notes.

Just as they finished, her daddy walked in the door. His shoulders seemed broader than she remembered. He filled the doorway.

She ran into his arms, taking comfort in the familiar smell of soap and Old Spice on his flannel shirt. "Thank you for coming."

"Like you could have kept me away." He looked around. "Speaking of that, where's your self-appointed protector?"

"Andrew?" She blushed. "He's at the hospital. I asked him to check on Luis."

He nodded. "Good." He turned to Jack. "Are you done with her?"

Jack nodded. "We've really turned up the heat on Zeke. We already had an APB out on him, but we've made catching him our top priority in Shady Grove and the outlying areas right now. I think we'll have him by morning."

As they walked out of the police station, Elyse motioned to the parking lot. "If you want to follow me home, that'll be great."

Her dad cleared his throat. "Actually, Luke came to take your Jeep home." Luke, leaning against her Jeep with his Carhartt jacket pulled tight around him, waggled his fingers. "I thought you might be too tired to drive."

"Thanks." She tossed her keys to her brother and climbed into her dad's truck. There would be other days to prove her independence. Tonight was a time for leaning her head back against the seat and trying to relax.

She opened her eyes and sat up when her dad slid under the steering wheel. "I'm really sorry I didn't tell you about Luis. It was just so weird seeing him again."

"I can imagine." He pulled out onto the highway behind Luke. "We completely understand."

"Really?" She tilted her head. "Because I don't even know if I can explain all the reasons I didn't want you to know. Partly because I had a crazy idea you might feel threatened by the fact that my biological father had shown up. But tonight when you walked into the police station, I realized that you know that you're my daddy and always will be. And no one can take that away from us."

He chuckled. "You're absolutely right. And you're also really,

really tired. Do you remember the second Christmas you spent with us?"

She glanced over at him. "What do you mean?"

"Cami talked you and Crystal into staying up all night so you'd be the first ones to get to the presents. Y'all were so tired that Cami and Crys were asleep by lunch. But you—our quiet, shy little girl—were wide-eyed and babbling about everything under the sun. We all sat and watched in amazement. I'm not sure I've ever seen you do that again until now."

She chuckled weakly. "I guess I lose my self-consciousness once I reach a certain point of tiredness."

He nodded. "Your mama will be sorry she missed it. She still mentions occasionally about how much you talked that Christmas." He glanced at her. "Speaking of your mama, she wants to fix breakfast for you in the morning. We need to talk to you."

"Is something wrong?"

He shook his head. "No. You get some rest tonight, honey, and try not to worry about things."

She laid her head against the seat again and closed her eyes. She could feel the bumpiness of the gravel road as they neared home. When the truck turned into her lane, she opened her eyes. "Thanks for driving me home."

"You're welcome." He pulled up in front of her house. Luke had already parked the Jeep and gotten out. Truck lights turned down the lane, and she squinted. Andrew, back from the hospital.

Her dad touched her shoulder. "Why don't you stay out here and talk to him while we go through your house and make sure everything's okay?"

She nodded. "Thanks. Just tell the dogs I'll be in soon."

"We'll tell them you found someone you liked better than them," Luke drawled.

She wrinkled her nose at her brother. "Go ahead. They won't believe you."

Her daddy laughed. "Nice to see some things never change. Lucas, leave your sister alone, and let's go make sure there's nobody in her house that isn't four-footed."

They walked up to the front door and let themselves in, just as Andrew pulled up beside her and opened his truck door.

She smiled at him. "Hey." He looked tired. She ran her hand through her hair. No telling what she looked like.

"Hey," he said, still sitting in the truck, his eyes never leaving her face. "Luis is going to be okay."

"Oh good." Her smile widened. It was so good to see him.

He climbed down and covered the distance between them in two broad steps. She didn't protest when he took her in his arms. For a few moments, she let everything fall away—Zeke, Luis, her parents, her shyness. All of it. She was right where she belonged.

She drew back slightly and looked up at him. "Thank you."

The moonlight danced shadows across his face, but she could see his crooked smile. "I missed you."

"Me, too." She felt her cheeks burn.

"You. I missed you." She knew what he meant. Tonight seemed like it had been an eternity long.

He stared into her eyes then bent his head until he was almost touching her lips. She didn't move, but in the depths of his eyes, she saw something unreadable. A little chill ran up her spine.

"Unless something changes drastically, I have nothing to offer you except this minute," he murmured.

She didn't understand exactly what he meant, but she believed him. And right now she didn't care. "Okay," she whispered, almost touching his lips.

Apparently he took her answer for what it was, because he kissed her fully and completely with no hesitation. And for the first time in her life she didn't feel ashamed of where she'd come from. Everything in her past, including the bad, had played a part in bringing her to this point. To this kiss. To this man. To this love? The thought shook her to the core, but she didn't pull away.

CHAPTER 23

Andrew stepped back suddenly and ran his hand through his hair. "I'm sorry."

"You're sorry?" She wrapped her arms around herself, suddenly cold. That wasn't what she'd wanted to hear after the most magical moment of her life.

"I had no right to do that."

A flash of irritation ignited her exhaustion, and she blurted out how she felt. "Last time I checked, I said 'okay,' so I guess that gave you the right."

"Yeah, but. . ." Andrew's words drifted off as the front door of Elyse's house opened and her brother and dad walked out.

"Thanks for going to check on Luis." Elyse was suddenly too exhausted to even think. "Good night." She turned and marched away without saying another word. Let him be sorry by himself.

"All clear?" she asked as she met her dad and Luke on the walkway.

"All clear." Luke slugged her shoulder gently.

Daddy gave her a one-arm hug. "What did Andrew say?"

"Uh. . ." She stammered for a second then realized he was

asking about Luis. "Oh. He said he's going to be okay."

"Good. See you at breakfast tomorrow."

"Okay. Thanks."

As days went, this had been one of the longest of her life. Maybe tomorrow would be better.

❦

Andrew slapped at his alarm and climbed out of bed, glad morning was here. It wasn't as if he'd had much sleep after the disaster last night with Elyse. He started the coffee brewing and peeked out the camper window at her house. Her Jeep was home, so she wasn't gone anywhere.

How had she gotten under his skin so quickly? He wasn't the kind of guy who fell hard and fast. He was the kind of guy—or at least he used to be—who eased into a relationship slowly and only committed his heart after making a long pros and cons list. Had Melanie's death changed him that much? Or was it just Elyse who had that effect on him? Since the first day when he'd leaped to her rescue, he hadn't been able to stop thinking about her.

After he was dressed and ready to face the day, he poured himself a cup of coffee and thought about last night. To say it had gone badly was an understatement. He sipped his coffee. The kiss hadn't gone badly. Not at all. But after. . . He'd tried to warn her, to warn himself. He cringed as he remembered his dramatic proclamation before he'd kissed her. But it had been true. He had nothing to offer her. Nothing lasting.

He took another sip of his coffee. Even if she could somehow overlook the fact that he'd been a suspect in Melanie's murder, he'd never want her to join him in the cloud of suspicion he'd been living under for the last three years. Nor would he expect her to understand his desire to see the killer brought down at any cost.

He finished off his coffee, letting the hot liquid almost scald his throat. For now all he could do was protect her. And be her friend, if she'd let him after last night.

❦

For the first time since he'd moved his camper in, Elyse regretted Andrew being her closest neighbor. She'd seriously considered never going out of her house again. But that would kind of put a kink in her plan to have breakfast this morning at her parents' house.

She reached over and rubbed the softest part of Majesty's ear. The dog pushed her head against Elyse's hand. "If I run out and jump in the Jeep," she explained to her canine cohort, "I can drive down the lane and out to the road then turn in the next driveway and go to Mama and Daddy's that way." She waved a hand in the air. "Voilà! I wouldn't have to take a chance on seeing him."

The doorbell rang, and the four dogs trotted to the door. Elyse got up and followed them. What if it was Andrew? She shook her head. Why would it be? She peeked out the window and sighed. It was him. She opened the door partially. "Hello."

He had the grace to look embarrassed; she'd give him that. "Hey. I needed to tell you something I found out last night. . . before you called me."

"What is it?" Inside her head, she could hear her mama's voice gently chiding her for her lack of manners, but she was not inviting him in.

He shifted from one foot to the other.

She stood without speaking. She'd already asked him what it was. That was better than she could have done.

"I heard from my contact in Texas yesterday. With some more information about Luis."

"I told you I don't want to hear any more about his con."

Andrew ducked his head and cleared his throat. "I don't see how this can be a con—"

"No. Normal people never do. That's the sad part." She knew her words were sharp. But she was tired of being nice. And just tired.

He stared at her top porch step and made no move to leave. She had a feeling that if she didn't let him tell her what he'd found out, he wouldn't. "Okay. What's the information?"

"You know Luis got out of prison two years ago?"

She nodded.

"Well, he did something unusual and served his whole term."

"Why?"

"Prison records show that he could have been paroled three years before that but he refused it."

"He stayed in prison?" Her mind raced, trying to make sense of that information. How could that have been a con? "Did it say why?"

"The letter he wrote asking not to be paroled stated that he felt that he could better serve the Lord from the inside."

"More than likely he just wanted to keep getting three squares and have a roof over his head."

Andrew met her gaze directly, and she was almost positive that she saw pity in his eyes. For her. "Do you really believe that?"

"Thanks for telling me. I'd better go. I'm supposed to go have breakfast with my *real* parents." She closed the door slowly, not wanting to actually slam it in his face.

"Wait."

She opened the door back.

"About last night. . ."

She shook her head. "We're going to forget that ever happened."

"I'm sor—"

She held up her hand. "Don't you dare apologize again."

His brows furrowed, but he nodded. "Okay then. I'll see you later."

She closed the door and wondered how hard it would be to get used to leaving through the back entrance of her house.

⤝

Andrew pushed open the big glass doors, clutching the small bouquet of flowers. After checking in at the reception desk, he walked down the wide, carpeted hallway and lightly tapped on Maxine's door.

A dark-haired woman in blue scrubs pulled the door open and motioned him inside the room. "We just got Miss Maxine bathed and back in her bed." She glanced at the watch on her wrist. "Her nephew usually comes in about this time." The nurse patted Maxine on the arm. "She's doing so much better. She'll probably be going home soon." She motioned toward Andrew's small offering. "Would you look at those flowers, Miss Maxine?"

Andrew set the bouquet on the night table and smiled at the woman lying in the barely wrinkled bed. Her face was nearly the same color as the pristine white sheets.

"Now, don't you wear her out," the nurse cautioned as she

pulled the door open. "She isn't really that strong yet," she added in a lower voice.

Andrew felt a moment of panic as he looked at the fragile woman lying in bed. She looked as if she would blow away at the slightest puff of wind. He could hardly believe she was well enough to be sent home anytime in the near future, but she had her eyes open and looked much more alert than when he had seen her last.

Before he could form a sentence, the door opened and Doug came in. He nodded at Andrew but went straight to the bed and leaned down to hug his aunt. "How are you today, Aunt Maxine?"

The older woman's face lit up as she looked at her nephew, and she tried to speak.

Andrew could only make out a few words, but Doug obviously knew what she was saying. "Now, don't you worry about anything. I'm going to quit my job and move here to Shady Grove to take care of you."

She frowned and shook her head slightly. Then she said something else that Andrew didn't understand.

"Yes, I am. I know I can find a job here, so don't you give it another thought." He leaned over and kissed her wrinkled cheek. "I wish I'd have moved here a long time ago so I could spend time with you. Remember how much fun we had when I was a kid and Dad would let me spend the summers with you?"

She nodded and smiled.

Doug stood and turned toward Andrew. "Thanks for coming by to visit her. She gets lonely, but some of her church friends visit during the week." He reached down and patted the old woman's gnarled hand. "I wish I could get here more often, but that's going to change as soon as I get my stuff packed up and move over here."

"That sounds like a good idea." Andrew admired this man's willingness to step up and take care of a relative. "I just stopped by to see how she was doing." He smiled at the woman. "You get well soon, Miss Maxine. I'll be back by to check on you again soon."

She nodded and said a long sentence Andrew couldn't quite make out.

Andrew opened the door, and Doug followed him out into the hall. "She thanked you for coming by and getting her to the hospital, and she appreciates your girlfriend for taking care of Pal."

"My girlfriend?" Andrew's brow raised.

"Elyse."

Andrew was sure he could see curiosity in Doug's eyes. Was the man interested in Elyse? If he was, Andrew wasn't going to make it easy for him. "Oh, okay. I'll tell her." He walked away and was almost to the door when he stopped and reversed course. He'd almost forgotten. He needed to make one more visit before he left.

⊱❦⊰

Breakfast at her parents' had always been Elyse's favorite meal, but today had been stilted and odd. Since Crystal had an early meeting at the bank about the drama studio loan, it had just been her and her parents. But back when Crystal lived in New York, they'd had plenty of meals, just the three of them. And it had never been weird. Had not telling them about Luis ruined her relationship with them?

"So what about Crystal's surprise shower?" she asked her

mama to make conversation. She had talked to Kaleigh and Bree both about it, so she knew it was still on—unless Crystal and Jeremy didn't work things out. But that was a possibility Elyse wasn't willing to entertain. "We're still planning that for Thanksgiving night at my house?"

Mama nodded, her face taut. "Bree and Aaron will be in for sure, and Bree is excited about the shower. And so is Kaleigh." She stood and scraped the remains of her breakfast into the trash. Elyse could see the tenseness in her shoulders. "It'll just be the five of us, but we'll have fun. Since the women at church are giving her a big one there, we won't have to be too practical with our gifts." She slipped her plate into the sink and turned around to face them. "Why don't we sit out on the porch and finish our coffee?"

Elyse nodded.

Her daddy picked up his mug. "Sounds like a good idea." He led the way, and she and Mama followed him.

Mama sat in the porch swing. She looked at Elyse and patted the place beside her.

Elyse smiled as she sat down. She used to love to swing for hours on the wooden slatted swing. She couldn't remember the last time she'd sat here.

Instead of claiming the chair next to them, Daddy stood looking out over the railing. "The hills are beautiful this time of year."

Elyse glanced out at the hills, rolling with autumn color. Reds, oranges, yellows, browns, and even purples mixed in together on the tree limbs to make a scene that always reminded her of melted crayons and grade school art projects. She shivered. Another thing she didn't get to enjoy until she was almost too old, thanks to her biological parents.

Her daddy turned around to face her. "You may not realize it, but Luis Reynolds contacted us years ago."

Her eyes widened. Why hadn't they told her?

"You were sixteen," Mama said quietly, beside her. "And we asked you if you would like to be in touch with him."

Just like that she remembered. She hadn't known that he'd contacted them, but she remembered what she'd thought of their question. "And I told you that I never, under any circumstances, wanted anything to do with him."

"Ever." Her daddy half smiled. "One of the rare times you stole the drama queen crown from Cami."

Elyse shook her head. "I didn't know you meant you knew how to reach him."

Daddy frowned. "Would it have mattered?"

"No. Not at all."

"You were so upset by us even asking that we didn't want to upset you further." Mama reached over and touched her hand.

"I can understand that." And she could.

"We did mention him through the years, but every time your reaction was basically the same."

She shrugged. "I guess I remember that. So did he keep harassing y'all?"

Her mama chuckled. "He never harassed us, honey. We ended up getting to know him fairly well over the years. But he didn't want to butt into your new life."

Elyse's heart sank. "You didn't give him money, did you?"

Her daddy gave her a stern look. "We offered to help support him in his prison ministry a couple of years ago, but he said we'd done enough for him by giving you the family you'd always deserved."

While she was trying to figure out the logic to that con, something suddenly occurred to her. "Y'all knew he was here, didn't you?" That was why they hadn't seemed that surprised last night when she'd called from the police station.

Daddy nodded. "After he saw the TV report, he called us and told us Zeke was bad news." He looked into his coffee mug but didn't take a drink. "Then he called again and said he was in town for a while. I told him you had more protectors than most, but he was determined to stick around and keep an eye on you." His gaze met Elyse's. "I'm sorry for not telling you. I thought he was being unobtrusive." He shook his head. "And I never thought about him getting himself beaten."

"Why would he do that?" Elyse wondered aloud.

Her daddy shrugged. "Because Zeke was going to hurt you?"

"This just doesn't make sense. And according to Andrew, he could have had early parole but didn't take it." She frowned. "I can't figure out his angle."

Mama reached over and patted her hand. "Maybe that's because he doesn't have one."

Elyse let that sink in. "You think he's turned over a new leaf?"

Mama smiled. "I think he's turned over a whole new tree. But what I think doesn't matter. It's your trust he has to win if he wants to be in your life."

"Be in my life?" She motioned around the ranch. "Even if I believed him, where is there room for him in my life? I have a family, in case you haven't noticed."

Her daddy pinned her with a gaze she'd seen very few times in her life—aimed at her, at least. "We didn't raise you to be stingy with love. There's enough to go around, and you know as well as I do that the more you give the more you get. Why wouldn't there be room in your life for him?"

She blushed. When he put it like that. . . "I'll think about it."

He nodded. "Good."

The rest of the day, she thought about what he'd said. And she knew he was right. But she wasn't ready to see Luis yet. She wasn't sure she ever would be.

CHAPTER 24

Y ou're Liza Who Little?" Chance asked, puzzlement evident in his voice. He was on the opposite end of the boat, watching his line.

"Eliza Doolittle." Kaleigh enunciated the words plainly as she pulled a night crawler out of the bait bucket and threaded it carefully onto the hook. "From *My Fair Lady*. Don't you remember, Cami and Crystal both loved that movie. They made us all watch it over and over?"

"What does that have to do with you?"

"Henry Higgins was trying to change a cockney flower girl— Eliza Doolittle—into a refined lady." Kaleigh made a perfect cast into the water.

"And she talked about rain in Spain, right?"

Kaleigh laughed. "Yes, but there was more to it than that."

Chance didn't say anything for a few minutes. Then he grunted. "That makeover didn't end well, did it?"

"No." Kaleigh sighed. "But I'm not following the analogy that far. I'm just saying that Carlton can help me be more refined."

"I've never even been able to talk you into switching from

live bait to artificial. What brought on this big change?"

She felt her shoulders tense. "You know what brought it on. I don't want to end up old and alone. Some eccentric old fisherlady who lives on a houseboat with a thousand cats. Or in the short term, I don't want to be sitting at Crystal's wedding, miserable with no date, while everyone else goes by in pairs."

"So, in order to avoid that, you need to be a different person?"

"Yes." She felt a tug on her line. Almost without thinking, she set the hook and reeled it in. "Got one."

Chance reeled his own line in and grabbed the net. He netted her catch then watched as she took the rainbow trout off the hook and threw it into the water-filled cooler. "This whole idea is crazy."

"You sound like Candice."

"For once, your roommate is right. And you know I don't say that lightly." He changed out his purple spinner bait for a neon green one. "Besides, look at how it is with the family. You're everybody's favorite."

A half grin tilted her lips. That must have been hard for him to say. They'd teased for years over which one of them was the family favorite. "That's just because I'm the baby."

"Actually, if you want to be technical, I'm the baby by about two minutes." He winked and grinned. "And maybe I *am* the favorite. But you're my twin. So you can't be too bad." He drew back and cast his line into the water.

Now there was the brother she knew and loved.

She cast, and they stood in silence for a few minutes.

"Bottom line," Chance growled, as if he'd been stewing about this, "if a man doesn't like you for who you are, then he's not worth wasting your time on."

Time to lighten up a little. Kaleigh looked over her shoulder at her brother. "I guess this means you don't think I should invite Carlton to go home with me for Thanksgiving."

That familiar mischievous grin tilted Chance's lips. "I wouldn't necessarily say that. Y'all are having that surprise girls-only shower for Crystal. We guys could use a little entertainment."

Kaleigh reeled her line in to recast. "Like I said, no to Thanksgiving, but who knows? Maybe yes to the wedding. You'll all be too distracted then to scare him off." And she'd be too distracted to worry about whether he approved of her or not.

❧

Andrew laid his paintbrush down for a minute and stretched his shoulders. It was hard to believe it had been almost a week since he kissed Elyse. But it was even harder to believe that she was so good at avoiding him. His calls to her—and he was embarrassed to admit there'd been several—had gone unanswered. He never saw her outside anymore. Daily, clients brought their dogs up the back path and came back to pick them up, so he knew she hadn't left the country.

After the chilly reception he'd gotten last time, he drew the line at going to her house. But if he didn't see her soon, he might be forced to cross that imaginary line and ring her doorbell.

The upside of her self-imposed quarantine was that he hadn't had to worry about her being a target for Zeke. He used the extra time getting the outside of the barn mostly painted. Another week and he'd be ready to move to the inside. Then a few weeks after that, he'd be ready to move on. He glanced over at Elyse's house. As far as work was concerned anyway.

His cell phone vibrated against his side. He plucked it out of the leather holder and flipped it open. Jack Westwood's voice boomed through the line. "Zeke's been spotted up in central Missouri."

"They didn't catch him?"

"No. But they will. I just wanted you to know that he's apparently left our area."

"For now, anyway."

"Yep. My contact thought he was going north, but for now this info only places him a few hours away. A half day's drive could change that. So keep an eye on Elyse."

"I will. Thanks for calling." Not only did the news give him relief, but it provided him with the perfect opportunity to go see Elyse.

"No problem. I already called Elyse." Jack cleared his throat. "I thought she might just tell you. But she said if I wanted you to know, I needed to call you and tell you."

Ouch. "Well, I'm glad you did. Thanks." He hung up and went back to painting with a vengeance. Yet again he chased the question in his mind. Was she mad because he'd apologized? Or mad because he'd kissed her?

❦

What would Victoria say if she skipped the 4-H meeting this week? She glanced in the mirror. Silly thought, considering she was completely ready. But she dreaded walking out the door. What if Andrew was waiting for her?

She brushed her hair back from her face and looked at her eyes. She could at least be honest with herself and admit that the big question was—What if he wasn't waiting? She felt like a sulky child. But she'd needed this time to process—the information about Luis and, also, the kiss.

She pushed to her feet and went to tell the dogs good-bye. After the others ran off to play, Majesty stayed, sitting regally by her side. Elyse stroked her soft fur for a few more minutes then bent down and dropped a kiss on her head. "Thanks, baby."

She grabbed her keys from the table and hurried outside. Andrew's truck was gone. Maybe he'd already forgotten her. She drove slowly into town and parked at Coffee Central, away from any shrubs this time. Instinctively, she glanced toward the far end of the parking lot. A familiar four-door red truck sat in about the same place that Luis's truck had sat last week. Even from here, she could see someone in the driver's seat. Her heart leaped and she smiled. Maybe Andrew hadn't forgotten her after all.

❧

Crystal stared at the calendar and shook her head. Her wedding was in a month, and she and Jeremy were barely speaking. She blinked against hot tears. It was crazy. Crazy to continue to plan to marry someone who didn't trust her enough to explain. Someone who could just cut her off on a whim. Anger burned in her chest, but confusion and despair snuffed it out as quickly as it came.

A tap on the bedroom door made her quickly wipe her eyes. "Come in."

Mama walked in, a white bag in her hand. "Delivery for you."

"For me? Who from?"

"Jeremy brought it by."

Crystal's eyes widened. "He was here?"

"Yes."

"But he didn't want to see me?"

"He just asked me to make sure you got this."

Crystal took the bag. "Thanks." She bit her lip to keep from crying.

"You want to talk?"

She shook her head, letting her hair shield her face from her mama.

"Okay. I'll be downstairs if you need me." Mama slipped out of the room and shut the door behind her.

Crystal held the small bag out away from her, not sure she wanted to know what was in it. Was he giving her back something she'd given him? Her heart, maybe? Her legs gave way, and she sank to the bed. Had he finally gathered the courage to end it once and for all, even if he couldn't do it in person? She'd known for a while that was the direction this was going. But knowing didn't make it any easier to bear.

Finally, she gingerly opened the bag.

CHAPTER 25

Crystal stared at the folded-up papers, almost afraid to pull them out. Curiosity got the best of her, and she slid the legal-looking documents into her hand and skimmed the information. She could tell they were land papers, but what did they mean? And why had he brought them to her? When she flipped to the last page and saw the signatures at the bottom and a blank spot for Jeremy's signature, it hit her. He was selling his ranch.

For the first time, she considered that maybe he had a brain tumor or some kind of mind-changing illness. He loved that ranch. It had been his dream all the years he'd worked in a factory in south Arkansas. And now he was going to sell it? He really had lost his mind.

She folded the document up and was about to put it back when a small square of paper in the bottom of the bag caught her eye. Her hand shook while she read it aloud to the empty room.

Dear Crystal,
    It seems like just yesterday that I found you sitting on the riverbank. I'm so sorry for how I've acted lately. But

I need to make you understand. Please meet me at the river. I'll be waiting.

A simple *J* was scrawled beneath the words.

Crystal glanced down at her faded jeans and turquoise T-shirt. Good enough. She grabbed a fur-lined denim jacket from the closet, slipped on her boots, and, clutching the white bag, ran down the stairs. "I'm going down to the river," she called toward the kitchen as she went out the door. She prayed as she drove her little car down the bumpy path.

She saw Jeremy's paint horse, Nacho, first. Then she saw him. Standing with his back to her, looking out at the river. She parked the car and jumped out. When he didn't turn to look at her, she froze. Why was she hurrying? So she could get her heart broken faster? She walked slowly toward him, her feet growing heavier with each step.

When she reached him, he turned and looked at her. His face lit up in the biggest smile she'd seen him have in a while. "Crystal, you came."

"Was there any doubt?"

He ducked his head and kicked at the ground. "After the way I've acted? Yes. I wouldn't have blamed you if you hadn't."

"Jeremy, what's wrong?" She wanted to scream, "Have you lost your mind?"

"Nothing is wrong now. I'm selling the ranch." He smiled again.

"I don't understand. Why?"

"Because I love you more than I love the ranch. There's no comparison, actually. And Beka has done so well adapting since she's been back with me. She'll do fine in New York. She can spend time every summer with her grandparents here."

Crystal could feel her legs start to shake. She sank down on the cold ground.

Jeremy came over and sat down beside her. He put his arm around her shoulders and pulled her against him.

Tears pricked her eyes again. She'd missed him so much. More than she'd ever dreamed possible.

He kissed her hair. "I love you, honey. Please forgive me for how I've acted." He took her hand in his and rubbed it gently. "I didn't understand before." He ran his finger down each of her fingers as if reassuring himself she was really here. "Oh, don't get me wrong. I knew that you'd worked hard and that you had a lot of talent. But until I saw. . ." His voice drifted off, and he tugged her tighter against him.

"Until you saw what?" Her voice was shaky.

"Until I saw all the different parts you played. All the bit parts, then the bigger ones. In plays where you obviously outclassed the others talent-wise, but you kept at it."

She frowned. He saw her?

"You kept at it because you were determined to get to Broadway." She could hear pride in his voice. "And then you did. You made it." He hesitated. "I took it away from you." He tilted her face to look at him, and the pain in his eyes was unmistakable. "I'm so sorry."

"What do you mean you 'saw' me in those parts?"

"On DVD. Mia sent me a packet filled with DVDs. A chronicle of your career, she called it in the note. She said they wanted you to come back. And I'm the only thing standing between you and your dream."

Crystal leaped to her feet. "And you believed her?" She

grabbed the white bag and yanked out the land contract. Tears poured down her face. She ripped the pages in half and ripped them again, sobs shaking her shoulders as she thought of how miserable she'd been for the last month.

Jeremy stood and watched her, his mouth slightly open.

When she'd finally spent her anger and frustration, she stuffed all the tiny pieces into the bag and shoved it at him. "Here's what I think about your plan." She pushed her hair back away from her face. "Why didn't you tell me about Mia sending you that?"

Jeremy looked down at the bag then back at her. "She said if I told you, you'd say she was wrong. But that she knew you were sorry you'd given it up."

Crystal didn't speak until her breathing evened out some. "She's an agent, Jeremy. She gets a percentage of what I make as an actress. She desperately wants to believe I'm sorry for my decision." She stepped closer to him. "But the truth is. . .I'm not. . .not even a little. Broadway was never really my dream. It was Cami's. I did it. . ." A realization struck her and a chuckle escaped her lips, still parched from crying. "I did it like you did this land contract. From some misguided attempt to fix things after she died. I love you. I love Beka. But I also love this place." She waved her arm to the river. "And our ranch." She nodded to the bag. "The one you were going to sell so you could make me happy."

He just stared at her as if he couldn't believe what he was hearing.

"I'm about to open my own studio for the arts in the barn. And if you move to New York, you're going to have to do it without me."

He stepped toward her and took her hand. She watched him

slide her engagement ring off her finger. Her breath caught in her throat, but before she could react, he slipped to the ground on one knee.

"What are you doing?" she whispered.

"Starting over." He looked up at her, still holding her hand. "Crys, I've been a fool. And it probably won't be the last time. But I love you more than life. Beka would love to have you as a mother, and having you as my wife is all I need, no matter where I live." He pressed his lips to her hand then met her gaze again, his blue eyes shining. "Crystal McCord, will you marry me?"

"Yes." Tears blurred her vision as he slipped the ring on her finger. He pulled her to her feet and into his arms. She was finally right where she belonged.

❧

Elyse took the coffee Victoria handed her and sat down at the table. They watched across the room as Allie's daughter, Katie, and Dylan had their heads bent together over a book.

"I've started something now, letting him do homework with Katie last week."

Elyse nodded. "Which is he more interested in? Homework or Katie?"

Victoria laughed. "It's funny how long they've been friends, but now suddenly he sees her through different eyes." She looked down at the table. "We need more creamer. Be right back."

Elyse watched her cross the room. The first thing she'd noticed when she'd gotten to the 4-H meeting was that Victoria was wearing a different perfume. In all of the years she'd known Vic, she'd worn only one perfume—Obsession. But tonight she had on something else. Something light and flirty.

And after the meeting, she'd almost insisted that Elyse drink a cup of coffee with her. She seemed nervous. Hands laden with creamer, Victoria wove between the tables and slid gracefully into the chair across from her.

"So what's up?" Elyse asked.

"Nothing." Victoria pulled the tab of a creamer and dumped it into her coffee. "Everything."

Elyse raised her eyebrow. "Which is it?"

"I can't quit thinking about you telling me about your childhood last week."

Uh-oh. And what? She'd decided that she couldn't be friends with a convict's daughter, after all? "And?"

Vic stirred her coffee. "And that took a lot of courage for you to tell me that. So I've been wishing I had that kind of courage."

Elyse blushed. "You run a large corporation, and I can't talk to strangers. I'm the least courageous person I know. What do you mean?"

Victoria laid her spoon down on the table and met Elyse's gaze. "I'm in love with Adam."

Elyse raised both eyebrows. "Okay. That was blunt."

Victoria choked out a little laugh. "Sorry. I've never told anyone before."

"No one? Not even him?"

Victoria shook her head. "Especially not him."

Elyse looked toward the front where Allie's husband, Daniel, was working the counter. "What about Allie?"

"Oh, yeah. I totally told her, 'By the way, I'm madly in love with your little brother. Yep. The one who was in kindergarten when we hit adolescence.'" She shook her head. "No, I haven't told her."

Elyse laughed. "Okay, I can see why you haven't, I guess. But don't you think she knows?"

Victoria looked panic-stricken. "Did you?"

Elyse shrugged. "Well, I kind of suspected at least. Do you remember that old show *Moonlighting*?"

Victoria nodded.

"I watched the first season of that on DVD not too long ago. And it reminded me of you and Adam."

"Really?"

Elyse nodded. "Y'all have a Bruce Willis and Cybil Shepherd kind of chemistry going on. You have ever since I've known you."

"So as long as none of my other friends have watched *Moonlighting*, my secret's safe." Victoria moaned and put her head in her hands. In a few seconds, Vic raised her head and peeked through her fingers at Elyse. "What should I do?"

"Do you know how Adam feels about you?"

A slight blush crept up Victoria's high cheekbones. "Yes. Actually I do. A year ago, he told me he was in love with me and had been as long as he could remember. I didn't say anything. So then he said that if I ever decided I returned his feelings to let him know."

"Then what?" Elyse was fascinated by a man who would make himself so vulnerable to the woman he loved.

Victoria shrugged. "Then I didn't say anything, and we went back to being friends like always."

"Are you happy?"

"Maybe." She gave Elyse a weak smile. "In a completely miserable way."

Elyse chuckled. "I don't think that counts."

"Yeah. Me either. But here's the thing. I can't tell Allie."

"Why? What's the worst thing that could happen?" Elyse knew she was echoing Andrew's words to her, but they were wise words.

"She could hate me. And call me a cradle robber."

"When one of you is thirty-two and the other one is thirty-nine, that's not nearly as big of a deal as it is when one of you is twelve and the other one nineteen."

"I know. I tell myself that all the time. But he's been Allie's little brother our whole lives. And that's exactly how I saw him until a few years ago."

"But that's not how you think of him now?"

"Not at all," Victoria drawled.

"Then I'd start by telling him how you feel."

"If I did that, he wouldn't be happy just being friends anymore." Victoria's smile was trembly.

Elyse was pretty sure Adam wasn't happy being friends, regardless, but she didn't say anything.

Victoria's smile slowly faded. "I'm not sure I can face what people will think." She picked up her coffee cup.

Elyse couldn't believe it. Victoria was one of the strongest women she'd ever known. "What would your life be like with Adam?"

Victoria stared at her, her cup halfway to her mouth. "What do you mean?" She set the cup down without drinking.

"Would you and Dylan be happier if Adam was in your family?"

A laugh bubbled out of Victoria's sculptured mouth. "Definitely."

Elyse could see her friend was considering her advice. She pressed on. "Do you think God sees anything wrong with you and Adam marrying. . .with the age difference between you?"

Victoria's eyebrows shot up. "What? No, of course not."

"Then why would Allie?"

"But telling her. . ." Victoria's voice drifted off.

"If you let Adam know how you feel first, the two of you can tell your friends together, including his sister."

"You make it sound so easy."

Elyse smiled at her. She, of all people, knew it wasn't easy. "It won't be easy. But it'll be worth it."

Victoria took a sip of her coffee and squared her shoulders. "I'm going to do it. I'll let you know how it goes."

"Be sure you do."

❧

Andrew looked up from the pencil sketch he was working on. The 4-H meeting had been over for forty-five minutes. He knew she'd seen him when she pulled into the parking lot. Was she trying to wait him out?

He snorted softly. She'd have to do better than this. He was in it for the long haul. As a friend, of course.

He glanced at the drawing balanced against the steering wheel. It was time well spent, anyway. Funny how getting something on paper helped him to get it out of his mind. He ran his finger over the rough sketch of Elyse, a hat perched on her head and her dogs playing beside her. He'd already titled it. With any luck, by the time he actually painted it, he'd be able to accept whatever the future held for them.

Suddenly there she was in person. He watched her walk out of Coffee Central, and his heartbeat picked up. She was the most beautiful woman he'd ever seen. And the kindest, most gentle person he'd ever known. And he was losing her. Throwing away a second chance at happiness. Because of fear.

He started the engine and buckled his seat belt. Just before she climbed into her Jeep, she paused and gave him a jaunty salute. He flashed his lights at her. She drove slowly on the way home, carefully, just as he would have expected. When she turned in the lane leading to her house and his camper, he was right behind her.

Should he pull into her driveway and say good night? Better not. He didn't want to ruin any camaraderie they might have developed with the whole salute/light-flashing thing. If she wanted to talk to him, she would seek him out. He killed the motor in his own driveway and sat in the truck for a minute. A week ago tonight she'd been waiting here for him when he'd gotten back from seeing Luis at the hospital.

His phone vibrated in the holder. He flipped it open and frowned at the caller ID. Elyse?

CHAPTER 26

"Hello?" Andrew could hear the hesitance in his greeting. Was she going to tell him not to follow her?

"Are you stalking me?" Her voice was husky with laughter.

He twisted in his seat, and by the light of the guard light between them, he could see her standing out by her Jeep in her driveway. She waved.

He lifted his hand. "I like to think of it as protecting you, but maybe I've just got it all wrong."

"Whatever you call it, thanks." The warmth in her voice was unmistakable and so was the relief he felt at being back on speaking terms with her.

"No problem. How did the 4-H meeting go tonight?" Not to mention, how did the last week go?

"Good."

"I'm glad." He slouched down a little and looked across the way at her.

She'd moved around to sit on the back bumper of her Jeep. "Something kind of weird happened."

He sat up straight. "Weird?" Had Zeke sneaked in the back

door of Coffee Central?

She chuckled. "Relax. Weird in a good way."

He felt his neck flush knowing she'd seen him tense. "What happened?"

"Remember how you wanted me to tell someone about my childhood?"

He glanced at her. "So you told someone tonight?"

She ducked her head and ran her fingers through the top of her hair. "Actually, I told Victoria last week at the meeting. But everything went crazy. . .and I didn't get a chance to tell you." She looked back up. He wished he could see her eyes.

"So what happened tonight?"

"Victoria shared some stuff with me about her life that no one else knows. Our friendship really grew stronger because I told her my secret."

"Wow. That's awesome." If she were next to him, he'd take her in his arms. He had no doubt she was staying several yards away on purpose. "I'm proud of you."

"I wouldn't have done it if you hadn't pushed me."

"Sorry if I'm 'pushy.' But by Thanksgiving, you're going to be able to tell Matthew yes."

She laughed. "You might be a little overconfident."

"Call it what you want, but I know, with God's help, you can do it."

"Thanks for believing that." She pushed to her feet. "I'd better get in." She gave him a little wave. "Night."

"Okay. Sleep well." He waved back.

"See you tomorrow," she said just as he hit END.

He sat in his truck and watched her go into her house. So she'd "see him tomorrow." That was the best news he'd had in a week.

❧

The McCords had a family tradition of going around the table on Thanksgiving Day and telling what they were thankful for. If Elyse had to answer that question right this second, the answer would be a hot shower. With the holidays coming up, all of her clients wanted their dogs to look nice, and she hated to let people down. That was the only excuse Elyse had for crowding her schedule as she had done today.

After her shower, she slipped into some jeans and an old Harding University T-shirt. Peanut butter and crackers for supper. She was too tired to go get groceries tonight. The doorbell rang, and she rolled her eyes. If this was her four o'clock no-show coming two hours late, she was out of luck. Most of her clients understood the significance of a closed gate in the back, but a few thought that meant they should come to the front door.

The dogs waited anxiously to see who the visitor was. Elyse brushed past them and peeked out the blind. All of her tiredness evaporated into sheer adrenaline. Luis. With a black eye and a faded scar on his lip. On her porch. Waiting to see her.

She put her hand to her heart. What would happen if she tiptoed back down the hallway, retreated to her room, and pulled the covers over her head? Would he go away?

Maybe for tonight. But not forever, she was afraid.

Her legs didn't want to move, but she guided the dogs back out of the foyer and closed the sliding doors. She turned back to the front door. For a few seconds, she examined the smooth wood surface. It was hard to imagine what would happen when she actually stood face-to-face with him. There was only one way to find out. Taking a deep breath, she grasped the cool brass knob and pulled the door open.

And stared at him. For the first time since he came back into her life, she really looked at him. His black hair was sprinkled with gray and the laugh lines around his brown eyes were deeper than she remembered, but other than that, he was still the same man who shared her high cheekbones. And her love of black walnut ice cream, a flavor she hadn't eaten since the day the police had taken her to social services.

"Elyse." His dark eyes were solemn.

She nodded, unable to speak.

"I came to tell you I'm really sorry." He gave a nervous shrug and half chuckle. "For everything. But right now, for butting into your life here."

Her life hadn't imploded like she'd thought it would if he ever showed up. So for that, she could surely forgive him. Still she couldn't say the words. She nodded again.

"After your"—he kind of flinched—"parents told me you didn't want anything to do with me several years ago, I never thought I'd come back here. But when I saw you on TV and the sheriff said that Zeke had threatened you, I had to take my two weeks' vacation and keep an eye on you for myself." Another self-deprecating laugh. "Not that I did that great a job of protecting you."

"I'm glad you're okay." She finally managed to get some words out.

Andrew's red truck came down the lane and immediately turned toward her house. She watched over Luis's shoulder as Andrew parked beside the yellow Toyota and jumped out. He didn't exactly run up the walkway, but he didn't meander either.

Luis turned, and Andrew nodded. "Luis."

"Andrew. Good to see you."

Andrew shook his hand. "Good to see you out of the hospital." As he was talking, he edged past Luis and positioned himself next to Elyse in the doorway.

Just like always, she drew strength from his presence.

"Thanks for the visits," Luis said. "It gets lonely in there."

Like prison? Elyse wondered. Then his first words hit her. *Visits?* She gave Andrew a quizzical look.

He shrugged and his face said, *I'll tell you later* as plainly as if he'd spoken the words aloud.

"I'd better go." Luis looked down. "I wanted to say I'm sorry. And see you one more time."

Elyse nodded. What could she say: "As long as it's only one last time"? "Don't make a habit of it"? She was capable of speaking now, but she didn't have the right words, so she still kept her mouth shut.

Luis turned and walked away. She thought of her mother— her first mother, as she'd been thinking of her lately—and any pity she felt for him faded into a familiar dull anger that she embraced. When he was in his little truck putt-putting down the driveway, she let the tension go out of her shoulders.

Andrew leaned over and dropped a kiss on her cheek. "Hard day?"

She smiled at him, surprised she could. He definitely brought out the best in her. "Once again you rode to the rescue." His presence in times of trouble was something she could get used to too easily.

"I'm not done yet." He motioned toward his truck. "Come make yourself useful."

"Doing what?"

"Helping me carry," he called over his shoulder as he strode down the walkway.

"Carry? Carry what?" She jogged to catch up with him.

"Are you going to stand around all night and ask questions, or are you going to help me?" He opened the passenger door on his red truck and pulled out three full plastic bags and shoved them in her arms.

"What is this?"

"Groceries," he said. "When I saw you at lunch, you said you were too tired to go get them tonight."

"But. . ." Was he kidding? He'd bought groceries for her? How would he even know what she wanted? The thought died a quick death when she glanced in the first bag and saw her favorite brand of coffee and the packets of dog food Nikki ate. Apparently he'd paid close attention the night he'd watched her put away groceries. "Thank you." She was blown away by how sweet he was. She blinked hard and hurried to the house with the groceries.

She paused in the foyer to let Andrew in and close the front door behind him. He carried four more grocery bags and a brown paper bag—her stomach growled—that looked and smelled suspiciously like it held Chinese takeout. "What's in the paper bag?" she whispered.

"Chinese," he whispered back, a grin playing across his lips. "Why are we whispering?"

She pointed to the sliding doors that kept the dogs in the hallway. "They know the names of every kind of takeout."

"Sure they do."

She opened the doors, and the dogs bounded over to Andrew, wagging their tails.

"I think they like me."

She shrugged and rolled her eyes. "What did I tell you? It's the Chinese food."

They laughed down the hallway, and by the time the groceries were put away and the sesame chicken demolished, Elyse had almost gotten over the shock of seeing Luis on her doorstep. "So you visited Luis in the hospital? More than that first night?"

He nodded. "I had a lot of time on my hands last week." He picked at a half-eaten egg roll with his fork. "He's easy to talk to." He shoved a little rice over to the side of his plate. "Humble and just a real nice guy."

She played with a fortune cookie, rattling the package but not opening it.

"You're normally so compassionate."

"And you think I should be able to just forgive him."

Andrew cut the half an egg roll into tiny pieces. "I don't think you *should*. . ."

She threw the cookie down. "You just wonder why I don't."

"You don't have to tell me." Andrew finally looked up to meet her eyes.

She listened to the dogs' even breathing and took a deep breath of her own. "My dad and mom walked out of that charity foundation building with *guns*. Guns. My mother was what most people nowadays would call a ditzy blond. She went along with whatever harebrained get-rich-quick scheme my dad cooked up. But she wouldn't touch a gun. Wouldn't allow them in her house." As she was talking, she wondered how accurate her memories were. Had eighteen years changed her perception? "My dad was a lot like you—he could defend himself with no problem. He'd done a lot of street fighting. But he never had a gun that I knew about. I remember he used to say something like if you used your head, you didn't need a gun."

Andrew frowned and pushed his plate toward the middle of the table. "That makes no sense. Did you see the police report? Did it say they had guns?"

Elyse pulled the fortune cookie back over to her empty hands. "I didn't see the police report." She looked up at him. "I saw them come out the door with guns in their hands."

"You were there?"

She nodded and squeezed the cookie between her thumb and index finger. "I was in the car."

"You saw your mother get shot?"

"Yes. My dad. . ." She laid the cookie on the table and pressed down on it with the palm of her hand. "Luis threw his gun down as soon as he saw the policemen outside. But my mother. . .I really think she forgot she even had the weapon in her hand and was just raising her hands. But she raised the gun straight up, and the police shot her in the chest."

"The police found you in the car?"

A tiny hole had developed in the plastic, and cookie dust scattered on the table. "An hour later."

He slid his fortune cookie across the table to her. "You sat there for an hour by yourself after seeing that."

"Not completely by myself." A bittersweet smile touched her lips. "I had the only kind of puppy my parents would let me have—a little stuffed dog named Friendly." She thought of Friendly, his black and white fur matted and thin with age, sitting on her bedroom dresser, watching over her. Someday she might show him to Andrew. But not tonight.

CHAPTER 27

Was it supposed to be this cold Thanksgiving week? Andrew pulled his jacket tighter as he stepped into the barn and shut the door behind him. Thankfully, he'd finished outside and was painting indoors now. And thankfully, there was a good heater in the barn theater. He plugged in his radio and tuned in a local channel. Outside, he preferred to listen to the cows bawling, horses whinnying, and even the crickets chirping, but when he was working inside, he needed a little background noise.

Thanksgiving was three days away, and as far as he knew, Elyse still planned to tell Matthew that she couldn't accept his offer. Andrew popped the lid off the nearest paint can and swirled the liquid slowly with a stir stick. If he could just get her to say yes, he felt sure she could do the job. The problem was that she didn't agree.

All morning he brainstormed as he painted, trying to think of ways he could build Elyse's confidence. He could bring in some dog owners who needed help and have her meet them. In theory that sounded like a good idea, but he wasn't sure it wouldn't just make things worse.

When he started putting things away for lunch, he still hadn't come up with a good answer. On the radio, the noon news announcer wrapped up the local news and segued into some good-natured commentary. Andrew reached over to turn the power off, but just before he slapped the button, the announcer's words caught his attention. "There's a town meeting tonight in the Hamlet Community Center concerning the fate of the dog shelter there. Apparently some members of the Hamlet City Council think the town is going to the dogs and too much money is being spent on maintaining the shelter. They've sent out an open invitation for anyone interested in speaking, for or against. After the meeting, the council will be taking a final vote on whether to allocate the funds needed to keep the shelter open." The announcer chuckled. "Too bad the dogs can't talk. Wonder what they'd say?"

Andrew grinned. Elyse knew what they would say. Hamlet was less than a half hour away, and he knew just the person to speak on the dogs' behalf.

❦

"So you're still not ready to give me a clue?" Elyse looked down at her brown slacks and turquoise top. She'd added some small dangly matching earrings at the last minute. It was hard to plan for an evening when Andrew refused to tell her where they were going.

"I gave you a clue."

"That it was something that would help me be able to say yes to Matthew's offer? That wasn't terribly comforting." She looked out the window. "Hamlet City Limits? Why are we at Hamlet?"

239

He kept his gaze on the road. In less than a minute, he slowed and turned into a parking lot dotted with cars.

"Hamlet Community Center? What are we doing here?"

"They're having a town meeting."

She grinned. "Like *Gilmore Girls?*"

He frowned. "Like what?"

She waved her hand. "Never mind. It's a TV show. I've always thought it would be so cool to go to one of those Stars Hollow town meetings where they stand up and yell out whatever is on their minds."

The frown disappeared. "Then this is your lucky night." He grinned.

"What are you talking about?"

"The subject of the town meeting is the fate of the local dog shelter."

Her eyes widened, and she covered her mouth with her hand. "I heard about that. They're thinking about closing it so they can put in a swimming pool with the money."

He nodded. "Something like that."

Just as she had the day she'd found Pal, she felt like hitting something—hard. "Surely the town won't allow it."

"Actually I made some calls this afternoon. Three of the council members are for it, three against it. One is undecided." He raised an eyebrow. "The town meeting tonight will probably decide the issue."

"And we're going to watch it?" He'd obviously put a lot of thought into something that would motivate her to hang out her dog training shingle. That was flattering, even though she didn't know how this would help. She glanced around the parking lot. Should she mention that she didn't like crowds? "There are a lot of people here." A blue truck pulled in beside them. "And more coming."

"We'd better go get a seat." Andrew unbuckled and climbed out. In less than ten seconds, he was opening her door.

She let him help her down, and when he didn't let go of her hand, she smiled. It was nice to have a hand to hold in a crowd. At least it *was* nice, until Andrew found two empty seats at the front and tugged her along after him. "I'm more of a backseat person," she murmured.

"Not tonight," he said over his shoulder. "Let's hurry while everyone is still milling around." He pulled her into a seat in the middle of the front row.

"Well, they have an advantage, since they actually *know* people here," Elyse said dryly. She glanced over her shoulder. "They're probably wondering why a couple of out-of-towners got front row seats at their town meeting."

"Shh," Andrew teased, "they might throw us out."

A balding man approached the microphone. He welcomed everyone and gave a brief summary of the two sides of the dog shelter issue. Elyse shook her head slightly as the man extolled the virtues of having a town swimming pool then a little harder when he played down the need to provide a safe place for the town's rejected dogs.

Andrew grinned at her. He looked as if he was ready to enjoy the show.

"I bet you wish you had some popcorn, don't you?" Elyse whispered.

He nodded.

Thirty minutes later, Elyse was squirming in her seat. So far the only person who had spoken in support of keeping the shelter open was the director. His heart seemed like it was in the right place, but she heard the woman beside her whisper, "He just wants to keep his job." Others nodded in agreement.

The emcee had the microphone back. "Lucille Harris, who volunteers at the shelter, is at home with pneumonia tonight. Since she couldn't be here, she asked me to say a word on her behalf. So I want you all to know that Lucille thinks the shelter should be kept open." He looked down at his note. "She says it's a worthy venture and serves a deep need." He glanced at the note again. "There's more here, but that about sums it up."

"What?" Elyse blurted out then blushed. She looked at Andrew. "That poor woman has pneumonia, and he couldn't even deliver her whole message?"

Andrew just shrugged.

She was more than a little irritated by how unconcerned he looked. She turned back to face the front.

"Is there anyone else here who wants to speak for keeping the shelter open?"

"What'll happen to the dogs if we don't have it?" one older man called from midway back.

The emcee shrugged. "I guess they'll have to do like the rest of us and fend for themselves."

Elyse jumped to her feet. "Fend for themselves?"

The man stuck the microphone out to her, and she took it, her mind still reeling with his last comment. "Dogs don't fend for themselves. They need humans for that." She kept her gaze locked on the emcee's face. "And I'll tell you some other things dogs don't do. They don't lie to you. They don't judge you or talk about you behind your back. And they don't ever. . .*ever* desert you in your hour of need. If they had a choice of playing in a giant dog bone maze or bringing you your newspaper, they'd choose to do what makes you happy."

The emcee put his hand lightly on her shoulder and turned her around.

A sea of faces stared at her. Her breath caught, and she looked down.

Andrew gave her a thumbs-up.

She focused on him. "They aren't able to provide food or water for themselves, but they can give you a lifetime of happiness and love." She finally looked up at the two older women directly behind Andrew. "Are you lonely?" One of them nodded. "Go down to the shelter and pick out a dog to love. If you can't commit to adopting a dog, do like Lucille does and volunteer at the shelter. I promise that you'll benefit from the gift of your time even more than the dogs will."

She glanced at a young woman next to them with a toddler on her lap. "Many of you came tonight in support of a swimming pool. But it doesn't have to come at the expense of helpless animals. Form a committee. Find another way to finance the pool. Common sense says it doesn't have to be one or the other."

The young woman nodded, and so did several other people. Elyse's stomach was churning, but the dogs needed her to say a little more. "How a town treats their helpless and needy residents—whether two-footed or four-footed—says a lot about its citizens. I've never been to Hamlet before tonight, but I've always heard it was a little town with a big heart. Is that true?" She turned and shoved the microphone back to the emcee.

Thunderous applause broke out.

Andrew stood and hugged her.

"I think I'm going to faint," she said against his ear.

"No, you're not. You did it."

"I've got to get out of here."

Andrew put his arm around her and guided her down the aisle to the back door. "Actually, I was thinking you might have a future in politics."

"Shut up before I throw up on you."

"Yes, ma'am."

Outside, she tilted her head back and let the wind cool her hot face. "I thought I'd die."

Andrew's hand was steady on her waist. "But you didn't. And that's the exciting thing." He looked down at her, his eyes twinkling. "That was epic. 'Little town with a big heart'? Did you just make that up on the spur of the moment?"

She looked sideways at him, her head still leaned back. "Like I would do that? I heard Mama say it one time when Hamlet was having some kind of walk-a-thon. She said they're always doing some good work." She wrapped her jacket tight around her and sank onto a park bench, grateful to give her noodly legs a rest. "I can't believe I did that." She hit at the air toward him. "You tricked me."

"Nothing you have to do as a trainer will be that bad."

"You've got that right," she blurted out. His words sank in, and she glanced over at him. "I'm going to tell Matthew yes?"

He nodded. "Definitely. Now let's slip back in and see how the council votes."

CHAPTER 28

"Y ou single-handedly saved a dog shelter?" Elyse's oldest brother, Aaron, looked at her for confirmation.

Elyse laughed. "Andrew's probably stretching it a little. I don't remember the applause being that loud."

Andrew shook his head. "I'm not exaggerating at all. She brought the house down."

Aaron's wife, Bree, leaned forward on the couch and smiled at her. "That's fantastic."

"We always knew she had it in her." Luke sat on the couch arm next to Elyse and ruffled her hair.

"We open our doors in February then, right, sis?" Matthew stood by the fireplace, studying the family pictures. He'd been excited when she'd told him the news, and yesterday they'd finalized the deal on a half-finished building on Main Street.

"If we get the office done by then."

"Was that a slam at your carpenter?" Luke asked, his eyebrow raised.

"Or your painter?" Andrew's blue eyes twinkled, and he winked at her.

Elyse grinned at him. She'd been thrilled when he'd offered to do the job. So he wasn't leaving immediately when the barn was done. That was good to know. "Nah, not a slam," she said. "Just a reminder that we're in a hurry."

"Speaking of hurrying, who's ready to eat?" Kaleigh asked from the doorway. "Mama said it's time to start putting the food on the table."

Elyse jumped up.

"I hope you brought your pumpkin pies," Chance said to Elyse as they headed to the kitchen.

"I wouldn't forget you." Most of the family enjoyed Elyse's pumpkin pies, but they were her little brother's very favorite part of the Thanksgiving meal.

Bree came up beside her and put her arm around her waist. "Girls' night at your house tonight after supper, right?"

Elyse winked at her. "I can't wait." Besides Crystal's shower, she knew they were all dying to know about Andrew. She wasn't sure what to say right now, but strangely, she didn't mind talking about him.

When the delicious meal was finished, her dad looked at Andrew. "It's our family tradition to go around the table and tell what we're thankful for. Guests are exempt unless they want to join in."

Andrew nodded, but he looked a little nervous.

Without really thinking it through, Elyse slipped her hand under the tablecloth and squeezed his hand. When she tried to pull away, he held on. She gave him a quizzical look. But he kept his gaze straight ahead, his thumb caressing the back of her hand.

Her infernal blush betrayed her, the heat creeping up her neck then into her face. Not that holding his hand didn't feel good. It definitely did. She wouldn't mind holding his hand for a long time. But in front of the whole family? Under the tablecloth?

He rubbed his thumb across the back of her hand one more time then squeezed and let go. She felt as if she were parachuting toward the ground and someone suddenly cut the chute strings. In that second, before her daddy started telling what he was thankful for, she knew the truth. She *was* falling hard without a parachute. In love with Andrew Stone.

❦

When it came his turn, Andrew considered passing. After Jonathan had expressed, with obvious sincerity, how thankful he was for his family, the guys had given mostly short answers, including pumpkin pie from Chance. But Andrew couldn't say what he really wanted to say—that he was thankful that he'd followed his wife's murderer to Shady Grove, because here he'd met Elyse McCord.

Instead, he took a deep breath. "I'm thankful that God has blessed me with the opportunity to see firsthand that there really are families who love each other no matter what. I'm honored to be included in this gathering today." He winked at Elyse then smiled at Chance. "And I'm pretty thankful for pumpkin pie, too."

Elyse was next. He was almost positive she glanced at him before she spoke. His heart thudded against his ribs. Would she mention him?

She smiled. "I'm thankful for new opportunities." She definitely glanced at him. "And for learning to embrace them."

His heartbeat picked up.

Chance and Luke exchanged knowing grins.

When the kitchen was cleaned up and everyone had rested, Chance sauntered into the living room and tossed a football across the room. Luke snatched it just before it smashed a lamp.

"Boys"—Jonathan, apparently snoozing in his recliner, opened one eye—"take it outside before your mama shoots us all."

Luke and Chance obediently headed for the yard. Matthew and Jeremy followed, and Aaron motioned to Andrew to go, too.

Andrew stood and stretched. A little touch football sounded good after their big meal. "Mr. McCord? You going to play?"

Jonathan opened his eyes and shook his head. "Call me Jonathan, please. And no, I guess not."

Aaron patted the back of his dad's chair. "C'mon, Dad, quit actin' like an old fogy. You know you want to get beat by the younger generation."

"Old fogy? You're going down, kid." Jonathan lowered his recliner and stood. "I'm going to get your mama to be on my team. She and I together could whip you all with one hand tied behind our backs." He disappeared into the kitchen.

In less than a minute, Kaleigh came barreling into the room, hands on her hips.

"Y'all aren't even thinking about playing football without us, are you?"

"We hated to mention it in case you weren't totally finished in the kitchen." Aaron grinned. "We didn't want to take a chance you'd put us to work."

Bree and Elyse appeared behind Kaleigh. "Just for that," Bree said, "the guys get to do supper dishes."

"How about the losers do supper dishes?" Aaron asked.

Kaleigh nodded. "Sounds perfect. Who's going to chose teams?"

"Y'all really do take your football seriously," Andrew remarked to Elyse as they lined up opposite each other.

"You better believe it, buddy." He barely saw her cheeky grin before she streaked across the line. Running behind her, he watched in admiration as she neatly caught a toss from her dad. He reached out to tag her on the back, but their feet got tangled. They fell to the ground in a heap.

Kaleigh's voice drifted to him. "All right, you two, this is called touch football, not tackle."

For a timeless moment, Andrew's gaze locked with the brown eyes just inches from his face. "Hey," he said quietly. "You okay?"

Elyse grinned. "Never better."

"You could at least give us the ball before you get friendly with the opposing team," Chance said loudly. "I guess that's what she meant about embracing opportunities."

"More like taking an opportunity to embrace, I'd say," Luke chimed in.

Andrew flipped the football up to Luke then pushed to his feet and offered a blushing Elyse his hand. "And you accused me of being corny."

She flashed him an apologetic smile as she took his hand. "How do you think I recognize it?"

"Hey, hey, no fraternizing with the enemy," Chance said and playfully tugged Elyse back over to their side.

As Andrew lined up again for the hike, he thought about Chance's words. Heaven forbid that Elyse really consider him an enemy. But if she found out about his past, she most likely would. Every time he felt as if he had to tell her, that thought stopped him.

"Stone! We're playing a ball game. How about you?" Luke yelled from down the field.

Andrew looked up and realized he'd missed the play entirely. "Sorry."

"Oh man, he's got it bad," he heard Chance mutter. He saw Jonathan and Lynda McCord exchange an amused look. This time it was Andrew's face that flamed.

❦

After supper Elyse walked over to her house to put the dogs in their playroom. Her mama loved her "granddogs," but since she'd been raised to believe that dogs were outside pets, she couldn't quite get used to the pandemonium of three big dogs and one small yappy one in the house, even if they were well behaved. Out of respect, Elyse usually put them up when her mama came to visit.

She'd barely let them back in from outside and closed them in the playroom with lots of toys and plenty of food and water when Victoria called.

"Hey, happy Thanksgiving."

"I'm sorry for interrupting family time, but I wanted you to know: Adam and I are getting married."

Elyse sat down. "Really?"

Victoria laughed. "Thank you so much. When I told him how I felt, he went with me to tell Allie."

"What did she say?"

"She said, 'Finally!' "

Elyse laughed. "Vic, I'm so happy for you. When's the wedding?"

"January, I think. Maybe early February. I'll let you know."

"Congratulations." The doorbell rang.

"Thanks. Talk to you soon."

Elyse said good-bye and went to let Kaleigh and Bree in. "Welcome to the party."

"Are you kidding?" Kaleigh held up a box with some streamers hanging out. On top of it perched a gift bag with wedding bells on it. "We brought the party."

"Mama is delaying Crys for a few minutes," Bree said. "I brought her gift, along with mine."

Elyse took the three gift bags and turned away to hide her smile, leading the way down the hall. At Aaron's urging, Bree had recently decided to call her in-laws Mama and Daddy. Bree had confided in Elyse back in the summer that she felt a little awkward doing it, but she'd do anything for Aaron.

Since meeting Andrew, Elyse could totally relate to that sentiment. Her smile disappeared. Where had that thought come from? "So Kaleigh, how's the wedding date quest coming?"

Kaleigh shrugged. "I've got a bite. We'll see if I can reel him in."

Bree raised an elegant eyebrow. "That sounds fascinating. What is this about?"

While Kaleigh filled her in on Operation New Me, they hung the banner and streamers in Elyse's living room.

When Kaleigh finished, a frown flitted across Bree's face. "Since Aaron insisted we couldn't have the Internet in the house with the boys, I'm missing all the fun stuff here. We've got to figure out a better way to stay in touch."

Elyse gave her a sympathetic pat on the shoulder. Aaron and Bree made a lot of sacrifices to be houseparents at an inner-city Chicago home for boys. They were true missionaries, as far as she was concerned.

A knock sounded on the front door, followed by the doorbell. Mama had remembered their agreed upon sign.

"Shh. . .they're here," Kaleigh hissed.

"Ya think?" Bree teased.

"Go let them in," Kaleigh whispered to Elyse. "Bree and I will stay in here to yell 'Surprise!' "

Elyse followed her little sister's orders and hurried to the door. Her mama and Crystal stood on the doorstep.

"It's about time y'all got here," Elyse said, winking at her mother over Crystal's shoulder. "Kaleigh and Bree are in the living room."

"It was my fault," Mama said and hurried on down the hall to the living room.

"She had to have my help getting the lint out of the dryer," Crystal murmured, her face puzzled. "I tried to tell her we'd do it later, but she insisted."

Elyse shrugged, fighting a blush. "Look at it this way: thanks to you, there's less chance of fire tonight." She went ahead of Crystal into the living room then turned and joined the others in yelling, "Surprise!"

Crystal's blue eyes widened, and she put her hand to her mouth. "Oh my goodness! I can't believe y'all did this."

"It's just a McCord girls thing," Kaleigh said. "Hope that's okay."

Crystal's smile was tremulous. "It's perfect." She hugged her mother then Kaleigh, Bree, and Elyse, in turn.

"I'm glad you and Jeremy made up," Elyse whispered as they hugged. "Otherwise tonight could have been really awkward."

Crystal laughed and let Kaleigh tug her over to the couch. "Presents first."

"Really?" Crystal grinned. "This is my kind of shower. Usually there are games and food first."

"Both of those come later," Elyse assured her. Kaleigh had a definite idea of how things should be done.

Crystal exclaimed over each gift, from Kaleigh's sassy terry-cloth robe with "Just Married" written on the back of it to the long, flowing white gown and beautiful royal blue one from Mama and Elyse. They all giggled at Bree's gift, a tiny red negligee. "From one newlywed to another," Kaleigh noted wryly. "Mama would have had a heart attack if you or I had gotten her that," she said in an aside to Elyse.

"Hey, I'm not primed for a heart attack just yet," Mama protested.

"And I'm not a newlywed." Bree put her hands on her tiny hips, faking disgruntlement. "I've been married more than a year."

Elyse stood. "Then you should both do great with the game we're going to play."

"Game?" Crystal moaned. "I'm awful at games."

"Whoever wins gets chocolate."

Crystal let out a sigh. "Okay. I'll play."

For the next several minutes, the five of them went around the room, each one naming a song with the word *marry*, *married*, or *wedding* in the title. Finally, they'd exhausted their repertoire and it was Kaleigh's turn.

"First comes love then comes marriage," she shouted.

"What song is that?" Crystal asked.

"You know: Crystal and Jeremy sitting in a tree, K-I-S-S-I-N-G. First comes love, then comes mar—"

They all started laughing. "That's not a song," Bree choked out.

"Yes, it is." Kaleigh was indignant, even though Elyse could see a smile teasing her lips. "I was just singing it."

Elyse grinned. No matter how much Kaleigh might want to conform, she marched to the beat of a different drummer.

"Chocolate all around," Mama said.

"I was robbed," Kaleigh grumbled good-naturedly as Elyse passed out Dove Chocolate Promises.

"I'm so happy." Crystal's face was beaming. She looked at Kaleigh. "Not about you being robbed. But about marrying Jeremy. I can't wait."

Elyse smiled. "It's wonderful to see you so happy." They'd all been through a lot when Cami died, but as her twin, Crystal had been especially devastated.

"I wish Cami were here," Crystal said, almost as if reading Elyse's mind.

"We all do." Mama reached over and patted her hand.

Kaleigh handed Crystal the last piece of dark chocolate. Her green eyes glittered with unshed tears. "Life is really weird sometimes."

Elyse thought about her childhood, then about meeting Andrew and all the things that had happened since. "But God gives us what we need to handle it, I guess."

"That's what Aaron always says." Bree brushed away a tear of her own.

Kaleigh rolled her eyes. "Then it must be true. Because we all know Aaron's perfect." Her grin took the sting out of her words. "I hope someday I love a man as much as you love Aaron."

"It'll hit you like a ton of bricks when you least expect it," Crystal said.

Mama smiled. "Yes, that's how it was with me and your daddy."

Elyse remained quiet as she remembered her earlier realization after dinner. She'd met her ton of bricks. But would she survive?

CHAPTER 29

Kaleigh smoothed her hair and glanced down at her black pants and matching blazer. If she weren't already late, she would stop by the restroom and put on more lipstick. No, better to forget the lipstick.

She pushed open the door to the Underground and scanned the darkened room. Carlton and a couple of his friends were at their normal places near the front, and she wended her way through the scattered tables and touched his shoulder.

Carlton turned and smiled up at her. "I was afraid you weren't going to show." He pulled out the chair beside him and patted it.

When the waitress came by and it was her turn to order, Kaleigh hesitated. *Operation New Me.* Even though she would normally order a caramel mocha latte, she forced out the words, "Black coffee." Her sacrafice was rewarded a minute later when the subject of Crystal's wedding came up and Carlton said it might be fun to go with her. Unfortunately, the poet stood before Kaleigh could answer.

Kaleigh leaned back in her chair, prepared to be bored. This morning the poetry reading was by Nicole Broome, a girl dressed casually in blue jeans and a red sweater. A contrast to the usual look and an unfamiliar face. To Kaleigh at least.

Nicole began reading, and Kaleigh straightened in her chair. Her eyes widened. The words seemed to speak directly to her.

The poem ended and the lights came on. Kaleigh blinked as the sudden brightness pulled her back to the present. "Wow." She breathed. "That poem was awesome."

"You must be kidding." Carlton narrowed his eyes. "I thought it was drivel. And who was that girl anyway?" He glanced around the table. "I've never seen her here before."

"Should we go and introduce ourselves?" Kaleigh looked over at the crowd surrounding the poet. "I think I'd like to meet her." And interview her for the school paper, although she hated to admit it, since Carlton obviously hadn't been impressed.

Carlton shook his head dismissively. "Maybe another time." He pushed his chair back and stood, offering a hand to her. "You working this afternoon?"

Kaleigh nodded.

"Well, I need to get to the library. Call me sometime and we'll get together." Carlton gave her a one-armed hug. "Maybe tomorrow?"

She nodded and watched as he headed toward the door, responding to friendly greetings from his fellow students. After she made sure the door closed behind him, she worked her way through the clusters of people surrounding the poet.

"Hi, I'm Kaleigh." She stuck out her hand. "And I loved that poem."

Ten minutes later Kaleigh had arranged to interview Nicole for a profile piece in *The Bison*. In only a few minutes of conversation, Kaleigh recognized a kindred spirit.

Heading toward the door, she glanced at her cell phone. Yikes. She should have left fifteen minutes ago. No time to change if she was going to make it on time to meet Chance for their afternoon fishing tour. She hurried to the dock to meet her brother.

Kaleigh was thankful for her haphazard car-cleaning skills when she fished out a pair of tennis shoes from the floorboard behind her car seat. She had neglected to put them away after her last hike. Pulling off her heels, she quickly laced up the more suitable shoes. She snagged a hoodie from the trunk before she rushed down to the landing where Chance was waiting with two flat-bottom trout fishing boats. And four impatient clients.

Kaleigh walked past a group of local fishing guides, friendly competitors, and a wolf whistle split the silence. Followed quickly by two more.

She glanced around to see who they were whistling at, and her face reddened as she realized she was the object of their attention. She stopped and put her hands on her hips. "I know you *didn't*."

"Kaleigh?" Jared Tolliver, one of the guides from Tolliver's Fishing Service, shot her an abashed grin. "Sorry, girl. Didn't recognize you."

She shook her head. "Better not happen again." She waved over her shoulder. "Bye. Good luck this afternoon."

Chance frowned at her and looked pointedly at his waterproof watch. He handed out life jackets to the four men. Two of them were outfitted in camouflage fishing vests and caps with lures sticking out of them.

Kaleigh hid a grin. Who was she to question the appropriateness of their clothing? She pulled off her jacket, put on her hoodie, and zipped it up over the silky sleeveless shirt. When her jacket was safely stowed in the small storage compartment, she climbed in and took her place at the back of the boat. Her two passengers settled themselves into their seats, and she pushed off the bank.

Chance motored up beside her with the other two men.

Kaleigh distributed the rods and reels, offered them their choice of corn, night crawlers, or power bait, and offered to bait their hooks with night crawlers, her preferred bait. They opted to do their own baiting and made it plain that they didn't need her help.

Wind in their faces, they headed toward Mossy Shoals, and she began her practiced spiel. "A world record brown trout was caught here in May 1992. It weighed forty pounds and four ounces." She guided the boat through the shoals. "And either of you could catch one just like it today."

After a couple of hours, they caught up with Chance at the Cow Shoals catch-and-release area where she rigged their poles with barbless hooks. "Anything caught in this area must be released, but I figure you'll catch your limit before we leave tonight." She checked the live well to make sure they were still legal as Chance glided up beside her in his johnboat.

"What happened to you?" he murmured, as quietly as he could.

"I was with Carlton. And I didn't have time to change."

"I don't have time for you to change, either," Chance snapped. "Into a different person, that is. This Operation New Me has got to stop."

Kaleigh glanced down at her black dress pants, looking ridiculous with her tennis shoes peeking out from beneath the hem. "Look, I want a date for Crystal's wedding. And this morning, after I ordered a black coffee instead of my normal caramel latte, he basically agreed to go with me."

Chance rolled his eyes. "Whoop-de-do."

"You ordered black coffee when you really wanted a latte? Just so you could get a date to a wedding?" The words came from behind her. She turned around to face her accuser. One of the doctors. His straight hair, not quite as red as hers, wisped sideways around his handsome face, in a look more befitting a rock star or a poet than a doctor. As a rule, she avoided fellow redheads. And this buttinski wasn't about to be the exception.

"So what if I did?"

He shrugged. "It just seems like being ourselves is the one thing we have that no one can take away from us. I don't know why you'd give that up voluntarily."

A childish taunt she and her sisters used to say to their brothers popped into her mind. *This is an ABC conversation,* she wanted to say. *It's between A and B, and you need to C your way out of it.* "Minding your own business is something else that you might not want to give up voluntarily."

He shifted in his seat. "You're probably right." He looked at her. "Nice fishing pants, by the way."

"Thank you," she said through gritted teeth.

Chance gave her a warning look and motored away from her.

For the rest of the afternoon, she thought about what the doctor said. She didn't want anyone to take away her right to be herself, so why was she giving it up willingly?

❧

The real thing beat those little tree-shaped air fresheners any-time, Elyse thought, as she bounced down the lane, the smell of fresh cedar surrounding her. Amazing how a particular scent could give her courage. Or make her temporarily lose her mind. She pulled up in front of Andrew's camper and parked. As soon as she'd smelled the Christmas trees, she'd thought of Andrew and his camper. She gripped the steering wheel until her knuckles were white. Maybe she should just leave the four-foot-tall tree in the Jeep as permanent aromatherapy.

The camper door opened slowly, and Andrew stepped out onto the top step. "Hey!"

She gave him a weak wave then climbed out of the Jeep.

"What's up?" A flicker of concern crossed his face.

"Nothing. I. . .um . . .okay, this is probably pushy." She walked around to the back of the Jeep and popped open the hatch. "But I brought you a little Christmas tree for your camper, if you want it."

A grin chased away the concern. "For me?"

She nodded. "I was buying a poinsettia to take by the rehab for Maxine, but then I smelled the trees, and when I saw this one, it had your name all over it."

He heaved the little cedar out and balanced it on his shoulder. "I love it."

She blew out her breath. In that case, she was glad she'd gone by and picked up the box of small ornaments she usually used for her grooming shop tree. She'd had too much on her mind to put one up in there this year, and this was for a better cause anyway. She snagged the box from the back and closed it with a bang.

Inside, Andrew propped the tree against the counter. "I can't believe you did this. It smells so good."

She set the box on the table. "It does, doesn't it?" No need to tell him the scent gave her courage. "I brought you trimmings so you can decorate it."

"You'll have to help me."

That's what she'd hoped he would say.

"The first thing we need is mood music." She set up her portable CD player and hit play.

The opening notes of "Jingle Bells" filled the camper, and Andrew smiled.

"So what kind of tree did you have when you were growing up?" Elyse glanced over at him as she laid the tiny ornaments out on the counter. She set the string of lights out and heaved a small tree stand from the bottom of the box and handed it to him.

He took the green and red tree stand and studied it. The screws that stuck out on all four sides seemed to captivate him. He twisted them back and forth, one at a time. He ran his fingers inside the small cupped-out area for water. "We didn't have a tree after my mom died." He moved a small table from in front of the window. "But my grandma and grandpa always did, and every year on Christmas Day, we'd spend about four hours there." A wry grin twisted his mouth. "When I was young, I'd look forward to those four hours all year long."

Elyse knew Andrew didn't want her sympathy, so she kept her mouth shut. But her heart ached for the little boy still lurking inside the man beside her.

She squatted and held the tree stand with her hands. He wordlessly lifted the tiny tree and put it into the stand. She tightened the screws.

She stopped and guided the tree with one hand. "To the left a little."

He tilted it to the left.

"No, no, to the right."

He pushed the tree to the right.

"Back a little. Okay, okay, perfect!"

She stood and dusted her hands on her jeans. Andrew was staring at her, and she was suddenly aware of how small the camper was.

He cleared his throat and picked up an ornament. "So what do we do? Just stick these all over?"

He'd never decorated a tree before. That reality hit her like a snowplow. "Not yet. The lights go on first." She pulled out a string of lights and handed one end to him. "Get that started at the top." She cast him another glance. "If you don't mind."

His fingers brushed hers as he took the end of the string of lights, and for a brief second, Elyse thought they were plugged in. They were standing almost shoulder to shoulder in the close quarters of the camper.

They slowly wrapped the lights around the tree. Every time their hands brushed, which was with each coil, Elyse felt the same electrical shock. Was he feeling that, too? She couldn't be sure. Maybe chatting would stop it. "Do you like Christmas?"

He glanced up and stared at her as if he were seeing her for the first time. For a second, she thought he wasn't going to answer the question. Then his blue eyes came back into focus. He gave his head a little shake. "What?"

"Christmas. Do you like it?"

"Oh. Yes. I like it. Especially this year." He patted the lights against the tree. "Thanks to the tree, of course."

Elyse stared into his blue eyes and blushed. "Of course."

"You're—" He stopped. "Nothing."

Her brow creased. "What?"

He straightened an ornament of a tiny mouse making a list then looked back at her. "I almost said you're beautiful when you blush. But the truth is, I think you're the most beautiful woman

I've ever seen, blushing or not."

"Oh." She stared into his blue eyes, mesmerized. What could she say—"You're pretty cute yourself"? That's what Kaleigh would say. But then what? Even though Elyse hadn't asked him about his wife's death, she was pretty sure he was still grieving. That would explain what he'd meant that night when he'd said he had nothing to offer her but the moment. If that was the case, she needed to give him space. Not stand three inches from him. She took a step back. Maybe bringing the tree had been a mistake. "Thank you."

Andrew took a step back, too, and carefully made the last two passes with the lights around the tree. Whether it was just a coincidence, or a plan on his part, his hand didn't touch Elyse's. When they were done, she dug into the box and picked up a tiny red Santa and handed it to him. "Hook this over a limb."

She lifted a tiny crystal snowman and looped the silver wire hanger over the limb nearest her.

Andrew reached back for a candy cane ornament. He gave Elyse a sideways glance. "Jeremy invited me to the wedding."

"Really?" *That will save me from having to ask you myself.*

Andrew nodded. "I'm flattered." He cleared his throat. "I know you'll be there in your official maid-of-honor status, but would you like to go with me?"

"I'd love to." She'd deal with the teasing from her family. It would be worth it. "I'm really nervous about the wedding."

"Walking down the aisle in front of everyone?"

See? That was one of the things she loved about him. He knew what she meant without her having to spell it out. "There'll be a big crowd, and for that few minutes, all eyes will be on me."

"I'll be there, and if you look like you're going to faint, I'll just stand up and walk to you. We'll pretend it's part of the plan."

She laughed. But she knew he meant it. He wouldn't hesitate to come to her, to embarrass himself in front of all the guests, if he thought she needed him.

She passed a tiny teapot to Andrew. He must have loved his wife so much. "How long ago did your wife die?"

He fumbled the teapot and barely caught it. "Whoa, that came out of nowhere." He carefully hung it on the tree. "Three years."

And he was still grieving enough that he wouldn't let himself commit to the obvious feelings he had for Elyse. She bent over the box to pick up another ornament. Somehow, it made the delay easier knowing that when he did commit to her, his heart would be hers for life.

She placed a little ornament that spelled out Joy on a top branch. That was what she wanted to bring into Andrew's life. He deserved it.

A few minutes later, they stood back to survey their handiwork.

"Wonder what it will look like with the lights out," Elyse mused.

He nodded toward the light switch by the door behind her, and she flipped it. The tiny Christmas tree was a beacon of multihued light in the darkness. The bright colors reflected in Andrew's eyes as he watched her across the small room.

Her heartbeat sped up. "What do you think?"

He still watched her. "Perfect."

CHAPTER 30

She flipped the light back on and started to gather the unused decorations into her box, studiously avoiding his gaze. She needed air. Unless she wanted to grab him and kiss him until he committed to more than this moment, she seriously needed air right now. "Want to see what the tree looks like from outside?"

"Sure."

She practically fell out the door.

Andrew stopped to turn the light out and followed her.

The small tree transformed the window of the camper into a twinkling stained-glass window. "Oh, it's beautiful." Her breath made tiny puffs of steam. She shivered. The air had cooled considerably since she'd gone into the camper an hour ago.

He put his arm around her, drawing her to his warmth. She couldn't resist—she rested her head against his shoulder.

"Thank you again," he said, close to her ear. "I love it."

"You're welcome." I love *you*. That's what she wanted to say. She stared up at the stars. So close and yet—in reality—so far. "I'm going to have to go."

"Let me get your box."

"You don't have to do that." By the time she'd finished saying it, he was coming out with the box in his hand. "But thanks." She rushed over to open the back door of the Jeep, and he set the box inside. She slammed the door shut.

He stood close again, facing her.

The look in his eyes didn't bode well for her promise to herself. If she stayed another minute, he'd kiss her. Or at least try. And she didn't want to do that again until he explained his cryptic words about not having anything to offer her. Yet she didn't want to ask him for an explanation. So she'd be patient. A virtue, after all.

She eased toward the driver's door. "Good night." Still keeping her eyes on him, she slid into the seat.

A grin darted across his lips. "Good night. And thanks again."

"You're welcome." As she drove away, she asked God to protect her heart. Her own defenses seemed useless when it came to the good-looking Texan.

❧

When Kaleigh woke up Monday morning, she turned over and slapped her alarm. No sticky note came away on her hand. Just like that, she remembered. She was done. There were no more steps to a "new her." For a few moments, she stared at the ceiling, mentally tracing a tiny crack in the Sheetrock. She could finally admit that her big plan had been flawed.

On the boat, when she'd tried to merge who she was pretending to be with who she really was, she'd felt like a fraud. Even though Chance had teased her, she knew he'd been embarrassed. That doctor had thought she was crazy. And she'd given

Jared Tolliver enough ammunition to use against her for the next decade. Of course, she wouldn't have been late to begin with if she hadn't been sneaking around, trying to keep Carlton from knowing she wanted to interview Nicole Broome.

She rolled over and fluffed her pillow. Since she wasn't going to straighten her hair today, she could doze a few more minutes.

She punched the pillow again then sat up. She'd get ready early and find Carlton. She needed to let him off the hook.

An hour later she found him in the cafeteria drinking black coffee and reading *War and Peace*. She sat next to him.

"Good morning," he said, barely looking up.

Then he did a double take. "Kaleigh?"

She smiled. She'd worn her neon green top with a matching tank over her faded flared-bottom jeans. Her funky potato shoes completed the outfit. And her hair flowed down her back in loose curls. It was good to be back. "It's definitely me."

"What happened?"

Her smile faded. She launched into her prepared speech with the enthusiasm of someone reading her own obituary. "I wanted to be someone I wasn't. And you got caught in the crossfire. But I finally realized that—even though I'd like to change some things—for the most part I'm happy being me. And the real me. . . isn't someone that you'd date."

He frowned. "How do you know?"

She laughed. "Trust me, I know."

His eyes scanned her, and he shrugged. "Then I guess I'll take your word for it." Typical. She stuck out her hand. "But we can still be friends, if you're willing."

He stared at her hand, and for a second she thought he was going to refuse it, but he gave her a firm handshake. Mild curiosity was the strongest emotion in his eyes. "So are you going to go to your sister's wedding alone?"

She shook her head. "I'm going with myself."

"That's what I said."

She started to explain the difference, but on second thought, she just smiled. "I'll see you around, Carlton."

He nodded, and before she'd pushed her chair all the way back, he turned back to his book.

She practically skipped to class. Operation Old Me was a big success.

Andrew set his coffee down on the table and took the extra few steps to plug the tree lights in. He loved having it, but more than anything, every time he looked at it, he thought of Elyse.

His pen and ink drawing of her lay on the table, and he ran his finger over it. He'd almost been busted the night she'd brought the tree. It had taken him forever to put the canvas and his small paint set away. Then he'd left the drawing out and had to shove it in a drawer while she was carrying the box in.

She hadn't suspected, though, and with any luck, she'd be surprised. It was fitting in a way to use the last of his paints and his last canvas to paint a picture of her. He just hoped he didn't run out before he finished.

He retrieved his coffee and sank onto the couch. The twinkling lights brightened the dull winter morning. His phone rang, and he glanced at the caller ID. His dad. Andrew had considered calling him on Thanksgiving but hadn't wanted to face the usual questions. Still, he couldn't *not* answer. He flipped it open. "Hello?"

"I thought you might be home for Thanksgiving."

"Didn't you work?" Andrew would have pulled the words back if he could have. They revealed too much of the hurt he'd always had that his dad pulled extra shifts on holidays. Sure, crime soared. But other people squeezed in family time. After Andrew's mom died, he'd always known that his dad hadn't really considered the two of them a family. *A self-fulfilling prophecy*, he thought wryly.

"No. I took off this year on the chance that you'd be here."

So they were going to play the guilt game. No winner there, that was for sure. They both had their fair share. "Sorry."

"Oh well, maybe next year. Unless. . .are you coming home for Christmas?"

Andrew frowned. "Since when do you want me home for the holidays? Our life isn't a Jimmy Stewart movie."

"Maybe it could be a little closer to one if you weren't off chasing the wind."

"Sorry, Dad. I'm going to be here through Christmas. I'll let you know what I'm doing after that." He took a sip of coffee.

"Does she know about Melanie?"

He froze with his cup still to his lips. "Who?"

"You know. Elyse McCord."

"How do you know about Elyse?" Andrew slammed the coffee cup on the table and bought time to answer a question he didn't want to think about.

"I can access online newspapers just like anyone else can. Looks like you played the hero."

Andrew didn't answer.

"You think this Zeke is the one who killed Melanie?"

"I don't know."

"They haven't found him yet?"

"No. Not that you need to ask me that." With his dad's Texas Ranger resources, any police information was at his fingertips.

"So Elyse McCord doesn't know you were a murder suspect?"

Andrew lowered his voice even though he knew he was alone in the camper. "Not yet."

"When are you planning on telling her?"

He should have told her the other night when she'd asked how long ago his wife died. But he hadn't wanted to ruin the moment. "After Christmas."

"Probably smart." His dad's voice grew sharp. "The holidays are an awful time to be alone."

And just like always, he was gone without a good-bye.

❧

Elyse had tried not to imagine this part of Crystal's wedding. But now it was here. She had to step out into the arched doorway and face the crowd. Walk up to the front with them all watching. She wasn't going to be a baby on Crystal's big day. And she definitely wasn't going to faint.

"Concentrate on walking in time to the music," her mama had suggested last night at the rehearsal. "Forget about the guests."

She stepped over to the opening and kept her eyes on the very front, purposely blurring her peripheral vision. Standing facing her were Jeremy and the preacher. To Jeremy's left stood all four of her brothers. Jeremy and Aaron, who was his best man, looked reasonably happy, if a bit nervous. But the other three all wore expressions more suitable for a funeral than a wedding.

Elyse forced herself to smile at them while the crowd watched Kaleigh glide down the aisle, a vision in her green dress, carrying a single red rose. To Jeremy's right, there was a blank spot for Crystal and ones for Elyse and Kaleigh. Bree and Crystal's high school friend, Phoebe, looked beautiful in green dresses, also, both of them beaming. They were married, so Elyse took it as a good sign that weddings were still a happy time for them. Finally, just before she stepped out into the aisle, Chance and Matthew returned her smile. Luke still scowled. She knew him well enough to know he was thinking about how glad he'd be to get out of that monkey suit and away from all the froufrou.

Her attempt at self-distraction worked until she actually started walking. She could feel the eyes on her. Her palms were sweating so much, she was afraid the white rose she carried against her red dress might slip from her fingers. What if she dropped it? Or what if she dropped it and stepped on it?

She was drowning, her lungs filling with her own fear. She was supposed to look at Andrew. That's what they'd agreed on. Her frantic gaze skittered across the spectators and locked with a familiar pair of blue eyes. Andrew, sitting near the front, in an aisle seat, was turned toward her. The smothering panic immediately washed away like the tide going out.

She kept her eyes on him and breathed evenly as she concentrated on walking in time to the music. How could one person make her feel so much more assured yet still make her stomach flutter? As she drew closer to him, she gave up on answering that and took her place beside Kaleigh.

"The Wedding March" blared through the building, and the crowd rose. In the doorway, arm locked with their daddy's, Crystal waited, her blond hair in an elegant twist on top of her head, a few loose wisps around her face. Her beauty was enough to take anyone's breath away, but Elyse heard Jeremy softly gasp.

She glanced at him, and the love written all over his face made her throat ache. What would it be like to have someone look at her like that?

No sooner had the thought formed than Andrew turned his head slightly and caught her gaze again. The expression on his face was so close to what she'd just seen on her future brother-in-law's that her heart stopped beating for a second.

Andrew loved her. She knew it as well as she knew that Crystal and Jeremy loved each other. A smile floated across her face, and Andrew responded with a broad smile of his own. The conversation they'd just had—though one with no words—was one they'd always remember.

CHAPTER 31

Kaleigh tucked the phone number into her tiny black purse and gave a wave to the guitar player as he went back up to the stage. She walked back over to where Elyse and Bree were sitting.

"Someone you know?" Elyse asked, her brow raised.

"A friend from high school." A friend she'd never have approached if Carlton had been here. She slipped into the seat next to Bree. "Anybody notice I didn't bring a date?"

"What's the right answer to this question?" Bree tossed a tiny bag of birdseed at Kaleigh.

Kaleigh caught it with one hand. "The right answer is yes, you noticed, and you're dying to know why."

"Yes, we noticed, and we're dying to know why," Bree and Elyse chorused.

"Good." She grinned and told them about her day at the boat.

Bree gasped. "You told a doctor to keep his nose out of your business?"

She nodded. "I feel kind of bad about that considering he really couldn't help being there. But he didn't have to react."

Elyse laughed. "You don't ask much, do you?"

Kaleigh shrugged. "The bottom line is Operation New Me is over. I've decided to be happy with myself. I didn't need a date for this wedding." She winked. "Besides, dates just get in the way of accepting cute guitar players' phone numbers."

"Good point," Bree murmured.

Kaleigh reached down and slipped off one black stiletto and rubbed her heel with her hand. "I'm so glad I don't have to wear these all the time." She snapped her fingers. "That's what dating Carlton was like. Wearing shoes that pinch your feet." She grimaced. "Of course, he could have said the same of me."

"Nice." Elyse slipped her shoes off, too.

Mama walked over to them and plopped down beside Kaleigh. "I think they're about to leave on their honeymoon."

"Feels weird, doesn't it?" Elyse said softly.

Kaleigh glanced at her sister. "We've still got each other."

"C'mon, guys," Bree protested. "Getting married isn't like moving to a foreign country and cutting off all communication."

"I don't know. Who was complaining earlier about not having Internet?" Kaleigh asked Elyse.

"I think it was our sister-in-law. The one who lives in a foreign country." Elyse kept a straight face.

"Chicago?" Bree asked.

"We're kidding," Kaleigh assured her. "Let's go throw some birdseed at the deserter and her new husband."

They walked, laughing, outside into the breezeway of the community building. Jeremy's truck sat over to the side.

Bree pointed to it. "Good to know the McCord boys found some way to keep from being bored to death during the reception."

Shaving cream letters spelled out JUST MARRIED. Empty cans hung from the back bumper.

"McCord *boys*?" Kaleigh drawled. "I'll have you know I helped."

Elyse gasped. "You did?"

She nodded. "It was a lot of fun." And something else she wouldn't have done if Carlton had been there.

Crystal and Jeremy came out the door behind them, their heads close together. Smiles lit their faces. Crystal, dressed in the turquoise top and brown skirt they'd all helped her pick out for traveling, said a word to Jeremy and broke away to join them. Over her sister's shoulder, Kaleigh saw her daddy speaking to Jeremy. What was he saying—"Take good care of my daughter"? Probably.

Still clutching her wedding bouquet in one hand, Crystal hugged each of them. "We'll be back next week sometime."

Kaleigh nodded. "Tell Cancun hi for us."

Crystal giggled. "I will."

Jeremy came up behind her and pulled her into his arms. "We'd better go, Mrs. Buchanan."

"I have to throw my bouquet."

Immediately Kaleigh was swept up into a throng of single females, ranging in age from seventy-year-old Mrs. Maxwell to six-year-old Beka. All of them clustered together behind Crystal. From the corner of her eye, Kaleigh could see the photographer snapping pictures.

Crystal kept her back turned and tossed the bouquet over her head. Everyone cheered as the cluster of white and red roses fell neatly into Elyse's hands. Kaleigh grinned as her older sister blushed. But she also noticed Elyse's eyes immediately sought out Andrew.

Kaleigh dropped her hands and reached in her pocket for the birdseed packet she'd opened earlier. She was glad she hadn't caught the bouquet. And glad that she hadn't brought a date to the wedding just for the sake of not being alone. Along with the crowd, she tossed birdseed on Crystal and Jeremy as they darted to their truck, beginning their new lives together.

Kaleigh was happy for her sister. She glanced to where Elyse beamed as she and Andrew examined the bouquet. Both sisters. But she couldn't remember the last time she'd felt more at peace. Alone. Or as she'd tried to tell Carlton—with herself.

Elyse paced in the foyer of her house, peeking out the window every few minutes. What if Andrew hated the gift she got him? What if he thought she was pushy? This morning at Mama's had been wonderful, but when everyone had settled in for an afternoon nap, Andrew and Elyse had split up to go home and get each other's presents. He was supposed to meet her at her house in five minutes.

She grabbed the bright red packages from beside the door and carried them into the living room for the third time. The dogs followed her curiously. "I can't decide whether to meet him at the door with them or bring him inside so we can sit down and open them."

Missy blinked.

"I know. I definitely should invite him in."

The doorbell rang, and leaving the gifts in the living room, she went to open it.

Andrew looked as nervous as she felt. The two packages in his hand were elaborately wrapped with curling ribbons and big bows.

"Wow. You did a great job."

He laughed. "I took them to the 4-H booth outside of Walmart and got them wrapped."

She nodded. "I should have done that. Come on in."

In the living room, he sat on the couch.

She sank down beside him then popped up again like a waffle in the toaster. Pasting on a smile, she moved over to the chair catty-corner to the sofa. "So I can see you," she murmured.

"You first," she said.

He nodded and took the first red package from her.

As he tore it open, Elyse scooted to the edge of her chair.

His eyes widened when he saw the compact but complete paint set. "I can't believe you did this."

"I'm sorry. I know you said you were going to use what you had and be done."

He shook his head and swallowed. "You have no idea what this means to me. To know that you believe in me enough to buy me paints."

She shoved the tall, skinny gift to him.

He opened it and laughed. "This is amazing. I left my easels behind when I—" His voice drifted off, and he ran his hand over the simple lines of the fold-up easel. "You don't know how many times I've sat out under the awning of my camper and wished I had an easel." There was something in his eyes she didn't quite recognize. Remorse? "I guess I've just been stubborn by not buying one." He stood and tugged her to her feet. "Thank you. You couldn't have gotten me anything I'd like better."

He hugged her, and she wrapped her arms around him and listened to his heartbeat. Steady and sure.

He released her. "Now it's your turn."

She sat back down, and he put the big square box in her

hands first. She lifted it. "It's light."

"Oh no, you're one of those."

"One of those whats?"

He winked. "A tester. One who shakes and prods and weighs gifts to try to decide what they are."

She shrugged and ripped the paper open then the box. "I don't have to be a tester if—" The words died on her lips as she saw a cream cowboy hat nestled in red tissue paper. "Oh, Andrew. It's beautiful." She pulled it out and put it on her head. "What do you think?"

"You look just like I imagined. Which leads me to your next gift."

He dropped a smaller package on her lap and remained standing.

She looked up at him. "You don't have to be nervous. I know I'll love it."

A wry grin twisted his lips. "We'll see."

She wanted to prolong the moment, so she slowly unwrapped this second gift, slipping the tape from the seams and gently opening it. Something inside was wrapped again in red tissue paper. When she pulled the paper back, she drew in an involuntary breath. "Andrew. . ." Tears burned her eyes as she lifted the small painting out. It was her, with a cowboy hat, leaning on the fence around her yard. The dogs played in the background. At the bottom were delicately filigreed words: Cowgirl at Heart.

She remembered when he'd told her she was a cowgirl at heart. From that moment on, her courage had seemed to increase exponentially. She wiped at her eyes with the back of her hand. "Thank you so much. It's perfect."

"I didn't mean to make you cry."

She jumped up and hugged him. "Want to go for a walk?" Maybe the cool air would dry her emotions some.

In the foyer, she stood the small painting up on the table underneath the hooks and turned to Andrew. "Looks good, doesn't it?"

He laughed. "I've never been any good at evaluating my own work, but I'm glad you like it. I had a lot to work with."

She blushed as she hung her cowboy hat on one of the hooks by the door and exchanged it for a toboggan. "Thanks."

Outside, they walked toward the river without speaking. Halfway down the path, she shivered.

"Let's head back to the house," Andrew said.

She nodded. They turned and started back. When they got back to her driveway, she briskly rubbed her gloved hands together and blew warm air into them. "I can see my breath."

Andrew put his arm around her shoulders. "Want to go inside?"

She shook her head, loving every detail of today, even the way the perky tassel on top of her knitted cap bounced when she moved. "Never."

"I think it might be a little cold to stay out here forever."

"Nope," she said. "It's not cold at all." She leaned her head against his shoulder. "You're all the warm I need."

He stopped and pulled her into a hug. "I agree," he whispered against her hair. "This is the best Christmas I can ever remember having."

"My family are pretty neat, aren't they?"

"Yes, they are. But one member stands out above the others."

She put her finger to her chin in mock concentration. "Hmm. . .that would be Luke, I guess. He's the tallest."

He reached up and took her hand and folded it into his. "As far as I'm concerned, it would be you."

She giggled. His eyes darkened, and he bent down and kissed her lightly on the mouth. She put her arms around his neck.

He drew back and looked into her eyes. "Elyse, I—"

A car came bouncing up the lane. Andrew let go of her, and she turned around to face the visitor. "Why would Jack be out here on Christmas day?" she asked absently.

Andrew shook his head. "I don't know." He glanced at the sheriff. "Unless they found Zeke."

"After all this time?" She figured they'd seen the last of him. And she sincerely hoped she was right.

Jack got out and walked up to them. "Merry Christmas, Elyse. Andrew." He frowned at Andrew. "This is difficult, but I need to ask you a few questions."

Andrew stiffened. "Why don't I follow you back to the station?"

"You can talk in my house," Elyse said. She looked at Jack. "What's this about?"

Both men stared at her, and a cold sliver of fear slid down her spine. "Andrew?" Her voice sounded unnaturally high-pitched, even to her own ears.

Andrew's shoulders slumped slightly as if someone had set a huge burden on them. He motioned Jack into the house. "We can just talk here."

When they were all three inside, Andrew took off his gray hooded jacket and hung it on the hook by the door with deliberate motions.

Elyse kept hers on. She was almost shivering already. She was suddenly reminded of the night of the storm. How could this be any worse than that? She put the dogs in the den and led the way to the living room. "Want me to wait in the kitchen?" she asked.

Andrew shook his head, his face drawn and pale. "Whatever it is, you might as well hear it."

He sat down on the couch, and Elyse sat next to him. She reached for his hand, and he squeezed hers then released it.

Her heart pounded. This was crazy. They'd been through so much already. What else could be lurking around the corner?

Jack cleared his throat and leveled his gaze at Andrew. "It's about the gun that Zeke had that day he attacked Elyse."

Andrew's brows drew together. "What about it?"

"I don't know how the report got delayed so long, but it finally came back. That gun was registered to a woman in Texas named Melanie Lawson."

Elyse thought she heard a small gasp come from Andrew. "I had that gun in my hand," he murmured.

Jack nodded. "Someone put two and two together eventually and figured out that it had been stolen in a house break-in."

"I can't believe it." Andrew's color had shifted from pale to slightly green.

Elyse looked at him. What did this have to do with him?

"Apparently the woman had recently married and hadn't changed her gun registration yet. But after some more research, her married name finally came across the fax machine today." He hesitated. "Melanie Stone." He looked at Andrew. "I sent back a request for more information. But I'm guessing this isn't a coincidence, is it?"

Andrew slowly shook his head. "Melanie was my wife," he said dully.

CHAPTER 32

"What?" Elyse couldn't process that information. Why had she assumed Andrew's wife had died of cancer? Or even a car accident? She hadn't asked because she hadn't wanted to pry or intrude on his grief.

Andrew looked at her. "We'd been married three weeks. We were supposed to go away that weekend with her friends from work. Everyone knew it. But I got a chance to display my paintings in a big art show that Saturday. I begged her to change her plans and go with me to the show. Or go on with her friends and let me go to my show and join her later. But she was so stubbornly against me pursuing my art that she wanted to make me sorry by staying home." His eyes had no tears, but the borders were red. "It worked. Someone broke in—no doubt someone who knew she was going to be gone—and killed her when she interrupted the robbery." He shook his head and wiped his hand across his face. "I've been sorry ever since."

"So you came here looking for her murderer?" Jack asked his first question.

Elyse just stared at him. That couldn't be right. Andrew, tired of being a reporter to satisfy his dad, had come here to paint houses.

Andrew nodded. "Right after the murder, I was the main suspect. But I hadn't done it, so I was determined to find out who did. I put out thousands of faxes to pawn shops with the missing jewelry information." He fidgeted with his keys. "The police eventually took me off the suspect list, but I've spent the last three years chasing false leads and making enemies of just about every Texas law enforcement agency there is. Last August I got a call from a pawn shop owner over on Fourth Street here in Shady Grove. A man had brought in a necklace that matched the description of Melanie's stolen necklace. He had a security video of the man and a possible address."

"Zeke," Elyse whispered. Every accident that had brought her and Andrew together had been a contrived move on his part to catch his wife's killer.

Andrew nodded. "I parked my camper at the river and painted all the houses in the neighborhood dirt cheap."

She suddenly remembered part of Zeke and Andrew's conversation on the porch that first day. "But Zeke wouldn't let you paint Maxine's."

"Right. So I had to satisfy myself with going by it several times a day, watching to see if he went to the pawn shop anymore or made any moves that seemed illegal or suspicious."

"Which is how you found me."

"Thank God," Andrew said. "It is."

She snorted. "Yeah, because that gave you the perfect opportunity to move yourself in here and keep an eye on me—the girl whose vehicle Zeke had stolen. And even after the Jeep was found, I was still good bait, considering all those awful threats he made to me." How could she, of all people, have fallen for a con?

He flinched and reached for her hand.

She pulled it away and caught a glimpse of Jack's face. He looked as if he wished he were anywhere but here. *Join the crowd*, she thought angrily.

"You were never bait." Andrew's voice cracked.

"I'm just going to step outside." Jack pushed to his feet. "We can talk out there in a minute."

"You don't have to leave," Elyse said, standing, too. "I'm going." Before she got the words out, the door had slammed behind Jack, and she was alone in the house with the man who had made her love him and then betrayed her.

"Elyse, I was going to tell you. But I was afraid it would scare you to find out that Zeke was probably a murderer."

"Oh." She snorted. "I get it. Your motives were strictly altruistic. You just wanted what was best for me."

He shook his head. "It was one of those secrets that took on a life of its own. There never seemed like a good time to tell you."

"That's funny. I can think of dozens of times that would have been better than me finding out this way."

He ducked his head and scuffed her floor with the toe of his boot. "Me, too." He looked back up at her. "I'm so, so sorry. I know it's hard to even think about forgiving me—"

"I'll never forgive you. You used me." Her voice shook, and she couldn't hold back the tears anymore. "I'm crying because I'm angry," she spat out. "Not because of losing you. This was all just a big con to you."

He looked as if she'd slapped him. "No, it wasn't. In the beginning, I did partly want to stay close to you so I could find

Zeke. In the very beginning. But within just a few days—by the time I moved my camper out here, my only thought besides protecting you was being with you as much as possible. And that had nothing to do with Zeke."

His lies almost got to her. But she knew from painful experience how con men operated. "I'm going into the den. Lock the door behind you when you leave."

"We'll talk tomorrow."

Her heart ached, but she ignored it. She shook her head. "We don't have anything to talk about. Ever." With that, she walked away from the man who, just an hour earlier, she'd been stupid enough to think she loved.

⚘

Andrew stopped and talked to Jack a little more. The sheriff seemed satisfied with his explanation. "Good luck," he muttered before he got into the car and left.

Andrew watched him drive away then walked on up to the main house before he lost his nerve. He didn't know what he must have looked like, but a rowdy board game came to a screeching halt when he walked in.

"Where's Elyse?" Matthew said, his expression already darkening.

Andrew stared around the room at Jonathan and Lynda McCord, Crystal and Jeremy with little Beka, Aaron and Bree, Luke, Matthew, Kaleigh, and Chance. How had he grown to love this family so much in such a short time?

"Where is she, man?" Luke growled and pushed to his feet.

Andrew told them the whole story, grateful to get it over with at once. Thankfully, they let him talk without interrupting. "I'm not proud of what I've done, but it quit being about revenge, or even clearing my name, a long time ago and started being about protecting Elyse." He shook his head. "I know she'll never believe that though. And I can't stand the thought of her being alone over there—" His voice broke, and he blinked hard at the grandfather clock beside him before he looked back at them. He drew the line at crying in front of Elyse's brothers. He'd save that for when he was alone in the camper. "I can't do what she wants and disappear. But I'll move my camper back down to the river campground early in the morning and keep an eye on her from a distance." He looked at Matthew. "If Zeke isn't apprehended by the time the office is completely painted, then I'll go quietly and leave it to y'all to protect her."

"Go where?" Jonathan asked.

Andrew shrugged. "If Elyse isn't there, it really doesn't matter. Merry Christmas." He turned and walked out to the camper. He didn't bother turning the lights on, but just sat in the darkness on the little couch and gave in to the heartache. Out the window, he watched Crystal, Bree, Kaleigh, and Lynda walk by going toward Elyse's. At least she wouldn't be alone.

❧

Elyse pulled the gray hoodie from the hook by the door where Andrew had left it on Christmas Day. Three weeks ago. How many times since then had she put it on? Every night when her customers were gone and the house was quiet, she made herself wait until the pain was so bad she couldn't stand it; then she'd walk in here and get it. But on Saturdays, like today, she couldn't make it through the morning without it.

She nuzzled her nose against the fabric as she slipped into it.

Any lingering smell of Andrew's soap and shampoo was almost gone. Shouldn't the same be true of his memory? What was wrong with her that she could be conned and then let her heart break over it?

As soon as she sank into her chair, the dogs came and gathered around her. She invited Nikki up onto her lap, and Missy, Majesty, and Pal moved closer to her. Majesty put her chin on Elyse's leg and pressed down, her big eyes looking up at her master questioningly. "I'm sorry, baby," Elyse whispered. "These are hard times. But we'll get through it."

Missy barked once, stood, then sat again. Elyse sighed. What Missy needed, Elyse couldn't give. She was taking care of their basic needs—food, water, exercise. But the dogs knew something wasn't right, and they always surrounded her when she put on the hoodie as if they were protecting her from her pain or at least sharing it with her. Nikki licked her under her chin.

"No," Elyse said halfheartedly. She hadn't been out of the house except for church since Christmas. She knew her family was worried. She'd taken a break from 4-H meetings, ostensibly to help Matthew get their office space ready to open in February. But she'd done little toward the decisions. She couldn't seem to care.

The doorbell rang, and she pushed to her feet. Probably Crystal or her mom. They'd been taking turns coming by, just to check on her.

She shuffled down the hall and opened the door.

Matthew stared at her. "You look awful."

"Thanks, bro." She stepped back and let him in. "Nice of you to stop by and cheer me up."

"I stopped by to get you. We're going into town to pick out the bathroom fixtures."

"Whatever you choose is fine with me."

"I have no idea what I'm doing, and this is supposed to be half your place, too."

She wanted to argue, but she knew she was being unfair. And from the determined gleam in his eye, she had a feeling he was ready to fight to get her to go. The last thing she wanted was a confrontation. She slipped off the hoodie and ignored Matthew's gaze on her while she hung it up. "Give me ten minutes to get ready."

"I'll be in the truck."

She put on her jeans and a brown sweatshirt, ran a brush through her hair, smeared on a little lip gloss, and went.

Thankfully, on the way, Matthew refrained from trying to make conversation.

She forced herself to block the future from her mind and just concentrate on this minute. By doing that, she was able to help choose faucets, mirrors, and lights for the bathrooms.

As she was signing the invoice, Matthew came over to the counter. "I'm going to run pick up something I need. Meet you at the truck."

She nodded absently. The cashier took the invoice and handed her a yellow copy. She turned around and almost bumped into Andrew. Her heart stopped for a second then wrenched painfully. "When I get my hands on him," she muttered under her breath. Matthew had sold her out.

"Elyse, I'm sorry. I just need to talk to you for a minute."

"Where's Matthew?" If he'd left her here without a ride, she was writing him out of her will. She barely let herself glance at Andrew's face. The pain she felt seemed to be reflected there. But con men were notoriously good for reflecting your own emotions back to you.

"He's on the other side of the store. He'll meet you in the truck. This isn't his fault. I begged him for just a second with you."

"He called and told you we were coming here?" Odd how things had flip-flopped. A couple of months ago, Andrew was one of the few people she felt comfortable around. Now she'd rather star in her own reality show than face him.

Andrew shifted from foot to foot. "I see Luke every day and Matthew almost every day. I knew you had to pick out faucets. I could have just shown up here and pretended to bump into you, but I didn't want to deceive you."

Elyse bit back a retort about it being a little too late for that. She took a deep breath and counted to five. "Andrew, will you do me a favor?"

"Anything," he said softly, his eyes tender like she'd seen them so many times before.

She bit her lip until it hurt. "Leave me alone." She brushed past him and hurried out to the truck.

❦

Elyse clutched the half gallon of black walnut ice cream and knocked on the door of the tiny log cabin. She'd stopped in Newport at Kroger's and bought it on an impulse. But now that she was here, she decided maybe grief over losing Andrew had made her go crazy.

The door swung open, and Luis's mouth dropped open. "Elyse. What are you doing here?"

She shoved the ice cream into his hands and tugged Andrew's gray hoodie tighter around her.

Luis glanced down at the ice cream, and when he looked back up at her, his dark eyes were filled with amazement. "Is black walnut still your favorite?"

She shrugged. "I haven't eaten any since that day. . ."

Pain flashed across his face. "I don't suppose I have either." He stepped back. "Won't you come in?"

She considered bolting for the Jeep. But she'd driven all this way. And brought ice cream. She stepped inside and looked around. The cabin was small but neat. "Nice place."

"Thanks." He held up the ice cream. "Could you eat some if I get us a couple of bowls?"

"Sure." Her legs shook a little as she followed him into the kitchen. "Mama and Daddy say you work in the prison ministry."

He pulled two bowls from the cabinet and snagged two small spoons and one big one from a drawer. "That's right."

"That must be exciting." Small talk was excruciating. But big talk would be worse, so she'd keep it up.

"Most of the time it's very rewarding." He set the bowls on the table. "I know I can never make up for what I did." He opened the carton of ice cream, and the sweet smell of black walnut filled the room. "But giving hope to the hopeless helps me to live with the unchangeable past." He carefully dipped out two equal portions. "You can choose."

"You taught me that. When one person splits it, the other gets to choose."

"Glad to know I taught you something that wasn't bad. I'm just so sorry. . . ." Luis wasn't good at small talk. He kept wanting to rush into big talk.

Of course, she'd brought it on with her reminiscing. What was wrong with her? She'd only wanted to make peace and get out. She picked up her spoon. It was the ice cream. She shouldn't have brought it. But her mouth watered as she took the first bite. She still loved it. After all these years and everything that had happened. It might not be her favorite anymore, but she still loved it.

She ate it quickly, nervously, then let the spoon clatter into the bowl.

Luis was already finished. Just watching her as if he couldn't believe she was there.

"Where did you get the guns?"

Confusion creased his brow. "What?"

"The guns. The ones you and. . .the ones y'all had when you came out the door that day. Where did they come from?"

He frowned. "Someone caught on to our con and called security. The first guard said the cops were on their way and he was going to need us to stay until they got there." He scraped his empty bowl with his spoon. "I didn't think I could do that. Nothing seemed worse than the possibility of going to jail. So I watched for my chance. And when the time came, I took his gun."

"And shot him in the leg?"

"While he and I were struggling—me to get it out of his holster, him to keep it in—the gun went off and shot him in the leg." He stood and rinsed his bowl at the sink. Then he turned back around. "Don't get me wrong. I'm sure I pulled the trigger. I deserved to go to prison, anyway, after all the things I'd done."

All these years and he couldn't spin a better tale of innocence than that?

"When he fell down, clutching his leg, I finally got the gun." He glanced at her and sat back down at the table. Then stood up again. "Your mom was furious at me. But when the other guard rounded the corner, I aimed the gun at him. He quickly put his weapon on the floor and kicked it to your mom, just like I told him to. Talking her into touching it was another thing."

"So she picked up the second guard's gun?" That made more sense than anything she'd ever imagined.

He nodded. "We backed up to the front door, not realizing there were cops behind us." His voice was as raspy as paper.

"You dropped your gun." Elyse stared at him. She couldn't believe after all these years she was getting answers. And even odder, she had a feeling they were the truth. "Why did she raise hers?"

His eyes were haunted as he looked back into the painful past. "She was just raising her hands. I know she forgot she had a gun in one."

"And they shot her."

He nodded. "It was all they could do, I'm sure. But you don't know how many times I wished they'd shot me instead."

"I did, too."

He sucked in his breath. "I don't blame you at all. You and your mom could have had a happy life."

"I've had a happy life. I wouldn't change anything about it." As soon as she said the words, she realized they weren't completely true. Of course, she'd rather her mother not have died. But if she hadn't, Elyse wouldn't have ended up with the McCords. And she wouldn't have met Andrew. Was that something she would change if she could?

"That's the beauty of God, Elyse. He can take our brokenness and make it beautiful."

"You're right." She stood. "I'd better go."

He looked like he wanted to protest, but he followed her to the front door. "Thank you for coming."

"I haven't figured this out yet, but if it's okay, I'll probably be back."

His smile was sweet. "I'll look forward to it. When you're ready."

In her Jeep, she took a deep breath and blew it out. She wasn't sure if she'd forgiven Luis or not, but she knew it was probable that she would. Maybe that reconciliation would take her mind off the giant hole in her heart that Andrew had left behind.

CHAPTER 33

"Going to a wedding by yourself must be the loneliest thing in the world." Elyse cradled the phone against her cheek. "I can see why you went so crazy trying to find a date for Crystal and Jeremy's wedding."

"A little too crazy. If I ever pull a stunt like that again, just knock me in the head." Kaleigh's laughter died away. "So, it was hard, huh?"

"Very hard. But the wedding was perfect. Lark was beautiful as the matron of honor. Allie and Rachel both had maternity bridesmaids'—or should that be brides matrons'?—dresses. They were adorable. Daniel and Jack both looked so proud."

"Sounds like the wedding party stole the show from the bride and groom."

Elyse sighed. "Not at all. Victoria was gorgeous. And her whole face was shining with happiness, just like Crystal's was at her wedding." Neither spoke for a few minutes. Elyse knew they were both wondering if they would ever have that kind of happiness. "They wrote their own vows. And when Adam told about how he'd been in love with Victoria for five years and how he'd just been biding his time, I actually cried a little."

"Aw. . .that is really sweet. I don't blame you."

"Then Dylan read a little note that he'd written to Adam, saying that he'd been a daddy to him for the last several years, and he was glad he was finally going to officially be able to call him Dad."

"Okay, that sounds like a wedding you'd have cried at even if you hadn't been alone." Kaleigh paused. "Do you ever see Andrew?"

Hearing his name was more painful than she'd thought it would be. She immediately thought of their run-in a few days ago. "Occasionally. He's still trying to contact me. I'm not sure why."

"Maybe he's biding his time."

"Don't you even try to catch me in a sappy mood and work that angle. Relationships are founded on trust and honesty. Mine and Andrew's was built on nothing except lies and deception."

"You really believe that?"

Elyse drew in her breath at the question. It was the same thing Andrew had asked her when she'd said that Luis probably stayed in prison for three meals a day and a roof over his head. He'd been right to doubt her. She hadn't believed it, even while she was saying it. Was Kaleigh right to doubt her, too? "I don't know what I believe anymore." *But I know I did tell him to leave me alone.*

"Don't wait until it's too late to fix this, Elyse."

"Did I tell you that they gave away handheld video games at the reception?"

"To all the guests?" Kaleigh handled the subject change smoothly, and Elyse was grateful.

"Yes. And the cool thing is it's a prototype of a new game

Adam has coming out in the spring."

"Cool. I can't wait to see it."

"Maxine's nephew, Doug, called awhile ago, and they're ready for me to bring Pal home."

"Ouch. That's going to be tough giving him up after all these months, isn't it?"

"A little. But I've always made myself remember that he wasn't mine to keep." Something she'd tried to keep in mind with Andrew ever since that night he'd told her he had nothing to offer her except that minute. The night he'd kissed her. Unfortunately, she'd allowed herself to be deluded into believing otherwise along the way.

"Are you going back to that house alone?"

"Yes." Elyse hesitated. "Between you and me, I did consider calling Andrew and asking him to go with me. Or at least asking him to follow me over there and make sure everything is okay. But I didn't want to give him the wrong idea."

"What's the wrong idea? That you love him?"

She started to protest, but she didn't want to lie. "I don't know." Elyse sank onto the chair and ran her hand over her eyes. "Kaleigh, this is so hard."

"Wanting to forgive him?"

She nodded even though she knew Kaleigh couldn't see her. Tears stung her eyes. "After all this talk of overcoming my fears. . .and of trusting God to see me through. . .the truth is I'm terrified."

"What are you so scared of?"

"That I'll make the wrong decision about him. That he'll deceive me again. Or that I'll miss my chance to be happy with someone who loves me." Elyse stopped short of sobbing, but barely.

"You've forgiven him, haven't you? If it wasn't for this fear?"

"Yes," she whispered.

"Deep down, even though you're hurt by the secret he kept, you believe he loves you, don't you?"

Elyse blew out her breath, determined to be honest with herself and her sister. "Yes."

"Then there's your answer."

"How did you get to be so wise?"

Kaleigh laughed. "The school of hard knocks."

"I'm going to call him when I get back from Maxine's."

"Why not call him now? That way he can go with you."

So tempting. . .but no. "I'm done living in fear. I can face this on my own. God will be with me."

"Good girl. Call me later, after you talk to Andrew, and let me know how it goes."

"Thanks, Kaleigh. Love you."

After they broke the connection, Elyse pulled the hoodie from the hook by the door and called Pal. It would be hard to let the dog go after all these months, but everyone had a place to belong. Pal's was with Maxine.

A genuine smile lit her face for the first time in three weeks. And she had a feeling that hers was with Andrew.

❧

"Come in, come in." Maxine's nephew, Doug, held the door wide open for Elyse and Pal.

"Thanks." Elyse smiled. It was getting so much easier to deal with people she didn't know well. And she had Andrew to thank for that. She had him to thank for a lot of things. Like helping her learn to face her fears. And for leaving his jacket hanging in her foyer on Christmas Day. When she'd gotten home from seeing Luis the other day, she'd hung it back on the hook and left it. But this morning, she'd needed it again for an extra dose of courage. She tucked her hands in the pockets, glad she'd worn it.

But she had herself to thank for the fact that he wasn't around. And every day his absence was getting harder to bear. This afternoon, maybe she could fix that.

In one of those embarrassing moments that sometimes happens with kids and dogs, Pal sat down on the welcome mat and refused to cross the threshold. "I'm sorry," Elyse said. "I think he remembers the last time we were here." Her own nerves were on edge enough that she wished she'd called and asked someone to come with her. She tugged on his leash, but he didn't budge. She slipped a treat from her pocket and set it down inside the house. Not as scientific as some methods, but the last thing she wanted was to make Maxine think Elyse had stolen the affection of her dog.

Pal walked cautiously into the foyer, and Doug closed the wooden door behind him.

"Where's Maxine?"

Doug motioned down the hallway. "She's in her room, resting. She should be out in a few minutes. Have a seat."

Elyse nodded and sat on the sofa. Here was the test. Could she make small talk with someone she hardly knew? Six months ago, she definitely couldn't. "How's she doing settling back into her house?"

Doug, still standing, glanced down the hall. "She's sleeping quite a bit. But I think she's just tired from the move."

Pal growled. Elyse cringed. She had a feeling that—even though he was nothing like his father—Doug probably smelled and looked a lot like Zeke to Pal.

"Are you going to move down here and try to get a job?" Elyse smiled at Doug. "I know Maxine would love to have you."

"My plans are up in the air right now." He walked to the window. "What's Andrew up to today?"

Elyse hated the pain that flared in her chest when she heard his name. How long would it take for that to go away? "I really don't know," she said softly. "We're. . .um. . .not seeing each other anymore." Her face grew hot as she suddenly remembered Andrew saying he thought Doug was interested in her.

She heard a movement in the hallway. "Isn't that just too bad?" a chillingly familiar voice said.

CHAPTER 34

Zeke came in, with a gun pointed straight at her. Pal's hackles rose, and he growled as he backed up against her.

Elyse gripped his leash tightly, needing something to hold on to.

"You said you'd let me find out what she knew." Doug didn't seem at all surprised to see his dad. "Why are you doing this?"

"I figured old Andy would come with her," Zeke snarled, never taking his beady eyes off Elyse's face. "But since he didn't, and if they're 'not seeing each other anymore,' " he mimicked in a high voice, "we'll have to be a little more direct in how we get him here."

"What do you mean?" Doug asked.

Elyse had a million questions of her own, but her tongue felt glued to the roof of her mouth.

Zeke motioned with the gun. "Get her phone. She'll call him and ask him to come over here."

Elyse suddenly found her voice. "I won't do it."

Zeke's maniacal laugh filled the room. "I think you will." He pointed the gun at Pal's heart. "Unless you want to see the dog die in front of you."

She glared at him, but she had no doubt he'd do it. "Where's Maxine?"

"Asleep," Zeke said.

"Doug?" Elyse asked the obviously nervous young man. "Where's your aunt?"

"After she called you, I gave her a sleeping pill mixed in with her vitamins. She doesn't know anything about this."

"So she's okay?"

"For now," Zeke growled. "But if shooting the dog doesn't get you to call, she'll be next."

"Wait a minute," Doug protested, his voice high-pitched with stress.

"You shut up and do what you're told, boy. Get her phone."

Doug walked over to Elyse. "I'm sorry," he said softly. "I need your phone."

Elyse looked up at him. "Your aunt was so proud of you. She said you'd turned your life around."

"You don't understand."

"Shut up," Zeke yelled.

Elyse handed Doug her phone.

"See if Stone's in her address book."

Doug obediently mashed the button to access her address book. "He's in here."

"Aww, isn't that sweet she didn't delete him? True love never dies, I guess." Zeke walked over to her and put the gun right next to her head.

Elyse's face grew hot, and she felt dizzy. This was what Andrew had tried to protect her from. And she'd thrown away what they'd had out of anger at him for not telling her.

"Here's what you're goin' to do," Zeke said in a soothing voice that was more terrifying than his ranting and raving. "You're goin' to call your boyfriend and tell him you've had a change of heart. Ask him to meet you at Maxine's."

"For what?" Elyse choked out.

Zeke shrugged. "I don't know. Tell him you're fixing some sandwiches and would love for him to be here, too, to share in the joyous reunion between dog and master." He grinned. "That right there about brings me to tears." His grin disappeared as quickly as it came. "But I promise you one thing. If you say anything. . .anything at all. . .that makes him suspicious or sounds nervous or scared"—he moved the gun to Pal's head, ignoring his growling—"then it's bye-bye, doggie."

Elyse nodded. "What are you going to do when Andrew gets here?"

"I just want to talk to him. Tell him I didn't kill his wife. Get him to explain it to the sheriff."

"That won't work."

"You let me worry about that. If my plan don't work, then I guess I'll turn myself in." He motioned for Doug to hand her the phone.

Elyse knew he was lying. But she couldn't see what he had to gain by getting Andrew over here. Andrew had disarmed him easily that first day. What was to keep him from doing it again? Unless Zeke shot him the second he walked in the door.

Her stomach churned. She'd always prided herself on being forgiving. Yet she hadn't forgiven Luis, even when faced with evidence that he'd really changed. And then when Andrew had shown her how sorry he was for what he'd done, she hadn't forgiven him either. Yet she'd accused *him* of having major trust issues. Something about staring into the beady eyes of death made her see life so much more clearly.

Doug put the phone in her hand, and she started to shake. "I can't do it."

Zeke pointed the gun at Pal again. "Really?"

"Wait," she stammered. "I'll try." She closed her eyes and silently begged God to help her.

"You'll do more than try if you want the dog to live."

When she opened her eyes, she relaxed more than she had since she heard Zeke's voice. This wasn't in her hands. It was in God's. He would handle it. She scrolled to Andrew's name and made the call.

Zeke sank down on the couch beside her and leaned close to hear the ringing.

She nearly gagged from the stench of him, but she forced herself not to react. She had more important things to think about. Like hoping that Andrew wouldn't answer.

He answered on the second ring.

⊱C

Andrew had just decided that if she didn't come out in two more minutes, he was going to the door. He knew that tailing Elyse after she'd ordered him to leave her alone would probably be the final nail in the coffin of their relationship. But Jack had called him this morning and told him Zeke had been spotted in Hardy but got away. Andrew had been on the way over to tell Elyse when he saw her pull out of her lane. Naturally he'd followed. He'd vowed to protect her, and he was going to do it.

His phone vibrated. He jumped. The caller ID said Elyse. Frowning, he flipped it open. "Hello?"

"Andrew, it's Elyse."

"Hi."

"Listen, I'm over at Maxine's bringing Pal home."

He stared at her Jeep in front of him in Maxine's driveway but still didn't step out from behind the tree.

"We thought you might like to come over and eat some tuna sandwiches with us. . .celebrate Pal's homecoming."

The adrenaline rushed through his body before his mind fully reacted to her words. "Tuna sandwiches. . .sounds perfect."

"Oh, good." He could hear the relief in her voice. "So you'll come?"

"Sure." He studied the yard. "It'll take me awhile to get there though. Maybe half an hour. Is that okay?"

She hesitated. "Thirty minutes will be fine, but don't be longer or the food might go bad, okay?" Her voice was considerably shakier.

He forced a laugh even though his throat ached with the effort. "No problem. I'll hurry. I can't wait for those tuna sandwiches."

"Okay."

The connection was broken.

He turned and walked away from the yard, keeping the front yard trees between him and the window. At the road he made a right turn and walked to where Elyse had parked her Jeep that day back in October. Then he cut through the woods. Since there was no foliage except for the evergreens, he could already see the chain-link fence. He stayed down low and kept his eyes wide open as he approached the back of the house.

The fence was partially collapsed from where Zeke had thrown Elyse onto it. Andrew easily stepped over it. The hair on the back of his neck stood up as he imagined someone watching him from the house. The windows appeared to have the blinds drawn, but if a person was in just the right place. . .

He shook his head and started praying silently instead. "My strength comes from the Lord," he whispered as he crept up to the busted basement window. He reached through the jagged glass and flipped the latch. It opened easily.

He slid his phone open and dialed the sheriff's direct line. Talking low, he quickly explained the situation. Without giving Jack time to argue, he laid out his plan, such as it was. "Give me fifteen minutes. Then do what you have to." He slid the phone shut and examined the open window. Just enough room to slip inside.

He landed softly on the concrete floor. Dust flew up around him like a cloud. He put his hands to his face and bit back a cough. When the dust settled, he squinted, letting his eyes adjust to the dim light. Stairs against the far wall led up to a closed door.

His movements were careful and slow, in direct contrast to his heart, which was beating wildly and faster than he could ever remember. He crept past shelves filled with jars of canned vegetables, arranged neatly by type. The shelf at the bottom of the stairs had old toys, coloring books, and other children's items. A large paper bag with handles overflowed with empty glass jars.

He stared at the lettering on the bag, the familiar logo of Melanie's favorite coffee shop. He'd only gone with her a few times, but she and her friends from work practically lived there. It was a local shop, though, so what would a bag be doing here? He choked back a gasp as his memory pulled the final pieces into place. Unfortunately, the realization only meant that Elyse was in twice as much danger.

CHAPTER 35

Andrew tiptoed up the stairs far enough that his eyes were level with the two-inch slit under the door. He could see most of the living room floor. He recognized Elyse's shoes. She was sitting on the couch facing him. One set of old work boots and one pair of loafers were standing on either side facing her. Occasionally the loafers paced over to the window and back. He couldn't see Pal's feet at all, so he was guessing the dog was on the couch next to Elyse.

If Andrew opened the basement door, even a crack, they would most likely all either hear a squeak or see a movement in their peripheral vision. He thought Elyse would guess that he would come from the basement, so even though he couldn't see her face, he felt sure she was watching the door.

He strained to listen. He could hear voices, but thanks to the old heating unit under the stairs, he couldn't make out what they were saying. He turned and made his way slowly back down the stairs. It only took a minute for him to find what he needed.

Back at the top of the stairs, he used the thick red crayon and scratched out the words BATHROOM—LOCK IN in big letters on the white cardboard. Then he put his eye back to the slit. The boots were gone, but Elyse's feet still faced him, and the loafers faced her. The boots walked back into view.

The heater stopped suddenly, and the silence was terrifying. He could easily hear what Zeke was saying. "If he don't come soon, I'm goin' to go ahead and kill the dog."

"You promised," Elyse said.

"It won't matter to you either way, nosy girl." Zeke laughed. "Once Stone gets here, he's going to go crazy and kill you and the dog. Then turn the gun on himself. After that, the police will figure out that he killed his wife three years ago and made it look like a robbery."

"No one will believe that." Elyse's voice was strong.

"We'll see," Zeke said. "But either way, Doug and I'll be long gone."

Both sets of men's shoes were facing away from him. Andrew slowly slid the cardboard under the door, being careful not to touch the floor with it. He tilted it with his fingers to where the words should be visible to Elyse if she was watching. He could only risk leaving it for a few seconds. Just as he pulled it back in, the boots turned around. "Did you hear something?" Zeke growled.

"I'll go check," Doug said. Andrew could hear the stress in the younger man's voice.

The loafers came straight toward him.

Andrew stepped soundlessly up the last few steps, ready to take the man down if he opened the door.

He heard footsteps go down the hall. In a minute, Doug's voice came again. "Aunt Maxine is still asleep, but she may have moaned or something."

Andrew lowered himself back to where he could see under the door. When he was able to see all three sets of feet again, he waited until the two men were turned away and flashed the sign for a count of five. Finally, after four times, he heard Elyse say, "I have to go to the bathroom."

She stood.

Andrew silently thanked God.

"Go with her," Zeke said.

"I—" Doug started.

"You've got my phone," Elyse broke in. "And Pal. I'm not going to do anything stupid. Can't I have a little privacy?"

"Hurry up. If you're not out when Stone gets here, I'm going to shoot him on the spot."

"Stay," Elyse commanded Pal.

"Watch her," Zeke barked at Doug.

Andrew watched Elyse's feet as she stood and walked toward him then turned and went by close enough for him to touch.

Doug's loafers stepped over right in front of the basement door, as he apparently watched her walk down the hall. Andrew heard the bathroom door close noisily and lock. Zeke's boots walked toward the window, with his back still to Andrew.

It was now or never. Andrew erupted up the stairs, opening the door with all his might.

He felt the wooden door connect with a body on the other side. "Oomph." Doug hit the floor with a bang.

Andrew went into a rapid series of forward rolls toward where Zeke's feet had been. Just as he came up low, he saw Zeke raise the gun. Andrew grabbed his arm and the gun went flying. He brought Zeke's arm up behind his body, and the big man went to his knees.

"Déjà vu," he murmured softly, and Zeke swore.

Andrew held Zeke easily. "Put the gun down, Doug," he said without turning around. He heard a gasp behind him and turned around to face the pistol, now in Doug's shaking hand. "You're not a killer."

"You don't know," Doug said, his eyes wide.

"Shut up, boy," Zeke growled.

Andrew yanked up on Zeke's arm a little harder. This was between him and Doug. "I do know. I remember why you look so familiar. You worked at the coffee shop." Andrew made no move toward Doug. "Melanie really liked you. She thought you had potential if you could get your head on straight."

Doug's eyes were red, but he didn't lower the gun. "I liked her, too."

"She knew you had a problem with drugs. That's why I remembered you."

"She said y'all were going to be gone for the weekend," Doug yelled, as if angry that she'd broken her word. "I was only going to take what I needed to score a hit then put everything else back. But I had it all in a sack to carry down to the living room to go through it when she came in and surprised me."

"And you had the pistol you'd gotten out of her nightstand drawer in your hand," Andrew guessed.

"I didn't mean to shoot. She scared me. When I saw her fall, I panicked. I used her cell phone to call 911, and I ran with the bag. All the way back here." Doug's eyes darted down the hall. "Aunt Maxine knew I'd done something bad, but she had no idea how bad. She let me stay here for a few days. I hid everything in the bottom of the closet. When I left, I started a new life." Now Doug's hand with the gun in it was shaking so badly that for the first time Andrew was a little afraid he might shoot.

"Put down the gun, Doug," Andrew said gently. "Before somebody gets hurt."

Doug lowered the gun slowly to the ground.

"Don't be a fool, boy. Shoot him. We can still get out of this," Zeke pleaded.

Doug shook his head. "I've spent the last three years trying to get out of the trouble you got me into by raising me like you. Now it's time you and I both face the consequences for what we've done."

"You're going down by yourself, boy. I wasn't even in Texas three years ago."

Andrew shoved Zeke toward the door. "But you've got plenty of crimes here in Arkansas to pay for. And there are policemen waiting outside to help you get started."

Andrew opened the front door and turned Zeke over to two of Jack's deputies. They walked him away, reading him his rights. Andrew looked at Jack and the deputy beside him. "You might want to call an ambulance for Maxine. They said she just had a sleeping pill, so she's probably fine. But just in case. . ."

Jack nodded.

"I'll do it," the deputy said and took off for the car.

Doug stepped out behind Andrew, tears evident in his eyes. "Sheriff, I killed Melanie Stone."

Jack looked over at Andrew with his eyebrows raised.

Andrew shrugged. "I'll be down to the station in a little while to talk to him if that's okay."

Jack nodded slowly. "As long as you don't bring any weapons."

Andrew gave him a sad smile. "Nothing sharper than a Bible,

I promise. And maybe a friend." He knew just the man who could help Doug see that his life wasn't over.

Doug stood without moving while Jack cuffed him.

Andrew watched them walk to the car. In the distance, he heard an ambulance. That was fast.

"Did you ever know that you're my hero?"

Andrew spun around to see Elyse standing on the porch step with Pal on a leash beside her. "Didn't I tell you to lock yourself in?" He couldn't believe how good it was to see her up close rather than just following her from a distance. It was all he could do to keep from running up the steps and pulling her into his arms.

"I did lock myself in." She gave him a sheepish smile. "Until I heard you tell Doug to put the gun down. Then I unlocked the door and cracked it open slightly so I could hear better. I thought you might need my help."

He returned her smile. "You're really brave."

She touched the gray hoodie she was wearing. "I had to wear your jacket for that."

"I'm glad I left it."

"Me, too," she said softly. She motioned over her shoulder. "I checked on Maxine before I came out here. She seems to be sleeping soundly but not unconscious."

"A deputy called for an ambulance. I almost dread her waking. This is going to be hard on her."

"She's strong though." Admiration filled Elyse's voice. "She has God and her friends." She rubbed the dog's head. "And don't forget Pal."

"How could we forget him?" Andrew said. "He got you into this mess."

Elyse's arched brow raised slightly. "That's not exactly how I look at it."

"Really? How do you see it?"

"He's the reason I met you." She reached in her jeans pocket and pulled out a dog treat. "And that's why you're a good boy, isn't it, Pal?" she cooed. "Here you go."

Andrew laughed as Pal eagerly ate the treat from her hand.

The ambulance came wailing into the yard. Andrew held his hand out for Elyse's. "We probably need to go down to the station and give a statement."

She smiled. "I'd better stay here and make sure Maxine is okay. I'll come down when the EMTs say she's okay."

"You sure?" He hated to leave her, even for a second, after just finding her again.

"I'm sure. Why don't you come over to the ranch later? I'm sure there'll be a big gathering at Mama and Daddy's."

"If you keep making a habit of getting kidnapped, they might stop throwing parties for you when you're rescued."

She grinned. "Somehow I doubt it."

It was so good to see her grin at him. "Yeah, me, too. You're always worthy of a party."

Her cheeks flamed, but before she could respond, two EMTs hurried up the walk.

"You should go," she said softly. "Jack will be needing information."

He took a step toward her then stopped. This wasn't the place. But Jack had better hurry and take his statement.

❦

Elyse didn't realize she'd been waiting for the doorbell to ring until she heard it. She stayed on the sofa between Kaleigh and Matthew and watched her mama walk to the front door.

"So I still don't see how you lived such a sedate life for all these years then suddenly turned into a danger magnet." Luke retrieved a chair pillow and tossed it onto her lap. He sank into the chair next to them.

"And let me guess," Kaleigh teased, "you also don't see why she didn't call you."

"You're right." Luke raised an eyebrow at Elyse. "Did you lose my phone number?"

She shook her head, her eyes straining to see who her mother was talking to in the doorway. Except for Aaron and Bree, the whole family was in the house. Even the newlyweds were here, sitting on—appropriately enough—the loveseat with their heads together and Beka coloring on the floor in front of them.

"C'mon, Lukey. . ." Kaleigh continued her teasing, using the name they used to pester him with when they were teenagers. "Give her a break. It took a lot of nerve to go back to where it all started."

Mama stepped backward, and Andrew came into the room.

Kaleigh's words buzzed in Elyse's head. "Where it all started" was exactly right. Maxine's house was where she'd met Andrew and started down a twisty path to today.

Everyone stopped talking, and silence fell over the room.

Andrew looked a little embarrassed, but then his gaze fell on Elyse.

Suddenly she felt as if she was the only person he saw. She felt the heat creep up her face. "Hey," she said weakly.

Her daddy stood and stuck out his hand. "Looks like we owe you another big thank you."

Andrew shook his hand. "You don't owe me anything." He glanced up at Elyse again. "But I was hoping I might steal Elyse for a few minutes."

Elyse pushed to her feet. "I need to go down and let the dogs out anyway. Why don't you walk with me?"

He nodded. "Sounds good."

Elyse almost giggled as she walked over to join him by the door. Her boisterous family was quiet enough that she could hear the seconds ticking by on the big grandfather clock. "We'll be back in a little bit." She waggled her fingers at them, and they all waved but still didn't speak.

Outside, she glanced up at Andrew. "I think we rendered my family speechless. And believe me, that's not an easy task."

He grunted. "Probably didn't think I'd ever have the nerve to show up here again."

She slipped her hand into his as they walked toward her house. "I'm glad you did."

"Really?" He squeezed her hand.

She nodded, glancing over toward the empty space next to the barn where Andrew's camper had been parked for so long. "More than you can imagine."

They walked in silence for a few minutes, and he looked across at her. "So is Maxine going to be okay?"

"The EMTs said she was fine. I didn't leave until we called her sister, Jane. She's coming to stay a few weeks."

"She took the news okay?"

Elyse cut her gaze at him. "About Doug?"

Andrew nodded.

"She didn't have much choice."

He cleared his throat. "I called Luis and asked him to help

Doug get involved in the prison ministry."

"What a wonderful idea."

"I was afraid you'd be mad that I contacted him."

"Did he tell you I went to see him?"

Andrew stopped walking and faced her in her driveway. "You went to see Luis?"

Suddenly shy, she nodded. "I took him some black walnut ice cream."

His smile was brilliant. "You forgave him."

She nodded again, her breath catching in her throat. She started up her walkway.

He fell into step effortlessly beside her. "Will you forgive me?"

"I already have," she whispered against the lump in her throat. "And I need you to forgive me now."

His brows furrowed together. "What for?"

"For refusing to talk to you."

"I forgive you for that as long as you talk to me now." He turned to her and pulled her gently into his arms. He brushed her hair back from her face, caressing her cheek with his thumb. "Remember how I told you once that I had nothing to offer you except this moment?"

Her heart pounded against her ribcage, and she nodded.

"I guess that's still true, in a way, considering we're not in control of the future."

She nodded again, unable to look away from his blue eyes.

"But now"—he moved his lips closer to hers—"everything I have is yours if you want it. My future, my life, my heart." He leaned down until his lips were touching hers.

She thought she might faint. But this was too nice to miss.

"I love you," he breathed softly against her mouth. Then he

kissed her with all the longing she'd seen in his eyes since that night at the barn so long ago.

She kissed him back without hesitation, and it was everything she'd ever dreamed it could be and more. "I love you, too," she murmured when she was able to speak. "Forever."

He pulled her tightly to him, and his lips were warm against her ear. "Forever."

CHRISTINE LYNXWILER

Award-winning author Christine Lynxwiler sold her first story in 2001 to Barbour Publishing. Since then she's written sixteen Christian romance novels and novellas, including three mysteries co-written with two of her sisters. She is currently working on *Cowgirls Don't Cry*, the third book in the McCord Sisters series.

Joy comes from many corners, and at this point in her life, Christine's list of blessings include a wonderful husband and two amazing daughters, a large family (including in-laws) who love God and each other, a close group of writer friends, a loving congregation of believers at Ward Street Church of Christ, and readers like you who encourage and support her dream of being a writer.

Please visit her Web site at www.christinelynxwiler.com, join her facebook page—Christine Lynxwiler Readers—or drop her an e-mail at Christine_Writes@yahoo.com. She would love to hear from you!

OTHER BOOKS BY CHRISTINE LYNXWILER

Arkansas
Promise Me Always
Forever Christmas
Along Came a Cowboy
The Reluctant Cowgirl